HOME ADVANTAGE

CATHRYN FOX

NEW YORK TIMES BESTSELLING AUTHOR

Daisy Reed of sound mind and memory, have
 as long as I can remember, with none other
nnon.

id it, and the next thing I need to do is go for
ean, come on, we're talking about a guy who
t, a guy who tricked me into touching a fish's
S EYEBALL, for God's sake!

se things when we were kids. But you know
d good things...great things, even. Like when
n vacation at Wautauga Beach, Washington,
ies had cabins. He saved my ass the night I
at Sebastian Wilson's house. I wasn't allowed
dy party at the end of the beach, but I snuck
 anyway. When I drank too much, I called
p. He pretended to be sick right along with
 both ate bad pepperoni on our pizza—
us food poisoning. He took me home, and
parents bought the bad pepperoni story.
 in the spare room that night, and kept
 every few hours. How could I not love him,

e him this, and despite how much it's going to
 to see him with my friend Naomi, Brandon
nd a chance at a future. You see, he friend
g time ago. I was the only girl allowed in his
the blanket tent, and while I thought it was
I realize now that the guys all thought of me
. The boobs and the hips that came along
't faze them one bit.

many years later, sitting at the Tap Room, the
inking hole, after my kick-ass hockey game,
two goals, and the guys—my buddies—are all

Discover other titles by Cathryn Fox at www.cathrynfox.com. Please sign up for Cathryn's Newsletter for freebies, ebooks, news and contests: https://app.mailerlite.com/webforms/landing/c1f8n1
ISBN: 978-1-989374-56-6
ISBN Print: 978-1-989374-55-9

D o I believe f Cannon, right best friend sir puck bunnies and settl school student?

Uh, how about no, with

Which raises the questi wingman? Or why am Sanders that he's a real well-known player—on a

Brain tumor?

Honestly, is there any c and I can't even believe these long and painful

Brandon. been in l than Bran

Okay, the a brain sc made me eyeball. A

Yeah, he what? He we were t where our went to a to go to th away and Brandon f me—saying claiming it fortunately Brandon s checking o right?

So, I guess break my h and I don't zoned me a tree house cool back t as one of t later... they

So here we local studen where I scor

ruffling my hair and telling me I did a great job. I keep scanning the place for Naomi. She had to run home after the game and said she'd meet me here later. Little does she know I'm Brandon's wingman and I'm going to try to set them up. Does that make me a bad friend? I guess not, especially if they end up married with kids.

Why does that thought bring pain to my stomach? Oh right... because I love him and never in this lifetime will he be mine.

As I swallow, hard, my friend Alysha nudges me. "Are you okay? You're quiet tonight."

I snort. I get it. I'm never quiet. "Just tired," I tell my new roommate. Alysha used to live with Piper, but moved out when Piper got together with Beck. Alysha came here from The Hampton's to study dance, and I like her a lot. She doesn't date, and is practically engaged to a boy back home. She never talks about him, which I find a bit weird. I also find it a bit strange how she's always stealing glances at Ryan. It makes me wonder if—

"I can imagine you're tired," Alysha says, cutting into my thoughts as she raises her beer glass and I click mine to it. "You kicked ass tonight, girlfriend."

I smile. While I do love hockey—heck, my dad was in the NHL—a future in the sport isn't for me. Over the summer, I spent every spare moment studying for the six-hour medical entrance exam. It's no wonder I'm exhausted. But it was worth it because I passed. Now I, along with Naomi, wait for the results of our interviews and whether we've been accepted or not, and I'm nervous as hell. I hold my hands out and examine my nails, which are faring worse than my nerves. I bring my fingers to my mouth and, catching me by surprise, my hand is slapped away from my face.

"What the—"

I look up and find Brandon shoving everyone away so he can sit next to me. "Stop biting your damn nails," he warns for the millionth time, and plunks down next to me, like a bull in a china shop. I shove him, but it does nothing to budge his powerful body as his hard thigh squishes the side of mine.

I shove him again. I realize it's futile, and can't help but think I'm doing it just to touch him. Yes, my friends, I am that pathetic. "Move."

He shifts, and scrubs his hand over his face, and I try to ignore the little shivers rushing over my skin as his scruff of a beard makes a little rustling sound that vibrates through me. It's a familiar habit and I wish I didn't like it so much.

"Hey, Duke."

"B," I respond. We've been calling each other by our nick-names for as long as I can remember. I'm still not sure why he calls me Duke. Maybe it's because he simply sees me as one of the guys, and Daisy is too flowery a name for me. Yeah, we'll never be an item, that's for sure.

But I can't think about that right now, not when he's practi-cally sitting on me, and I like it. I take a quick breath at his closeness and try to pull off casual, but his warm familiar scent of fresh soap and something uniquely Brandon curls around me and messes with my hormones. Good lord, when I'm around him I'm like a dim-witted moth. Not that he'd notice and maybe I'd be horribly embarrassed if he did. When push comes to shove, the last thing in the world I want is to risk losing his friendship. He means everything to me.

"Why are you chewing your nails again?" He takes my hand in his, and his stupid warmth invades my skin and curls around my heart. "I told you, you'll get into medical school." I nod, and he goes quiet, thoughtful before adding, "Want to do something next Wednesday? Go shopping or something? Grab dinner?"

My throat tightens. God, he can be so darn sweet. Next Wednesday is when the interview results come in and I find out if I've been accepted to Dalhousie Medical School here in Halifax. I hadn't mentioned it to him in ages, I don't want to think about it, but he didn't forget the date.

"Yeah, that sounds good," I reply casually. "But you might be on a date with Naomi that day."

His face lights up. "She said yes, she'll go out with me?"

"I'm still working on it. You have a reputation that a professional PR firm with years to spare would have a hard time cleaning up. You gave me—a girl who knows nothing about PR—one week to sell you to Naomi." It was at Piper's birthday celebration that Brandon set eyes on Naomi, and I foolishly agreed to help set them up. Not because I don't think they'll be good together, but because maybe he is ready to settle down, and they might be a great couple. Could I be any more of a masochist?

He takes a swig of beer and a fat drop clings to his bottom lip. He swipes it away with the back of his hand and I try not to stare at his mouth or think about how many times I wondered what it would be like to kiss him—on his lips. Yes, we cheek kiss me all the time. We're pals like that.

"She's not into hookups, B." I stare at him, gauging his reaction, and for a moment he seems like he's a million miles away. "B?"

"Yeah."

"She'll want to go to nice places—places that aren't your bedroom."

"Are you saying my bedroom isn't nice?"

"It's disgusting, but that's another story."

He toys with the label on his beer bottle, his big fingers tugging at the paper and I try not to imagine them toying with my panties in much the same manner.

He arches a brow, looking totally offended. "Then you're saying you think I don't know how to treat a girl."

"Fish eyeballs!" I shoot back.

He laughs. "Well, okay, maybe you're right. I guess it's good that I have you. To get insider information, so I don't mess this up."

"Insider information?"

He shrugs. "Yeah, find out what she likes, what she doesn't... things like that."

"You've really never been on a real date before?" I ask even though I already know he hasn't. He shakes his head. "The first thing you need to know is that on a real date, with a girl you like, you have to put real work in, B. It doesn't just come to you. I realize you had it easy, girls throwing themselves at you, but this is different. Naomi isn't a puck bunny, infatuated with you." How crazy is it that I'm giving advice when I haven't been on a real date either? But I'm a girl, one who doesn't sleep with hockey players, and I know how I'd want to be treated, so maybe I can be of value to him. Okay, and maybe there's a secret girly part that would like to go on a real date with him.

COPYRIGHT

Discover other titles by Cathryn Fox at www.cathrynfox.com. Please sign up for Cathryn's Newsletter for freebies, ebooks, news and contests: https://app.mailerlite.com/webforms/landing/c1f8n1
ISBN: 978-1-989374-56-6
ISBN Print: 978-1-989374-55-9

DAISY

October

Do I believe for one small second that Brandon Cannon, right winger extraordinaire and my very best friend since childhood, is ready to give up the puck bunnies and settle down with a soon to be medical school student?

Uh, how about no, with a capital N.

Which raises the question: why the hell did I agree to be his wingman? Or why am I showing my good friend Naomi Sanders that he's a real catch and that she should give the well-known player—on and off the ice—a chance?

Brain tumor?

Honestly, is there any other explanation? Maybe there's one, and I can't even believe I'm admitting this to myself after all these long and painful years of doing 'buddy' things with

Brandon. But I, Daisy Reed of sound mind and memory, have been in love, for as long as I can remember, with none other than Brandon Cannon.

Okay, there. I said it, and the next thing I need to do is go for a brain scan. I mean, come on, we're talking about a guy who made me eat dirt, a guy who tricked me into touching a fish's eyeball. A FISH'S EYEBALL, for God's sake!

Yeah, he did those things when we were kids. But you know what? He also did good things...great things, even. Like when we were teens on vacation at Wautauga Beach, Washington, where our families had cabins. He saved my ass the night I went to a party at Sebastian Wilson's house. I wasn't allowed to go to the rowdy party at the end of the beach, but I snuck away and did it anyway. When I drank too much, I called Brandon for help. He pretended to be sick right along with me—saying we both ate bad pepperoni on our pizza—claiming it gave us food poisoning. He took me home, and fortunately my parents bought the bad pepperoni story. Brandon stayed in the spare room that night, and kept checking on me every few hours. How could I not love him, right?

So, I guess I owe him this, and despite how much it's going to break my heart to see him with my friend Naomi, Brandon and I don't stand a chance at a future. You see, he friend zoned me a long time ago. I was the only girl allowed in his tree house and the blanket tent, and while I thought it was cool back then, I realize now that the guys all thought of me as one of them. The boobs and the hips that came along later... they didn't faze them one bit.

So here we are many years later, sitting at the Tap Room, the local student drinking hole, after my kick-ass hockey game, where I scored two goals, and the guys—my buddies—are all ruffling my hair and telling me I did a great job. I keep scanning the place for Naomi. She had to run home after the game and said she'd meet me here later. Little does she know I'm Brandon's wingman and I'm going to try to set them up. Does that make me a bad friend? I guess not, especially if they end up married with kids.

Why does that thought bring pain to my stomach? Oh right... because I love him and never in this lifetime will he be mine.

As I swallow, hard, my friend Alysha nudges me. "Are you okay? You're quiet tonight."

I snort. I get it. I'm never quiet. "Just tired," I tell my new roommate. Alysha used to live with Piper, but moved out when Piper got together with Beck. Alysha came here from The Hampton's to study dance, and I like her a lot. She doesn't date, and is practically engaged to a boy back home. She never talks about him, which I find a bit weird. I also find it a bit strange how she's always stealing glances at Ryan. It makes me wonder if—

"I can imagine you're tired," Alysha says, cutting into my thoughts as she raises her beer glass and I click mine to it. "You kicked ass tonight, girlfriend."

I smile. While I do love hockey—heck, my dad was in the NHL—a future in the sport isn't for me. Over the summer, I spent every spare moment studying for the six-hour medical entrance exam. It's no wonder I'm exhausted. But it was worth it because I passed. Now I, along with Naomi, wait for the results of our interviews and whether we've been accepted or not, and I'm nervous as hell. I hold my hands out and examine my nails, which are faring worse than my nerves. I bring my fingers to my mouth and, catching me by surprise, my hand is slapped away from my face.

"What the—"

I look up and find Brandon shoving everyone away so he can sit next to me. "Stop biting your damn nails," he warns for the millionth time, and plunks down next to me, like a bull in a china shop. I shove him, but it does nothing to budge his powerful body as his hard thigh squishes the side of mine.

I shove him again. I realize it's futile, and can't help but think I'm doing it just to touch him. Yes, my friends, I am that pathetic. "Move."

He shifts, and scrubs his hand over his face, and I try to ignore the little shivers rushing over my skin as his scruff of a beard makes a little rustling sound that vibrates through me. It's a familiar habit and I wish I didn't like it so much.

"Hey, Duke."

"B," I respond. We've been calling each other by our nick-names for as long as I can remember. I'm still not sure why he calls me Duke. Maybe it's because he simply sees me as one of the guys, and Daisy is too flowery a name for me. Yeah, we'll never be an item, that's for sure.

But I can't think about that right now, not when he's practi-cally sitting on me, and I like it. I take a quick breath at his closeness and try to pull off casual, but his warm familiar scent of fresh soap and something uniquely Brandon curls around me and messes with my hormones. Good lord, when I'm around him I'm like a dim-witted moth. Not that he'd notice and maybe I'd be horribly embarrassed if he did. When push comes to shove, the last thing in the world I want is to risk losing his friendship. He means everything to me.

"Why are you chewing your nails again?" He takes my hand in his, and his stupid warmth invades my skin and curls around my heart. "I told you, you'll get into medical school." I nod, and he goes quiet, thoughtful before adding, "Want to do something next Wednesday? Go shopping or something? Grab dinner?"

My throat tightens. God, he can be so darn sweet. Next Wednesday is when the interview results come in and I find out if I've been accepted to Dalhousie Medical School here in Halifax. I hadn't mentioned it to him in ages, I don't want to think about it, but he didn't forget the date.

"Yeah, that sounds good," I reply casually. "But you might be on a date with Naomi that day."

His face lights up. "She said yes, she'll go out with me?"

"I'm still working on it. You have a reputation that a professional PR firm with years to spare would have a hard time cleaning up. You gave me—a girl who knows nothing about PR—one week to sell you to Naomi." It was at Piper's birthday celebration that Brandon set eyes on Naomi, and I foolishly agreed to help set them up. Not because I don't think they'll be good together, but because maybe he is ready to settle down, and they might be a great couple. Could I be any more of a masochist?

He takes a swig of beer and a fat drop clings to his bottom lip. He swipes it away with the back of his hand and I try not to stare at his mouth or think about how many times I wondered what it would be like to kiss him—on his lips. Yes, we cheek kiss me all the time. We're pals like that.

"She's not into hookups, B." I stare at him, gauging his reaction, and for a moment he seems like he's a million miles away. "B?"

"Yeah."

"She'll want to go to nice places—places that aren't your bedroom."

"Are you saying my bedroom isn't nice?"

"It's disgusting, but that's another story."

He toys with the label on his beer bottle, his big fingers tugging at the paper and I try not to imagine them toying with my panties in much the same manner.

He arches a brow, looking totally offended. "Then you're saying you think I don't know how to treat a girl."

"Fish eyeballs!" I shoot back.

He laughs. "Well, okay, maybe you're right. I guess it's good that I have you. To get insider information, so I don't mess this up."

"Insider information?"

He shrugs. "Yeah, find out what she likes, what she doesn't... things like that."

"You've really never been on a real date before?" I ask even though I already know he hasn't. He shakes his head. "The first thing you need to know is that on a real date, with a girl you like, you have to put real work in, B. It doesn't just come to you. I realize you had it easy, girls throwing themselves at you, but this is different. Naomi isn't a puck bunny, infatuated with you." How crazy is it that I'm giving advice when I haven't been on a real date either? But I'm a girl, one who doesn't sleep with hockey players, and I know how I'd want to be treated, so maybe I can be of value to him. Okay, and maybe there's a secret girly part that would like to go on a real date with him.

He nods this time and when a plate of cheesy fries is set on the table, he snags one. I try not to stare at his mouth as he takes a bite and holds the cheesiest part out for me. I open my mouth and he feeds it to me.

"You never did tell me what you wanted in return for your help," he reminds me.

The only thing I want in return is him and I can't have it. I sigh and say, "To see you happy, B." He smiles at me, and while this might sound cliché, the truth is, it truly takes my breath away. His hand goes to his temple and he rubs slightly and I narrow my eyes as he frowns. "Are you okay?"

He plasters on a smile, and while it looks genuine, I know him well enough to know something is bothering him. Is he worried about making it into the NHL? Most of the guys are, but most of the guys don't have the kind of pressure Brandon does. His father was one of the greats and Brandon is expected to follow in his footsteps.

"I'm fine," he answer cheerily, and leans into me again. "What about you?" I'm fully aware that he's changing the subject and I'm about to call him on it until he shifts ever so closer and my brain nearly shuts down. Geez, I wish he'd cut it out—I think. "What can I do to make you happy?"

God, if he only knew.

"Naomi is here," I say instead of answering and I lift my hand to wave her over. She comes toward me, dressed in a long pantsuit that looks amazing on her lithe body. Her hair is loose, framing her pretty face, and her makeup is absolutely on point. Everything about her reminds me I have no game— outside of the rink. I do, however get asked out a lot, but I'm beginning to believe it's a competition between the guys now.

I shove Brandon. "Go. I can't say nice things about you if you're sitting right here."

He leans in and gives me a friendly kiss on the cheek. "Thanks, Duke."

"Yeah, yeah, now go."

He stands and everyone grumbles and pushes him as he ambles his way from the booth. He heads to the bar, where our friend Ryan Potter is sitting, and Naomi moves in beside me to take Brandon's place.

"Great game tonight," she tells me, and I grab the pitcher on the table, fill an empty glass with beer, and set it in front of her. "Did I scare Brandon off or something?" she asks.

I laugh at that. "No, he needed to talk to Ryan."

"He's cute, huh?"

Maybe this will be easier than I thought. At the birthday party, she didn't seem to have the time of day for Brandon. I guess maybe she's changed her mind. I've yet to meet a girl who wasn't interested.

"Yeah, he's cute."

"You going to go for it then?" she asks me, and judging from the confused look on her face, I should probably pick my jaw up from the table.

"Me, go for it?"

"You two are always together, and it's easy to see how comfortable you are around one another."

I take a big gulp of beer—like, a huge gulp—hoping I don't say something crazy and give myself away. I set my glass on the table. "We're friends. We go way back." I hold both hands up, palms facing Naomi. "Trust me, there is nothing between Brandon and me." She eyes me, her head angling. She's far from stupid, which makes me want to babble on, and say more to convince her, but she who protests too much...

"Oh, I just thought you liked him."

"I do like him. He's one of my best friends, and I'm so not his type. I'm a tomboy and he's into girly girls, you know." *Stop rambling, Daisy*. I take a breath and go for it. "Actually, it's you he likes."

Her big dark eyes stare at me in disbelief. "Me?"

"Yeah, he's been asking me about you."

She lifts her head and turns to look at Brandon, who is looking back. "I don't think I'm his type either, Daisy. I mean, his reputation..."

"Yeah, apparently, he's played out and is looking for a nice girl...like you."

She puckers her lips and runs her finger over the rim of her glass as she considers my words. "He really told you that?"

"Yup."

She stares at him for another second. "I don't do hook-ups."

"He's not looking for one. You know, underneath it all, he's a pretty great guy."

"Didn't he make you touch a fish's eyeball?"

I can't help but laugh as my mind goes back to that day on the lake. We were sixteen, out on the boat, and he caught a speckled trout. He wanted me to touch the scales and when I did the boat moved and I ended up poking the eyeball, and got so freaked out I jumped up and fell into the water. He abandoned—and lost—the fish when he dove in to save me, and it only solidified my love for him.

I snort. "The story isn't as bad as it sounds."

She turns to me. "I trust you, Daisy. If you think I should go on a date with him, then I will."

I angle my head, catch Brandon's gaze, and if I'm not mistaken, he's a little wobbly on his feet. Was he drinking before he came to the pub? I'm not sure, but something is off about him. Heck, maybe he's in love with Naomi or something and it's messing with him. Lord knows it's messing with me.

"Yeah, I think you should," I say. Just because I mean it doesn't mean I don't hate everything about it.

"Okay, I'm free tomorrow. Next week, I'm away for reading week." She leans into me and her warm vanilla scent fills my senses. "You're a good friend, always helping others. You're a real caregiver, Daisy."

"Yeah, that's me." If I'm thinking about others, I don't have to think about myself—or how I was abandoned as a baby so my biological mother could snag herself a hockey player, one who wasn't my dad. Crazy I know. It was my dad who got her pregnant, but she wanted his best friend. But the simple fact is, I'm a pawn. People use me to get what they want—just like Brandon is doing right now. But he's not all to blame. I agreed to this, because deep down I have horrible abandonment issues and I'm terrified of losing him. One thought dances around inside my brain as I fill my glass up again, wanting to drown out the emotions rising in me.

When it comes to setting up Brandon, I'm damned if I do and I'm damned if I don't.

2

BRANDON

"Thoughts?" I ask Daisy as she snatches a book off my shelf, and plops down on my bed. I spin around and wait for her opinion on my pants and dress shirt.

"Good," she says, as she peels open one of my mother's romance novels. I always buy a copy, wanting to support my mother, and I do read them—skipping over the sex scenes of course, because that's just weird.

"Good?" I huff. "That's all I get?"

Looking exasperated, she drops the book and sits up. "Okay, fine, you clean up nice."

"That's better." I blink as the vision in front of me doubles, and I try not to wobble as vertigo threatens to overcome me. Nausea hits, and I curse under my breath as I try not to run to the bathroom to vomit.

"Do you like it?" I ask.

"I just said you looked nice." Daisy huffs and rolls her eyes again. "Always fishing for compliments."

I laugh, even though it throws me off balance. "No, I'm asking if you liked the book." Daisy always reads my mother's books too, but she doesn't skip the sex scenes, and sometimes when I'm pissing her off—which is a lot—she threatens to tell me about them.

"Have you read that book?" I ask, redirecting her, and she stares at me in the mirror. I shift under her scrutiny, not wanting her to see my dilated eyes. She's going to be a doctor, for Christ's sake. She knows the sign of a concussion when she sees it, and I can't let anyone, or anything, keep me from the game. I've been taking good care of myself, getting rest, and hanging out in the dark whenever I can and next week is reading week, so I'll have lots of downtime. I just need to get through tonight—this date—without incident.

Turning her attention back to the book, she snatches it up and flips it over to read the blurb. "No, is this her latest?"

"Just out last month. You can read it if you want."

She shrugs. "I guess I have nothing better to do tonight."

"You know, Jared has been asking about you." She flips the book open and reads, ignoring me. I laugh. "What is it you have against hockey players again?"

The book drops enough for me to see her pretty blue eyes. "Did you forget my two best friends are players, and not just on the ice."

"Hey, come on, Chase is married now..." I stop to wave my hand over my clothes. "And look at me, all grown up and going on a real date."

"Naomi is smart, B. She's not going to fall for any of your ridiculous lines."

"Maybe you and I should have gone out on a practice date."

She laughs but I'm serious. I'm a little worried that a brilliant, sophisticated girl like Naomi is out of my league. She's a soon to be medical student who probably dates professionals—not hockey players. The guys she goes out with are no doubt well-read and care about their studies more than sports.

What people don't really know about me is that I'm well read and care about my studies too, even though my professors would give me an easy ride. But I want a good education—for private reasons. But no one knows that, not even Daisy, and I'm not about to tell her or anyone why I read my mother's books and care so much about my classes. I have no desire to be the laughingstock of the academy. And honestly my dreams—my true passions—aren't important. I need to make it to the NHL. Not making it, and disappointing my father, would be the worst thing in the world.

"Oh wow, this is spicy," Daisy says, and I put my fingers in my ears when she pretends like she's about to read the scene out loud.

"Stop!"

She laughs, drops the book and stands. Her ponytail bounces as she comes close and I turn to her, our bodies inches apart. A smile touches her lips as she fixes my collar, and runs her hands down the front of my shirt to smooth it out.

"Knock her socks off, B." Her eyes move back to mine. "But not her panties." As soon as the words leave her mouth, her head inches back and she shakes her head. "I just mean that I don't think you should try anything on the first date."

I put my hands on her shoulders, partly to reassure her that I'm not going to jump Naomi's bones, and partly because I'm dizzy again.

"I won't," I promise and because I don't want her noticing the size of my pupils, I lean into her and kiss her cheek. "You're a good friend, Duke."

Did she just suck in a breath?

"The best, you mean."

I inch back to see her, but she's already turning around and picking up my mom's latest romance novel. I don't usually tell people my mom writes sexy books. I'm not sure I could live up to any of the heroes she pens. I'm a good guy, don't get me wrong, and girls know what they get when we hook up, but I want to be a better guy and need to start thinking about my future.

I can't deny that I'm a little jealous of my friends. Most of them are all about serious relationships and family now, and I'm feeling a little lost and left out. Do I think Naomi is the one? I don't know, and if I don't go on a real date, I'll never know. So that is what I'm doing. She's a girl who knows what she wants in life and looks like she has herself together, and Daisy really likes her.

"You should get going. Are you driving or walking?"

"Walking." I'm not sure I'm in any shape to get behind the wheel. I'm really glad Naomi picked a place right around the corner from her place and wanted to meet me there.

"Come on, it's on my way home. I'll walk with you." She tugs her coat on, slides the book into her bag and we head downstairs. Tank is on the sofa in front of the TV, shoving popcorn into his face. It's Saturday night, and since he moved out of

Scotia Storm house and in with me, he's been partying less. I guess the newer generation has taken over the place, and we all seem to be okay with that. Cheddar spends a shit ton of time here too. I think he's as sick of the partying at Storm House as the rest of us.

"Hey Daisy, want to grab a drink later?" he asks.

"As much as I'd love that, Tank, I already have plans."

Tank laughs. "It was worth a shot."

I smile at Daisy. She might not date hockey players—or anyone for that matter; I honestly don't remember the last time I saw her with a guy—but she always lets them down nicely. She's kind like that and there's this weird strange tingling jealousy swirling around in my gut. She's my friend, my closest female friend, and I like having her to myself. Wow, okay, that's a real shitty thought, and I'm a real shitty, selfish guy for even thinking it.

I want to see Daisy happy. She deserves love and happiness like the rest of us, and while we talk about everything under the sun—almost everything, I guess—we never talk about her love life, or lack thereof. I know she puts a lot of focus into hockey and academia, but I'd like to see her enjoying life a little more. She hasn't even asked for anything in return for helping me.

We step outside and the end of October air is cold. Soon enough snow will be flying and I'll be flying back to Seattle to visit the folks for reading week.

"Do you have any plans for next week?" I ask Daisy and when she shivers, I put my arm around her and pull her closer. She sinks into me, a perfect fit, like always.

"Not really. Mom and Dad are vacationing in Mexico. They invited me, but I'm so stressed out about next Wednesday I think I might just stay here and hibernate until I hear if I'm accepted or not."

"You've got this, Duke." She chuckles, and I tug her closer to offer my support.

Her head lifts, her eyes full of questions. "Are you going home?"

"Yeah, actually, I'm headed to the cottage tomorrow."

"Wautauga beach?" I nod and she frowns. "Why did you ask me if I wanted to do something next Wednesday if you weren't going to be here?"

"I would have stayed." I make a fist and give her a fake, best friend punch to the jaw. "That's what friends do." Something moves over her face, something soft and vulnerable—it's not a look I often see on her. "Daisy?"

"That's sweet, B. But not necessary. I'm a big girl." A beat of silence and then, "You're staying at the cottage, not with your family?"

I glance at the pavement and focus on it. I love my family and miss them, but early in my father's career, he was down and out with a concussion, and one look at me and they'll know. Like father, like son, I guess. He went on to do great things after some rest and I know I can too.

"I'll see them, sure. I'm just going to decompress at the beach for a few days." Hopefully that's all it will take to get me up to par.

"Sounds like fun. Maybe you can catch a big fish and touch its eyeballs."

I laugh. "That's no fun without you. Come on, what are you really doing for reading week?"

"Stressing."

"You'll get in, I know it."

She exhales a shaky breath. "Casey graduates from high school this year." It's a statement not a question and a way for her to get the focus off her. "He still planning to go to Stanford?"

I nod as I think about my younger brother, then a laugh bubbles in my throat. "Hard to believe how much that kid hates hockey."

"Like his mom."

I laugh. Growing up my mother hated hockey—even though her brother was in the NHL, and that's how she met my dad. My dad and her brother were best friends. But honestly, I think Daisy would be shocked to realize just how much I'm like my mom. Not in my hate for hockey, I don't hate it, but in my love for other things. But there are some secrets that I won't—can't—share with anyone. I was groomed for hockey and with my little brother wanting to be a software developer —he's an ace at coding—I'm my dad's only hope that that one of his offspring makes it in the NHL.

"Casey might hate hockey. It's the only thing he has in common with Mom, but as far as everything else, you'd think he was adopted, really." I'm joking, making an observation, but as I angle my head to glance at Daisy, I realize the joke has fallen flat. Shit. What a stupid fucking thing for me to say. "Daise..." I begin.

Christ, I know my insensitive words hit a sore spot with her. Even though she was raised and loved by her biological father and his wife, who adopted Daisy as her own, and thinks of her as her own. Her fucking biological mother left her on the doorstep of a hockey player she was trying to trap. She was used as a goddamn pawn, and even though she was too young to remember any of it, that kind of shit stays with you, after you learn about it.

She bumps me, letting me know she's okay, and I stumble a bit on the curb. "Jeez girl, sometimes you don't know your own strength."

She laughs, letting my adoption comment go and I'm grateful it didn't conjure up painful memories. "I do know my own strength. I had to in order to compete with you and Chase and everyone else when we all summered together at the beach."

I laugh, missing those summer days. "Casey is a good kid who knows what he wants, that's all."

I nod in agreement. I like that he chose his own path. As the oldest, I feel the responsibility to follow in Dad's footsteps because I was good at hockey. I hope that somehow paved a way for Casey to be whatever he wanted. That would make it all worth it.

"You know what you want, too," I say.

She eyes me. "So do you right?"

I look straight ahead. "Yeah, of course. Hockey." It's not a lie. I do want hockey. I just want something else—something I can't pursue—more. "The goal is to play for the Seattle Shooters."

"Like your dad did." I nod and her steps slow. She waves ahead to where the restaurant sign is hanging. "Here we are."

"Thanks for walking me, and thanks...you know, for setting this up."

She pokes my chest. "I didn't set it up for you to mess it up."

I shake my head and feign hurt. "You have such little faith in me, Duke."

She jerks her thumb over her shoulder. "I'm going to grab a latte and go read. Text me later."

"Will do."

"If you don't, I'll start texting you snippets of the sex scenes."

"Jesus, Daisy. That is just wrong."

She laughs and I stare after her a second, a huge smile on my face as she bounces away and heads to the coffee shop. Numerous people call out to her, and at the door she meets up with our buddy Cheddar. That's his nickname because he's a ginger. No, it's not an insult. I think he gave it to himself. He chats up Daisy and they step into the little café together, and I turn and walk into the restaurant.

The second I enter, and the bright overhead light shines down on me—instant headache. I tug a bottle of pain pills from my pocket and knock a few down. I glance around the restaurant and find Naomi sitting, watching me. Shit, did she see me take meds? I talk to the hostess and I try carefully to put one foot in front of the other as I walk to the table.

"Hey," I say and drop down into the chair.

"Are you okay?" Naomi asks, her eyes narrowing in on me, much the same way Daisy's had.

I touch my temple and brush it off. "Yeah, just a small headache." Shit, my words sound a bit slurred, like I might have been taking meds, *and* drinking. I can't even imagine what kind of impression I'm making here. Turning the conversation to her, I admire the pretty blue dress she's wearing. "You look really pretty."

She smiles and moves her shoulders, wiggling them happily. If she were standing she'd probably be spinning around right now, which would make me really dizzy. "You look nice too."

"How are you liking the city?" Daisy told me she moved here from British Columbia a short while ago.

"I love Halifax. It's a great city. Daisy tells me you're from Seattle, and your Dad was in the NHL and your mom is a romance novelist."

"Yeah, all true."

"I'll have to read one of your mom's books."

"I have some at my place, if you want to check them out." Shit, wait, did that sound like a pickup? Judging from the way her body is stiffening, I'm guessing it did. I'm about to backtrack but the server arrives and sets the menus in front of us. I blink as the words blur, and order a beer when Naomi asks for white wine. I probably shouldn't be drinking, but I don't want her to think there's something wrong.

The server leaves and I excuse myself to make a quick trip to the bathroom. I splash water on my face and take a few deep breaths to pull myself together. Once the dizziness passes, I head back to the table. People walk by the restaurant and for a second I think I spot Daisy shading her eyes and peering inside. But I must be wrong. She was heading home to read. No way is she peeking into the window of Naomi's favorite Italian restaurant, because that would just be strange behavior. Unless she's watching to see if I mess this up. I focus back on the table, and stutter a little as I try to speak.

The server brings our drinks and before she can take our orders, I reach for my beer bottle, and knock the damn thing over. It spills across the table, and unfortunately, Naomi's dress soaks it up like a paper towel.

Way to do everything wrong so far, dude.

She yelps and jumps up. "I'm sorry," I burst out. "My place is just around the corner..."

She glares at me as she snatches up her napkin. Oh, God, now she thinks I'm trying to get her out of her dress, and that I might have knocked my drink over on purpose.

"I'm going to go."

"I'm sorry, Naomi." She drops her napkin on the table, and I want to tell her I'm not well because of my concussion, but I can't admit that to anyone. "Can I call you?"

"Are you serious?"

"I'm sorry." I pinch the bridge of my nose. "I'm having a bad night."

She pauses for a second. "Are you okay?"

"Yes...no."

Her eyes narrow in on me. "I'm calling Daisy."

"No, don't, please..."

She eyes me for a second longer, and I glance down, averting my gaze. "Do you need a ride home?"

"I think you've had one too many to be driving."

Okay, so she thinks I'm drunk and I can't believe I'm happy about that. But I am because it means she doesn't know it's a concussion.

"No, I walked, but I can get you an Uber."

"I'm good." She pauses for a second. "You might want to go sleep off...whatever this is."

She disappears, and I sit there for a second, trying not to vomit. A few minutes pass and I'm about to pay the bill and get my sorry ass back to my place when Daisy appears before me, concern all over her face.

"Daise..."

She leans into me, a full-on inspection of my eyes. "Jesus, Brandon."

3

DAISY

"**S**he called you, huh?" Brandon says, quietly, looking lost and forlorn as he avoids my gaze, but it's too late. I already saw his dilated pupils, and yeah, I'm mad—at him and myself.

"Who, Naomi?"

"Who else?"

"No, she didn't call me."

"What are you doing here then?"

Dammit, I can't tell him I was hanging around outside to see how their date was going, or that I was fighting down waves of jealousy and envy. "I was walking by and saw Naomi leave, and her dress was soaked. When you didn't surface, and I saw you sitting here with your head down, I came in to see if you were okay, and clearly, you're not." I put my arm under his and help him up. "Why didn't you tell me?"

"Tell you what? That I drank too much?"

"Save it, B. I'm not an idiot."

"I never said you were." He reaches for his wallet. "I need to pay the bill."

"I got it. You can pay me back later." I pull open my wallet and toss some bills on the table. His lids fall a little more as I guide him outside, and we slowly walk back to his place. "I should be walking you straight to a clinic," I grumble, angry that I hadn't noticed his condition earlier. "But I know you wouldn't go." If he hid this from me, and we don't keep secrets—okay well, I have a big one that he doesn't know about—then he's not going to get checked out by a doctor.

"I just need to lay down for a few minutes, then I'll be fine."

"Fine, my ass."

"Are you saying you have a fine ass?" He tries to look over my shoulders and I smack him—gently. "Oh, maybe you're saying I have a fine ass.'

"Not funny."

He snorts. "What happened to your sense of humor?"

"It died with your concussion."

His face twists up in that adorable way that always gets to me, and softens me when I'm mad. "Shit, Daise...don't say anything."

"I won't," I assure him. He has enough to worry about. "For now." If he doesn't get better, it's not a promise I can keep.

I use the key he gave me ages ago to let us in, and I stay by his side as I walk him up the stairs and into his bedroom. He plops on his bed, and puts his forearm over his head and I let my gaze move down his long stretched out body. Okay, now is not the time to be admiring my best friend's physique. Not when he just bungled a date he was really looking forward to and is laid up with a head injury.

Any other time, sure, fine. Just not tonight.

I walk to his closet and close the door tightly. I have a weird thing about open closet doors when going to sleep, thanks to all the scary movies Brandon, Chase and the others made me watch.

"Still afraid of the boogeyman?" he teases.

"Careful, B. Didn't anyone ever tell you that you should always be nice to the girl who's taking care of you...and cooking for you."

"Hey, when aren't I nice to you? Wait, you're going to cook for me? You hate cooking."

I just laugh and untie his shoes and tug them off. His socks are next and I'm not a foot person, but his toes are kind of cute. He falls quiet. "You okay?"

"I really fucked it up with Naomi, didn't I?"

"If she's who you really want, I'll talk to her." He goes quiet again, and I glance at him. "She's who you want, right?" Why on earth am I holding my breath, hoping he gives me a different answer.

"Yeah," he mumbles.

"You need some rest." I pull his blinds closed, and darken the room. "Can you get undressed or do you need me to help?"

"Help, please."

I huff like undressing the hottest man on the planet is a hardship. It's not. I pop the button on his pants, and his boxers start sliding down with the pants as I tug. I try not to stare at his delicious oblique muscles or the light trail of hair that leads to the promised land. Except I'm one of the few women on campus who has yet to find great happiness in Brandon's garden of Eden, and it's likely to never happen in the future either.

I get his pants off, leaving him in his boxer shorts and he just lays there waiting for me to unbutton his shirt. "I know you're not that useless, B."

"Fine."

He starts unbuttoning at the top and I start at the bottom and I try not to react every time my knuckles brush his hard muscles. There's nothing I can do however, to keep the heat he's stirring up inside me, from flushing my cheeks. I'm glad it's dark in the room.

Once I have him naked, save for his boxers. I lift the blankets. "Get in."

He shifts on the bed, and I'm about to cover him when his strong arm wraps around my body and he pulls me down.

"You have to stay."

I land with a thud, and he turns me, his body a big spoon to my little spoon, and I'm pretty sure I no longer know how to breathe. I close my eyes, not wanting to think about how many women he's had in this bed—and how it was never me.

"Why do I have to stay?"

"Come on, you're the doctor."

"Not yet," I remind him and try to move but he wiggles against me to hold me closer and I like it, a lot.

"Remember when they were worried Kennedy's daughter had a concussion and they had to check on her every few hours."

"I remember."

"Come on, help a friend out, Daise..." God, when he says it like that. "I need someone to check on me..."

Once again his words remind me that I'll forever be friend zoned. "As your very best friend, I'll keep an eye on you and keep your secret, unless it gets worse and you need real medical attention."

"Thanks, Duke."

"Shouldn't we at least make a pillow wall?" I wait for an answer, but the room falls silent and a moment later his breath is warm on my neck as his breathing slows and he drifts off to sleep. I exhale and since my body is a jittery mess of nerves, I practice breathing exercises and will myself to fall asleep. Like that's going to happen. The hottest guy on the planet is half naked behind me, with his arm around me, and I'm supposed to play it casual.

Not that I'd know what to do if he wanted to have sex. I mean I know a thing or two—in theory. God, how am I still a virgin? Oh, probably because the only guy I've ever wanted has never wanted me in return, and every other guy has paled in comparison. I'm going to have to work extra hard to get him together with Naomi. Once he's in a serious, committed relationship, maybe it will knock some sense into me and help me move on.

He makes a noise in his sleep and moves closer. Wait is that... OMG!! He's sticking me with his...parts. Well, one part in particular. He's clearly having some amazing dream, and I'm pretty sure I'm not the star of it. I try to move away as his erection grows and nestles against my backside. Wow, it's kind of impressive really. Not that I have anything to compare it to—in real life anyway. Okay, fine, I've watched a bit of porn on my laptop, until I got a virus and almost died when the technician chuckled quietly to himself, knowing exactly what I'd been up to.

Where's a pillow wall when you need it?

I shift, and ever so slowly, slide out from beneath his arm and set it on my pillow. I tuck him in, and tip toe to his desk chair. I drop into it, checking my phone to find a dozen or so messages from Naomi. She really wasn't impressed tonight, telling me Brandon showed up drunk and was taking pills.

I glance around the dark room, my stomach tight. I promised I'd keep his secret and I can't tell her what's really going on. Instead, I message her back and let her know he wasn't himself tonight and that he's a really good guy. I ask if she'll give him another chance and she answers that she'll think about it.

As I consider that, I think about ways I can help Brandon get his girl. At first, he asked me to pretend to be his girlfriend to show Naomi not all hockey players are jerks who sleep around. I decided against it, and took a different path, and simply built him up in her eyes, but now, after he screwed up the date, maybe I went about it all wrong. I should be fake dating him, teaching him how to treat a lady and that he should reschedule when he's ill, and dizzy with a concussion, to avoid disaster like tonight.

I do a quick search on my phone, once again convinced I'm a masochist, but go ahead with my plan anyway. Once that's done, I turn on my flashlight app, grab the book Brandon lent me, and settle in to read.

An hour passes and I stand, about to check on Brandon when he moans and jackknifes up. "Daisy," he begs his voice thick and deep. Everything inside me goes on high alert, and I drop my book and aim my flashlight app at him. "Jesus, don't."

Instantly realizing the light might have made things worse for him, I shine it on the floor and hurry to him. "Are you okay?"

He gulps. "Bathroom."

I help him off the bed, and he leans on me as I rush him from his bedroom, hurrying him down the hall to the bathroom. I'm about to flick the light on and stop. Instead, I shine my light on the floor to guide his way. He drops down onto his knees in front of the toilet, and starts vomiting. Worry wells up inside me. I sink to the floor next to him and rub his back. Thank God he has the next week off. If he doesn't improve, he'll have to seek proper medical help.

He groans and goes back on his heels. I jump up, flush the toilet, and race to the kitchen to get him water and grab a cloth from the hall closet. He's on the floor, knees bent, his back against the wall when I come back.

"Hey," he groans, his voice tired, and low.

"Rinse your mouth." He takes the glass, rinses his mouth, spits, and when he settles against the wall again, I press the cold cloth to his forehead and flush a second time.

"That feels good." He leaves the cloth on his head and tilts his face upward. "You don't have to stay. I shouldn't have asked."

"I'm your best friend, doing what best friends do, so shut up already."

A long, silent moment passes, and he turns to me. I reach out and adjust the cloth on his forehead. "I have to play, Daisy. You know that."

My heart squeezes tight. I realize the pressures he has on him, the pressures he puts on himself. It's not easy being the children of NHL superstars. Less expectations were put on me because I'm a girl—ridiculous, I know—but for Chase and Brandon and all the other guys in our NHL family circle, life is hard.

"You'll play, Brandon. I'll make sure of it. That's why I'm flying to Washington with you tomorrow."

His eyes go wide as surprise registers on his face. "Yeah?"

Oh, God that look, that sweet, adorable look on his face takes me back to when we were kids, and he taught me to ride my bike without training wheels. When I nailed it, he was so happy, he gave me a great big hug.

"Yes."

"Wait, no." He puts his elbows on his knees and holds his forehead. "I can't ask you to do that." His eyes meet mine in the dark. "I'm a big boy."

"Way to throw my words back at me, but you're not asking, I'm offering, and this is far different than me waiting to hear if I'm accepted to med school or not."

"Not really. That decision affects the rest of your life, and if I don't get better, the rest of my life is affected too."

Okay, he's right. The worst thing that could happen to me is I don't make it, and the worst thing that could happen to him is he gets cut from the team, and the truth is, I'd love to have him by my side when the acceptance notices start going out.

"I'm going."

He reaches out and takes one of my hands into his and simply holds it. "You're a good friend."

"I know." A beat passes between us and I say, "I was also thinking about that proposal you made at the birthday party." He frowns like he doesn't remember. "You asked me to pretend to be your girlfriend to show Naomi not all hockey players were, well...players."

"What were you thinking?"

"While we're away, we could do things that real couples do."

"But Naomi won't be there to see it."

"No, but we can go on dates and things like that, and I can tell you when you do something she might like and when you do something stupid—like going on a date when you're not well."

He groans. "Not my best move."

I laugh and lean into him and he throws his arm around me. "Do you even have any moves?"

He chuckles and I'm about to tell him he has at least one, and it's the way he's holding me to his body. "Maybe not. Do you?"

"I don't think I do." We both laugh, and I say, "All I can tell you is what a girl who isn't infatuated with hockey players might like and might not like when on a date."

"Why the hell couldn't Naomi be infatuated with hockey players?"

"Because you don't want that, right? You're looking for the real deal."

"Yeah, I'm looking for the real deal." His arm tightens around me. "I'm pretty sure Naomi is never going to go out with me again, though."

"I'll do what I can."

"In the meantime, it looks like it's just you and me Daisy, learning things together."

"Guess so," I answer quietly, and try not to think about how grooming my best friend to get the girl he wants will either help me get over him, or be my demise...

4

BRANDON

"Holy fuck!" I sit up fast, my head spinning and it's not from my concussion. Nope, my rattled brain isn't spiraling out of control because I hit my head one too many times—it's spinning because my mind went down a path it never should have gone.

I swallow, hard and slowly turn my head to my right, and my heart beats even faster when I spot a sleepy Daisy coming to life—fast.

"B," she says, panic in her voice as she sits up and puts her warm hand on my bare chest. Her touch travels all the way through my body to curl around my hard cock.

What the hell is happening to me?

"Are you okay. Are you sick?" She wipes her eyes and is about to climb from the bed, no doubt to hurry me to the bathroom again.

Before she can put her feet on the floor, I blurt out, "I just had a sex dream...about you." She gulps loudly, clearly horrified by the thought and I shake my head and try to back-track. "I mean, I think it was you. You were in it, anyway."

She was in it all right. She was the star of the show and I have no idea why I just blurted that out. Although it could be because it surprised the hell out of me. I've never had sex dreams about Daisy before. Well maybe once, when I was going through puberty, but that was a long time ago. She's my best friend, and there's a line I'm not going to cross. Not just because she doesn't think of me like that, but because I am not about to jeopardize what we have. She's far too important to me.

"I...I was in it?" Her voice is low, unsure, and I grip the blankets, and let the cotton absorb the moisture from my hands.

Trying for casual, I answer with, "Yeah, maybe you were like a secondary character or something."

Her nose crinkles, and her blue eyes narrow. "Like I was the third in a threesome or something."

I laugh but it comes out harsh and strangled. Why did I have to open my big mouth? "No, I'm not into threesomes."

She pulls the blankets up to her chin, covering her body. "Was I naked in this dream?"

Naked and on full display.

"You know what, it's fading now. I can't even recall it."

Oh, but I can, and it was sinful, and unbelievable.

"Oh, okay. Maybe your concussion is messing with you."

"Yeah, that has to be it." I snort like an idiot. "How crazy would that be, right?" *Shut up, Brandon. Shut your mouth right now.* "You and me, you know...doing it."

"Craziest thing I've ever heard," she says, her cheeks turning a bright shade of pink. Dammit, it takes a lot to embarrass Daisy, and I hate how awkward I've suddenly made things between us. But yeah, I get it, she's mortified that I had a sex dream about her.

"Right, okay, let's get moving." I shove my blankets off, and that's when I realize my early morning boner is on display. Jesus, could this day get any more embarrassing? I toss my feet over the side of the bed to hide my erection, but I'm pretty sure it's too late for that. "Our flight is in a few hours."

"I need to go home and pack, but I don't want to leave you alone."

"Let me throw some things together and then we'll go to your place, but first coffee."

"Yes, please..."

I glance over my shoulder as my cock jumps as she whispers those two simple words. Why the hell am I suddenly picturing Daisy beneath me moaning...*yes, please...?* Holy shit, I need to get myself together. My concussion is clearly messing with me if I'm thinking about Daisy in my bed, naked. She stands, and my eyes follow along as she snatches up her phone and circles the bed.

"Coming?" she asks, when I remain motionless.

Oh, if she only knew.

Get your shit together, bro.

I try to work out some math problem in my brain, anything to get my dick to deflate. To buy myself some time, I gesture to the door. "You run to the bathroom first." She nods, and I'm grateful to be left alone with my erection. It needs a good scolding. Once my dick shrinks, I adjust my boxers, grab my suitcase from my closet and start tossing things in.

Daisy reappears, her hair a mess of curls that she tries to tame with her fingers. "I couldn't find a brush."

I point to my dresser. "Will a comb do?"

As she walks across my room, I dart to the bathroom and once done, I head down to make coffee, but Daisy is already in the kitchen chatting it up with Cheddar. He's here so often he should be paying rent, but I don't mind. Mom and Dad bought this house as an investment, and plan to rent it once I'm done with school.

"When do I get an invitation to the cottage?" he asks as I step into the kitchen.

I shrug. "You're welcome to come anytime."

"Hey," Daisy pipes in. "Maybe we can send an invite out to everyone for next weekend." She nudges me. "You know, for when the Wautauga Beach association does the big summer closing bash on the lake. Everyone could join in for one last blowout before we all have to come back for exams. We could accommodate everyone at the cottages so it would only cost airfare." I hadn't planned on taking part in the activities, not with a concussion, and since, before last night, Daisy had no plans to go to Seattle—and it's always more fun with her there—I didn't feel like I was missing out.

"Great idea," Cheddar agrees. "I'm down for a blowout."

Daisy eyes him, her brow arched because he put way too much emphasis on the word blow, and he just gives her a grin. She turns to me, and her face goes serious. "If you're up for it, that is."

Cheddar scoffs. "Why the hell wouldn't he be up for it?"

"No reason at all," I tell him.

"That's my man." Cheddar makes a fist and holds it out to me. I fist bump him and he says, "Brandon is always up for a bash. At least he used to be when we lived on campus. Hey, how come we don't have any house parties anymore?"

Daisy hands me a big mug of black coffee and I take a big slurp of it. Instead of answering Cheddar, who clearly isn't quite as played out as I am, I murmur, "I'll shoot the group a message and send out invites."

"Don't forget to send one to Naomi," Cheddar says, and fist bumps his own hands together this time. I just roll my eyes at him, and turn to Daisy.

"She'll probably come, if I ask her," Daisy tells me. "She's in British Columbia next week so it wouldn't be far for her to go."

I nod and take another big drink of my hot coffee. "Okay."

Cheddar leaves the kitchen, and Daisy leans into me. "Then you can try out all the new moves we'll learn over the next week."

I chuckle and to be honest, I'm not sure if I'm more excited to fake date Daisy or really date Naomi. What I do know is we need to get a move on it. "We better go."

We hurry outside, and I toss my bag into the back as she slides into the driver's seat. I settle in beside her, and even though I usually drive, I know better than to argue. She drives to her place, which isn't very far from mine. It's busy downtown, everyone headed to the waterfront market on this warm Saturday morning.

"I'll be right back."

"I'll give you a hand to carry your bag," I say and step from the car.

"I'm capable of carrying my own bag, Brandon."

"I know you are, and I'm capable of helping you. It's the least I could do after you spending the night to help me."

"Yeah, I guess. It was quite the hardship."

Hard being the key word, but I keep that to myself. We reach the door, and she puts her finger to her lips. "Alysha is probably still sleeping. She's flying home later today to spend the week with her boyfriend. They're practically engaged."

"If she's practically engaged, why is Ryan's truck parked across the street?"

She turns, her eyes wide. "Ohmigod, you don't think..." Her words fall off as the door yawns open and as we step inside, and I see Ryan on the sofa, I point.

"Yeah, I do think."

Daisy bites her bottom lip, and I can almost hear her brain going a million miles an hour. "I'm going to need all the details on that," she says, staring at a sleeping Ryan, his body far too big for the sofa.

We go up to her room quietly, avoiding all the creaking steps —yes, I've been here enough to know which ones make noise. In her room, she gets her suitcase from her closet.

"Are your mom and dad going to be upset that you're coming with me and not going to Mexico?"

She rolls one shoulder. "What they don't know won't hurt them."

I sit on her bed next to her open suitcase and she opens her drawers and starts tossing things in. I'm about to flop down and wait until her white lace panties land on my lap.

"Oh, sorry."

I pick up the panties and twirl them around my finger. "Wow, my little tomboy wears white lace." I shake my head. "And here I thought I knew everything about you."

She walks over to me, snatches them from my finger and tosses them in the suitcase. "There are things you don't know." She tucks the panties under her pajamas. "Things that might surprise you."

Intrigued, I sit up a little straighter. "Really, like what?"

Why the hell am I baiting her? This is Daisy, and we don't flirt. Like ever.

She gathers her hair and ties it into a ponytail. "Not your business."

"Come on, tell me." Wanting to get a rise out of her, I dig in her suitcase and find her panties. "What don't I know about Daisy Reed?"

"Things..."

I laugh. "Nah, I don't believe you."

"I don't care."

"Yeah, you do. Come on, tell me."

"No."

"I'll tell you something about me you don't know." What the hell am I saying. I am not telling her my biggest, darkest secret. I do not want to be ridiculed.

Would she ridicule you, Brandon?

I don't know, probably not, but I'm not taking that chance.

"You're an open book, Brandon. The only secret you had was your concussion and now I know all about that."

I shrug, and give in, letting her believe she's right. "Is there a guy in Seattle you're looking to hook up with? Is that why you're packing sexy panties?"

"Maybe, maybe not." She turns to me and if looks could kill, I'd be a dead man. She marches back to me, and snatches the panties. "What is your problem? I know you've seen white lace panties before, plenty of times."

"I've never seen yours."

"If you like these so much, maybe you should buy yourself a pair." She tucks them back into her suitcase and mumbles something about my concussion doing weird things to my personality, and that's when I realize she might be right. I also realize that I could try to hook up with my best friend and if it didn't work out, I could blame it on the injury.

But that would be too risky, and when it comes to Daisy, I can't risk losing her. I just wish I hadn't had that stupid dream, because now I can't stop imagining what it'd be like to have her in my bed, beneath me.

She opens her nightstand and pulls out her birth control pills. She tosses them into the suitcase and glares at me. "Do you have something to say about that too?"

"Nope, just glad you're being careful."

"I use them to regulate my cycle." I angle my head, and then as if it's an afterthought, she adds, "And well, you know, for safety."

When I think about it, really think about it, I realize there is a part of me that knows she's not been with anyone—ever. I've never met a guy who wasn't interested in her, and while she's always nice to everyone, I'm almost certain she's never hooked up.

She reaches into her nightstand for something else, and I tug her until she's on my lap. "Hey Daise...If you're into girls, that's cool."

She rolls her eyes so hard she gives me a headache. We've talked about everything under the sun over the years, but her sexual preferences never came up. Mine are well known and documented. "I'm not, you big dummy."

"You can tell me."

"I'm not, B." Her voice is strained, full of frustration, her eyes pleading me to believe her when she adds, "There's this guy that I..." Her words fall off and she swallows as she shakes her head, and her ponytail whacks my face.

"Do I know him?"

Wait, is that jealousy coursing through my blood? Jesus, it shouldn't be. What right do I have to be jealous? She's my best friend, and I've been with dozens of girls. I can't be upset if she wants to be with some guy. Okay, yeah it's totally true. I am a selfish bastard, wanting Daisy for myself, wanting her to always be there for me when I need her. Have I been there for her too? Have I been a shitty best friend? Fuck, maybe I haven't been a good friend.

She pushes to her feet. "It doesn't matter. He's not interested."

"Make him interested." I take her hand in mine and give it a squeeze as I push back the jealousy and work to be a real best friend by putting her needs first. "I could talk to him, build you up like you did for me with Naomi."

She gives an unladylike snort. "You said it yourself, B. I'm a tomboy." Is that sadness in her eyes? "Guys on the hockey team go for puck bunnies, and look at me, I'm anything but."

"You're gorgeous, Daisy. Everyone loves you." Wait, what did she just say? I jump up, and wobble a bit. Daisy reaches out and puts her hand on my arm. "You're telling me it's someone on the hockey team that you like?"

She curses under her breath, like she's given too much away, and retorts, "No, I didn't say that."

"I think you did."

She lightly taps the side of my head. "And I think your concussion is messing with your hearing."

"There's nothing wrong with my hearing, Duke."

"Then it's messing with your understanding."

I slowly shake my head. "Nope, don't think so."

She puts one hand on her hip, frustration on her face. "Did anyone ever tell you how annoying you can be?"

"Yeah, you have, many times, and we have a long plane ride ahead of us. Which means I have hours to interrogate you and find out who you're crushing on."

She closes her suitcase and nearly tears the zipper as she tugs it shut with more force than necessary. I grin at her and take the suitcase from her hand.

She shakes her head and mumbles under her breath, "Dear God, I truly am a masochist."

5

DAISY

"If you keep it up, your concussion isn't the only thing that's going to lay you up." I glare at Brandon, and the grin he gives me in return nearly turns me inside out. No man deserves to be that hot—without even trying—and damn my body for reacting.

He nudges me with his broad shoulder, and deep between my legs, I vibrate with want. "I'll cut it out when you tell me his name."

I walk to the luggage carousel and cross my arms. Brandon practically spent the entire flight from Halifax to Seattle trying to get the name of my crush. There were times however, that he was so engrossed in his laptop, tapping away on the keyboard furiously, that I'm sure he didn't even know I was beside him. It's crazy to think how fast he went from playful to serious—like he had some sort of epiphany and had to write it down, which made me wonder what he was working on, and honestly, I never knew he could type so fast.

It looked like he had a Word document open, although he wouldn't tell me what he was doing, and he even turned his laptop away from me so I couldn't see the screen. No doubt he was typing out the names of the guys on his team, going through the roster trying to discover who I might like. Maybe I should just tell him it's Tank or Cheddar, or someone... anyone. Maybe then he'd leave me alone. What am I saying? If he knew who it was, he wouldn't leave me alone. Unless of course he knew it was him, then I could probably kiss our friendship goodbye. But I don't want to just give him a name. He'd likely do his best to try to set us up, and I can't risk him telling a guy I like him when I don't.

Damn you, Brandon.

A loud buzzer cuts through my dark thoughts, and the carousel starts turning. Everyone starts pushing in closer, and Brandon stands by me, an immovable force, preventing anyone from knocking me over. I sigh like a teen with a schoolgirl crush. But you can see why I like him so much?

He finds our luggage and pulls them from the belt. I reach for mine, but he extends the handle and brushes my hand away. I don't argue. I should, since he's the one with the concussion, but when Brandon sets his mind to something, there's usually no changing it.

"Are we getting an Uber?" I ask, as we make our way outside.

"Yeah, for now. Once I'm feeling better, I'll borrow Dad's car. I didn't want to rent something and risk getting lightheaded on the drive."

I lift my chin an inch. "I have a license you know, and I'm quite capable of driving."

"I didn't know you were coming until last minute."

"True."

People stare and point and talk in whispered words as he pulls out his phone and gets us an Uber. Sometimes I forget that he's so well known—not just because he's a great hockey player, but because his dad was in the NHL. I don't get the same fanfare as he does, and I'm okay with that. A group of girls take pictures of him and he takes it all in stride as our car pulls up to the sidewalk. The driver and Brandon put our luggage in the trunk and I hop into the back seat with our backpacks.

Brandon's laptop is sticking out, and I glance over my shoulder, and consider taking a peek at what had him so focused. I'm not sure I'd ever seen him concentrate so hard outside of the rink. Before I can open it, he slides in beside me, his big body eating up the back seat.

"Move over." I shove him but he doesn't budge and honestly it's insane how much I like the way our legs touch.

"Be nice, I have a concussion," he whines.

"First you hide it from me, and now you're embracing it just to get sympathy."

"I do what I can."

The driver eases the car into traffic, and Brandon and I fall silent. I briefly close my eyes, tired after the long flight and Brandon puts his arm around me and pulls me to him so I can sleep on his shoulder. I breathe in the scent of his skin and put my hand on his chest, reveling in his strong heartbeat beneath my palm. I'm anxious to get to the cottage, but I like being held like this so much I don't want the drive to end.

He lightly brushes my hair from my face, and I moan as he runs his fingers through it, the way I like. It's true, Brandon knows a lot of things about me, but there is one thing he can never know.

I drift off as he holds me, and the next thing I know his mouth is close to my ear, his breath warm on my face. "We're here," he whispers quietly, and I sit up and blink my eyes back into focus. As soon as I see the cottages coming into view, and the wide expanse of sandy beach, warm memories bombard me and a sense of contentment curls through my blood.

"I love it here," I murmur as the crashing sea soothes my soul and washes away most of my worries. My gaze searches the other cottages, and I spot Sebastian Wilson. We've hung out many times over the years. He goes to Penn State and it looks like he's back for reading week too—and the year-end blowout. It was his party I snuck away to all those years ago when Brandon covered for me.

"Me too." I turn to Brandon, and that's when I realize I'd spoken out loud. "You're staying in my cottage, right?" he asks.

I laugh. "I never even thought that far ahead." Our family cottage is two doors down from his, and I do have a key, but I'm here to keep an eye on Brandon.

"You can't nurse me back to health two doors down."

"Ohmigod, you're really going to milk this, aren't you?"

He holds his fist up and starts lifting one finger at a time as he lists things off. "I figure I need a cook, a cleaner, a doctor, someone to sponge—"

I hold my hand up and cut him off. "I am not sponging anything."

He laughs, and when the Uber comes to a stop in front of his cottage, he opens the car door, and the salty air washes over me. He climbs out and his chest expands as he breathes in. I try not to stare, but that's like asking a fish not to swim.

I glance at Brandon and frown. "Did I pack my bathing suit?" After he toyed with my panties, I was so frazzled I wasn't even sure what I was tossing in my suitcase.

He wags his brow. "Your panties will be fine." I stare at him for a moment. Is my best friend flirting with me, or am I reading this all wrong? I've seen him in action with other girls, he just never really turned on the charm with me before, and I don't know what to make of it. He doesn't see me as anything more than a friend—his buddy Duke—and I'm his wingman where Naomi is concerned. He straight up asked me to hook them up. This strange change in personality has to have something to do with his concussion. Either that or he's suddenly, miraculously, seeing me as more than a tomboy. But I'm sure that's just wishful thinking on my part.

He tosses his arm over my shoulder and we stand there as the Uber drives off and simply stare at the ocean. Cottage country is much different in October. Most people have packed up and gone home for the school year, but a few stragglers remain, and many do come back for the last weekend for the big blowout. Luckily for us, the forecast calls for a gorgeous week of sunshine. The rainy season is holding off and for that I'm grateful.

"Let's get you to bed."

Brandon grins at me. "You're not even going to buy me a drink first?"

"God, you're so annoying."

I push off his body reluctantly, and snatch his keys from his hand. I head to the front door, slide the key in and open it. Brandon comes up the stairs behind me, carrying our luggage. He turns off the alarm system, kicks the door shut as he crowds me in the hall.

I take in his weariness, and concern gnaws at me. I'd never forgive myself if there were long term repercussions that could have been avoided by seeing his doctor. I could try to force the issue, but short of carrying him to the emergency department myself, I'm pretty certain I'm not going to get him there and I honestly do think he just needs rest.

"Are you going to call your parents?" A deep sense of sadness, or worry, comes over him, and I put my hand on his arm. "You're going to be okay, B. A week of rest and you'll feel better. If not, we'll deal with it then." As I say the words to him, in my heart I really hope they're true. This man has a lot of pressure on his shoulders, and as his best friend, yes, I'm going to cook for him, clean for him, and sponge...no wait, I draw the line at sponging anything. As much as I might enjoy that, I'm his wingman for God's sake, helping him get another woman, so no, sponging is off the table.

"Maybe later. Let me take these to our rooms first."

I grab my suitcase and start up the stairs before he can protest. He stomps up behind me, and I stand outside Casey's room. "Do you think he'll mind if I crash here?"

"What he doesn't know won't hurt him, and of course he won't mind. He loves you too."

Too...

Yes, I know Brandon loves me, just not the way I want him to.

God, get over it, girl.

"Hungry?" he asks me.

"That little bag of pretzels on the plane didn't cut it for you?" I ask and laugh as his stomach takes that moment to grumble.

"I'll order us a pizza. I need to check the cupboards too. I can make a trip to the grocery store."

"I can do it," he says his voice tired and lacking conviction.

I stand and walk up to him as he hovers in the doorway and poke his chest. "You...need rest."

He yawns, and I note the dilation in his eyes. It sends shards of worry to my heart. "Are you sure it was a good idea to invite everyone here next weekend?"

"It seemed like a good idea at that moment." He wags his brow in that playful way. "That way, I'll have the home ice advantage."

I stare at him for a second, not understanding. "Oh, you mean with Naomi?"

"Yeah, with you showing me the ropes this week, I'll be able to try my new moves on her, on my own turf, and really be able to impress her."

"You never told me ropes were going to be involved, B." My God, now I'm the one flirting. Maybe I should check myself out for a concussion. I did get hit pretty hard last game. But no, I can't use that as an excuse for my odd behavior. Right?

It takes him a second to figure out what I'm saying and when he finally clues in, he laughs and steps closer. "You're the one who's showing me how to properly treat a girl who isn't infatuated with hockey players, so ropes or no ropes, that's entirely up to you."

Ropes! I want ropes!

"There will be no ropes," I tell him pointedly, and pray to God my cheeks aren't turning red and giving me away. "But hey, playing on your own turf is smart." I put my hand on his chest. Honestly, I really need to stop touching him. "Your team always wins when you have the home ice advantage."

"I plan to win, Duke." He waves his phone. "I'd guess I'd better let my parents know we're here. I'll tell them we're decompressing and will stop by in a couple days."

"I'll order pizza."

"Hawaiian with extra cheese," he blurts out. "From Mario's. I've been craving it since last summer."

I shake my head. "You and your Hawaiian pizza from Mario's."

"We can get a different kind if you want."

"No, what the sick boy wants the sick boy gets," I say, and sigh heavily like it's a hardship, but it's not. I like pizza, all pizza.

He leaves my room and the wheels on his suitcase rattle as he drags it across the hall to his bedroom. I stand still for a second after his door shuts, then I dig into my suitcase and pull out a pair of shorts and a V-neck T-shirt. I glance at the ocean, and consider taking a swim to cool down my hot body, but first, food.

I step into the hall and hear Brandon on the phone with his folks. I should probably let mine know I'm here too. Brandon's voice is joyous, and I can't help but think he's putting on a show for his family, not wanting them to know the real reason he's here. I'm glad I figured it out—although I'm still mad that he didn't tell me. But Brandon needs a friend right now. I'll neuter him for keeping his concussion from me when he's better.

Moving quietly, I tiptoe downstairs, check the cupboards and the fridge, which are both mostly empty. I grab a pint of ice cream from the freezer and jam a spoon into it and surf through my phone to find Mario's and order our pizza.

As I wait for it to arrive, I walk around the cottage that I know so well. I grin as I enter the living room, my heart full of happiness as I reminisce about the fort tents we all used to make. There is no doubt we all had a great childhood, and I'm glad we all have each other as we navigate our college years.

I hang out downstairs and walk to the floor-to-ceiling bookshelf as I wait for Brandon to join me. I grin as I scan all the romance novels on the shelf. One thing is for sure, Brandon's mother is a prolific writer. I run my fingers over the spines as I read the titles and tug one that looks promising—maybe because it has a friends-to-lovers trope—off the shelf to read later. It's funny, his mom does love that particular trope. Maybe because she was friends with her husband before they fell in love—although according to Cole Cannon, he says his wife Nina hated him at first. I would love to hear their true story.

I take in the hot couple on the cover. Hmm, maybe reading a hot romance in bed, when the guy who fills all my fantasies is between the sheets in the room across from me—dreaming about another girl—might be my undoing.

The doorbell rings, and I hurry to get it, and the delicious scent of Hawaiian pizza with extra cheese fills my nose as I open the door and pay the delivery driver. Darkness has fallen over cottage country as I carry the pizza to the kitchen and stare at the doorway. Is Brandon still on the phone? I walk to the foot of the stairs and listen for sound, but it's dead quiet.

Did he...pass out?

My heart jumps into my throat and I take the stairs two at a time. I try to push back the panic as I hurry to his room. His door is ajar, and I nudge it, and find him flat out on his bed. His breathing is soft and even, and I step closer to him. I consider waking him, but I think sleep is the answer to helping him heal.

His laptop is open beside him, and I lift it, so he doesn't roll on it or knock it off his bed. It comes to life as I carry it to his small desk, and without really meaning to, I glance at the open document. Okay, it's possible I'm nosy—err, curious— and I really truly didn't mean to snoop. My gaze scans the words, and as my brain speeds up, air tangles in my lungs. Taking in a breath becomes almost impossible as I read faster, the room spinning before my eyes. What the hell am I reading? I work to slow my racing thoughts, to piece the sentences together and comprehend the words on the screen.

Wait...is Brandon...oh my God, he is!

6

BRANDON

"**B**randon," Daisy whispers, her voice low, saturated with lust and need. I moan, and turn, and her hand lands on my chest. "B?" she gasps again, and this time there's something else in her voice, something trying to break through my addled thoughts, but I won't let it, not yet.

"Yeah," I murmur, some part of my brain registering that I'm still dreaming, and Daisy is not sitting on my bed, her hot hand pressed against my hard, needy body.

"Are you hungry?" she asks, and my dick twitches, because yeah, I'm hungry...hungry to taste her mouth, or between her legs. Lick every fucking inch of her.

"I'm hungry." I reach for her, and pull her to me and there's nothing gentle in my greedy touch. Her mouth crashes against mine and I grab a fistful of her hair, tugging harder than I normally would, but I'm all twisted upside down, a hot mess overflowing with an unfamiliar need for my best friend.

But this is a dream, and I can do whatever the fuck I want. I eat at her mouth with a hunger that defies logic, plunging my tongue inside to taste the delicious depths of her. Ever since my last sex dream—and where the hell are these coming from —I can't seem to stop thinking about her, craving her. It's wrong, all kinds of wrong, but in my dreams, it's so goddamn right.

Her body falls over mine as I slide my arm around her back, and cup her ass, pushing her against my starving cock. Yeah, sure, it's been a while, and even though I've been jerking off, nearly nightly, my cock is like a rigid power tool, and if I tried, I'm sure I could drill through steel.

She moves against me, warm and pliable and so sexy, I'm sure my wet dream is about to come to fruition. When was the last time I ejaculated in my sleep? Don't know and don't care, not when her soft moans are curling around me and seeping under my skin. Christ, she sounds all too real, like her little purring noises aren't coming from inside my brain.

"B," she whispers, and that's when some working brain cell kicks me in the nuts—hard—and snaps some sense back into me. As I become fully alert, my lids fly open, and my eyes take in the image before me. Horrified, I pull my hand from Daisy's mess of curls, and inch back to break the kiss. Reality comes back in a whoosh, and my dick deflates almost as fast as my lungs.

"Oh, shit!"

I scramble backward and Daisy nearly topples off the mattress as I shift my weight. She yelps and I capture her arm before she faceplants on the floor. My eyes lock with hers, and I note that her breathing is erratic—much like mine— her lips full and bruised from my hungry mouth, but it's her wide blue eyes that I focus in on and I know in an instant I fucked up.

"I'm so sorry," I apologize quickly and try to blink away the lust that continues to linger. "I...I was..."

"Dreaming," she explains, finishing my thoughts. Her brow is arched in question, and I can't quite figure out if she wants me to agree or disagree with her fast conclusion. What am I saying? Of course, she wants me to agree that nothing about this is real. That dream is still messing with me, making me see—hope—for things that aren't true, and honest to God, I shouldn't be fantasizing about Daisy like this.

I nod and add, "It has to be my..."

"Concussion."

"Yeah, my concussion." I rake my damp hair from my face, and glance around my room. That's when I realize I'm at the cottage. As the tumblers click into place, my gaze jerks to the pillow beside me. After talking to my parents, I popped a few pain pills and as I waited for them to kick in before I joined Daisy for pizza, I added a few words to my manuscript. But my laptop isn't where I left it.

Oh, fuck no.

I'm not sure which is worse, kissing my best friend with outright want and hunger, or her finding out what I've been secretly doing with what little spare time I have. That one working brain cell niggles in the depths of my mind, a message of sorts, and I reach deeper into my brain to pull it forward.

Was Daisy moaning...or was that all in my head? Fuck knows I'm not about to ask and make this worse than it already is. I shift again on my pillow, putting a measure of distance between us, and the smell of cheesy Hawaiian pizza plays havoc with my churning stomach. Blood drains, pools in my gut, and judging from the way Daisy is staring at me, I'm pretty sure I must look like death.

"What?" Daisy asks.

I kick the blankets off. "I'm going to be sick."

She moves quickly, clearing a path to the bathroom, and I hurry to the toilet and lose what little I have in my stomach. Once I'm done, I lean against the wall and hang my head in my hands. Daisy comes hurrying in with a glass of water and turns on the tap to wet a cloth as she flushes the toilet.

She drops down next to me, and puts the cloth on my head, and my heart pinches. It's really nice to have her here with me. I angle my head, and find concerned eyes studying my face. What would I ever do without her in my life? I don't want to find out, which is why I need to get my shit together, and in order to do that, I need to play this all off like it was nothing.

"We need to stop meeting like this," I joke. She laughs and it holds no humor. "Seriously though, the smell of pizza...uh...it nauseated me."

"Are you sure it wasn't the sex dream?" She's joking, I think. Or maybe she isn't. Maybe I hit a sore spot with her. I realize she doesn't date, but it's not because guys don't like her. They do. She's just never interested. Now I guess I know why. She has a crush on someone on the team—someone who's never hit on her before. Since she won't tell me who, when I get back home, I'm going to poll the guys. Not that it's my business. But she's helping me, so I want to help her too.

"I'm positive it wasn't the dream. It was the smell of the pizza." I point to my head. "Concussion."

Her blonde curls bounce as she nods in agreement. "Yeah," she whispers, and glances away.

I put my hand on her knee, and realize she changed her clothes. "You say that like you don't believe me."

"I believe you. Here, rinse, and I'll go get rid of the pizza." She pushes to her feet, and I reach up and thread my fingers through hers.

"Daisy, I'm sorry." Why the hell did I open my stupid mouth and tell her about my dream? All it did was put a strain on our relationship. "My dreams are fucked up. Just know, I never would have kissed you if I was awake." Her face pales a bit. "Not because you're not beautiful or desirable. You are. It's just...we're friends, right?" Why the hell did I add the word 'right'? Am I feeling her out, trying to figure out if she'd like to get naked with me? Which would, no doubt, be the biggest mistake of my life, and I still have a lot of life left to live.

Brandon, you are such a dumbass.

"I found some bread in the freezer and a jar of peanut butter in the cupboard. Let me go make you a sandwich."

I nod, grateful that she's letting the kiss go—I think. "Thanks, Daisy. You always know exactly what I need."

She pauses for a second, like she wants to say something, but she simply nods and I listen to her footsteps as she goes downstairs. That's when I remember my laptop and another wave of nausea grips me.

Did she read my work in progress?

If she snuck a peek, surely to God she would have said something. It's not like Daisy to hold anything back and I can just imagine the razzing. I rinse my mouth, brush my teeth and step back into my room. My laptop is closed, and as soon as I open it, my document pops up.

I scan what I've written and my heart drops into my stomach. Why oh why did I have to jot down that sex scene before I fell asleep? If she read it, there's no way she would have kept that to herself. She wouldn't have been able to stop herself from saying something, especially if she read the line where I called a man's erection his turgid manhood. I'm sure that's a stupid thing to call it, but it was just a place holder until I could think of something better.

It's probably crazy that I, Brandon Cannon, a *man* no less, is trying his hand at women's romance. What do I know about romance, in fiction or in real life? Nothing, really. Which is why Daisy is going to help me figure out how to impress Naomi.

I could buy more books. The only ones I keep around my place are my mother's—no one questions that—and I don't read the sex scenes. I wanted to buy more from other authors, but how the hell would I explain it if my buddies found them in my room or on my ereader? Nothing is private with the guys on the team, they're always coming and going from my place, and they'd demand I hand over my man card.

But you know what, I really like writing romance, and the story is about more than sex, so maybe me writing them isn't so crazy after all. I just have to learn how to write intimacy, and I'm not great with the happily ever after, either. Honestly how could I be? A few of my friends might have found their happy ever afters, but I haven't. Maybe it's going to take me falling in love with Naomi to figure out what love and romance really looks like. Maybe being in a committed relationship will help me be a better writer.

But none of that is going to get me into the NHL.

At that disheartening thought, I shut my laptop and follow the sound of clinking dishes to the kitchen. I realize I'm still fully dressed, and it's hot here in Seattle.

Daisy pulls the chair out from the table. "Peanut butter sandwich up."

"You're the best."

"You know it."

I smile and sit, and dig into my sandwich, thankful that my stomach has settled. I notice that Daisy only has the lights under the cabinet on, keeping the place dim so I avoid another headache. She cracks a bottle of water and hands it to me.

She picks up her phone. "I'm going to run out later and restock."

"I'll come with you."

She looks like she's about to protest, but instead asks, "How are the folks?"

I chew, swallow, and take a drink. "Surprised."

"You told them I was here."

I nod and finish half the sandwich in one bite. They weren't at all surprised by that. People are used to Daisy and me hanging out. "They offered to run us groceries, but I told them we were decompressing. They'll want to see us, though. Did you call your folks?"

"Not yet." She nibbles her lips. "I don't want to explain why I flew here and not Mexico."

I exhale. "I'm sorry, Daise...I shouldn't have—"

"You didn't, I offered."

I gobble up the rest of the sandwich. "I'll make it up to you. You just have to tell me what you want." She takes my plate when I finish and I wait for her to answer.

"I told you, to see you happy." The dish clangs as she sets it in the dishwasher. "And to help you get over this concussion with no long term affects."

She swipes her hand over her brow. "I was thinking about going for a swim before getting groceries."

I push back in my chair. "Sounds like a plan. I'll join you."

"Do you think that's a good idea?"

"No, but I'm going to go cool off anyway. I won't exert myself."

"You have to wait twenty minutes."

"Okay, doc." She laughs, and I say, "If I promise not to go in deep will you stop giving me a hard time?"

As soon as those words leave my mouth, I resist the urge to follow up with something sexual. I steal a glance at Daisy, and she turns from me but not before I catch the blush crawling up her neck. What is going on with her? Daisy never blushes. Maybe she's still embarrassed by the kiss.

"Go get your suit on then."

"Did you pack one?"

She turns back to me, and tugs the shoulder on the T-shirt to show me the suit she's wearing beneath. "Found it. I'm sure we could have found one at my cabin, anyway."

"Okay, give me a sec."

I head back upstairs, find an old pair of swim trunks in my drawer and tug them on. Shit, I don't remember them being this loose last time I was in them. I guess I have been working out and trimming down over the last few months, wanting to be in peak condition for the season. I grab us two towels and head back down to find Daisy waiting for me at the door. Her hair is pulled back and her face is makeup free. As she stands there, looking sweet and sexy in her one piece, with that whole girl next door look about her, I grin. What a contrast to the girl who shows up in my dreams. What would Daisy be like behind closed doors?

"What?" she asks.

"Nothing. Ready?"

I tie my trunks tighter as they slip lower on my hips and I don't miss the way Daisy's eyes just dropped. She turns quickly and we head outside, not bothering to lock up. The beach is only a few feet away.

"Maybe we can have a bonfire later," Daisy suggests as we walk by the pit shared by all our families when we gather in the summer. I nod and wince as we reach the water. Daisy laughs. "You always were a baby when it came to cold water."

"Oh yeah." I pick her up, and she starts wiggling and screeching as I trek deeper into the water, ready to toss her, but she slips lower in my arms, and my goddamn cock takes that moment to make its presence known.

Down, boy.

I let Daisy go, depositing her on her feet.

Moonlight falls over us, and it's hard to tell, but I'm pretty sure her cheeks are pink again. Her gaze drops. Great, she's aware of my fucking hard-on.

Brandon?"

"Yeah?"

"You might want to adjust your boxers. Your turgid manhood is showing."

7

DAISY

As Brandon's eyes open wide, and his gaze jerks downward, I turn, dive into the water and swim until I'm exhausted. I'm far from shore as I turn to see Brandon, but he's no longer standing up to his knees in water. Shoot, maybe I shouldn't have teased him. Why do I blurt things out like that without thinking? Honestly, I wasn't even going to say anything about his manuscript, but when I felt his bulge, and am still high from that kiss, the words just spilled out of me, and let's face it, he gave me the perfect opening.

Wait, why was he hard? The water is cold, and by rights he should have had shrinkage. Then again, I was pressing up against him. Not that he finds me attractive, but he's a young, red-blooded man, and likely gets aroused the second anything touches his...turgid manhood.

But now he's probably embarrassed and upset and I'm mad at myself for making fun of him. Or maybe he took another dizzy spell and is drowning. They say you can drown in less than two inches of water.

Oh God, do not think about Brandon and inches in the same sentence. Shit, I'm thinking about it, and dammit, even in cold water he was sporting a hell of a lot more than average. I'm about to kick my legs out and swim back to shore to apologize, when something grabs my leg and drags me below the surface. I gulp and hold my breath. Please don't let it be a shark.

Two arms wrap around me, and I realize I'm doomed, because it's Brandon tugging me to him, and after teasing him about his turgid manhood, my survival might be better against a great white.

I push his arms off me and surface. "Brandon," I scream, my voice carrying over the water in the night. He pops up in front of me and puts his hand on my head. "You're supposed to be taking it easy."

He dunks me, and I nearly drown because I can't stop laughing at his horrified expression. I choke, and he reaches down and pulls me up.

"Daisy, I'm sorry. Are you okay?"

I choke a bit, and the next thing I know, he's swimming me to shore like I'm a drowning victim. I am coughing and sputtering and I'm sure after calling him out on his writing he'd like to drown me. We get to the sand, and he lays me out and kneels over me. I want to talk, I try to talk, but as his big, near naked body hovers, his mouth close to mine, I can't seem to find my words—especially since my brain is still stuck on our earlier kiss. Christ, what was that? I don't know, but I do know I wouldn't be opposed to it happening again, and sure, let's just blame it on the concussion. Why the hell not? Then again, what other explanation can there be for his sudden change of character?

He tilts my head back and his lips close over mine. He breathes into my mouth, and I let him. After a few breaths he puts his hands on my chest, about to perform CPR, and while I like his palms on my body, between my breasts, I reach out and squeeze his shoulder.

"I'm okay," I squeak out, my body warming beneath his. He inches back and blows out a relieved breath.

"Thank God, I thought I'd drowned you." Worried eyes move over my face. "I'm so sorry, Daisy."

"No, I'm the one who should be apologizing. I never should have said anything about your turgid manhood."

"It's not...I don't have..."

"B," I reassure, to quiet him and he falls silent. "You know what? I think it's awesome."

"My turgid manhood?"

I can't help but laugh as he slicks his wet hair back, his eyes assessing me beneath the moonlight as sand gets into parts I'd rather it didn't. "No," I begin. "I think it's awesome that you're writing." Groaning, he flops down onto his back beside me, the waves lapping against our feet.

"Go ahead, get it all out now."

I roll toward him and admire his hard body as I crook my elbow and brace my head on my hand. "Okay, I will. I had no idea you liked writing."

He goes quiet for a second and then turns his head toward me. "That's it? You don't have some other smart-ass comment?"

"Just that we could probably come up with a better word than turgid manhood, but honestly, I think it's fantastic. How come you didn't tell me?"

He shrugs. "Embarrassed, I guess. I mean, I'm a hockey player, not a writer."

I consider that for a moment. Maybe his talent comes from both parents. "Maybe you're both."

This time he rolls toward me, and our bodies are close, close enough for me to feel the heat radiating off him. "I get these stories in my head. I need to get them down, but I don't really know much about writing. It's stupid."

I put my hand on his arm and his muscles bunch as I give him a supportive squeeze. "No, there's nothing stupid about it. I play hockey and I want to be a doctor. Do you think that's stupid?"

"Not at all. You'll be a great doctor." He looks off into the distance, like he's considering that and I add, "Maybe you could ask your mom for tips."

"No," he blurts out quickly, too quickly as he rolls away from me, staring up at the sky, like that's the last he wants to hear of that idea.

"Okay. I read a lot. Maybe I could help you."

He sits up and crosses his legs. "Really?"

I sit up and mimic his position. "Yeah, but you'll have to let me read what you have so far. Are you comfortable doing that?" It's crazy how excited I am to read Brandon's words. We were in English together and he always had better grades, but I had no idea beneath the hockey jersey he was a budding novelist.

He rolls one shoulder and exhales. "Are you going to make fun of me?"

"No," I say honestly. "I wasn't even sure I was going to mention that I saw your manuscript, until—"

"Until I gave you a great opening." He groans and shakes his head. "Sorry, my dick has a mind of its own these days."

"Dick," I state and his gaze jerks to mine, like I just told him my deepest, darkest dirtiest secret.

"What?"

"That's a better word than turgid manhood. So is cock."

"Jesus," he curses under his breath and I kind of like messing with him like this. Or maybe I like the dirty talk and the way it makes him all jittery, like he's trying to hide an erection. Either way, I should probably cut it out.

"Tell me you don't call a woman's clit the pearl of her oyster."

His jaw drops open and it's all I can do not to laugh. "Pearl of her oyster? Jesus Daisy." He pushes to his feet and angles his body away and I'm dying to know if he's erect.

"You used that, didn't you?"

"No," he blurts out as he walks into the water, turning his body away. I follow him. "That's ridiculous. I...I just..."

He who protests too much. I think about other words I've read in novels and continue with, "What about honey pot, or door of femininity....or..."

He turns to me, his eyes wide, and shakes his head vehemently. "No, I don't use those words." He bites his lips. "At least I won't anymore."

I burst out laughing and he laughs with me. "Thank God I discovered your little secret before you tried to get it published."

His smile dissolves and there's a new seriousness about him. "You really want to help?"

"I do. I think it will be fun, but you're supposed to be resting this week." Water splashes against my feet and I squeeze my toes into the sand. "You could dictate, and I could type it out for you. I'm faster on the keyboard."

"Aren't you doing enough for me?"

I blow his words off. "What are friends for?"

He nods, and goes quiet as he looks off into the distance. What is going through his head? "You're going to teach me how to go on real dates, *and* write a book. I'm going to have to do something epic in return. Tell me or I'll do something on my own."

"Such as?"

"Find out who you like on the team and set you up."

I toss his words around inside my brain. I realize he's not going to let this go. "How about I tell you when this week is over."

He smiles, satisfied with that answer, and the way I see it is this, Brandon will be engrossed with Naomi by the end of next weekend, and will likely be less interested in my crush. If Naomi even shows, that is. What I didn't tell him was that she no longer seems interested after our last few messages, but if this is what he wants, I can't give up so easily. So hopefully I can talk her into changing her mind about Brandon, and if he still insists on knowing who I'm hung up on, I'll tell him I'm over it. Heck, maybe I'll pretend I fell for Sebastian Wilson since he's here this week. I make a mental note to spend a bit of time with him, just to make it believable. I don't want him to get the wrong idea, though. I'd never want to lead anyone on just to cover my feelings for Brandon.

"Maybe we can combine those two things. As we discover what a girl who isn't infatuated with hockey players might like on a date, we can incorporate that into your romance."

He grins. "That could work and what was that about ropes?"

His teasing grin plays with the needy spot between my legs. "No ropes..." I shake my head. "You know," I begin as I turn and head back toward the cottage, "for a guy who knows a lot about sex, I figured you'd know how to write about it."

He arches a brow at me, and he doesn't need to say anything for me to get the gist. Yeah, he knows I'm inexperienced, and I guess I deserve that look after my comment.

"Okay fine, I might not have experienced sex, but I've read about it a lot. I guess we'll just have to discover what works together." His steps slow and I realize what I've said. "What I'm trying to say is we're not going to discover *sex* together... we're going to discover dating together."

"I knew that's what you meant?"

Great, now I sound like I want to have sex with him, which I do, but he can never know.

"Yeah, I was just clarifying." I start to walk faster, but his legs are long, allowing him to easily keep pace, and stay close. "How much do you have written?"

"Half, but it's not my first book. I've shelved all the others. I learned a lot writing those drafts and I'm putting everything into this book. It will be great to have your help writing the rest."

"I can't wait. Are you getting your appetite back?" I ask, changing the subject.

"Yeah, I'm hungry."

My head swivels at the heat in his voice. Has all of this talk about sex made him hungry for...something other than food?

"Still don't want pizza, though."

Oh, okay, I'm just reading too much into his tone because clearly all this talk about sex has made me hungry. "Maybe you shouldn't go to the grocery store. I think the swimming was enough exertion tonight." Honestly, I want him to stay home because I need a break.

"We can wait until tomorrow. I'm good with another peanut butter sandwich, and you're probably tired too."

"Yeah, I am, and I wouldn't mind getting a start on your manuscript tonight." He nods and remains quiet as we enter the house. I hurry to my room, get changed into my pajamas and I open my bedroom door, about to go across the hall and get his laptop, when I find him standing there in a pair of dry shorts, no T-shirt, his laptop in his hand.

"Oh, thanks." I take it from him and he follows me into the bedroom. "What are you doing?" I ask as I shut the closet door tightly, because you know, monsters.

"I just thought I'd hang out while you read. In case you have any questions." He plunks down on the bed, and puts his arm over his eyes, like the room is too bright. "Is that okay?"

I turn the lights off. "I...guess." He falls quiet and I sit beside him on the bed, and open his laptop, letting my eyes adjust so I can see in the dark.

I'm instantly drawn into the story, realizing he's using the friends to lovers trope, and I'm so engrossed, especially in the delicious bathroom scene—my God, the man has a wicked imagination—I don't even realize he's fallen asleep beside me. I finish the first sex scene, and can't get it out of my head. From his description of the room, I can't help but wonder if it's the ladies' room at Tandoor, my favorite Indian restaurant here in Seattle. But that would mean he's been in the women's bathroom. Heck, maybe he has.

Brandon Cannon, you are a dirty, filthy guy.

Why do I like that so much? I don't know and I never expected his book to be this hot, like I should be wearing oven mitts while holding his laptop. Even his strange bodily descriptions—turgid manhood—didn't take away from the scene. I steal another glance at Brandon as my body temperature jumps from simmering to inferno and I'm really glad he's asleep because when I crawl between the sheets, I just might have to touch myself.

8

BRANDON

I wake to the sound of seagulls squawking in the distance, and I slowly peel one eye open. I wince against the brightness and wait for the nausea. When none comes, I roll to my side, memories of last night filling in the blanks in my brain.

I open the other eye, and I'm about to jackknife up, but stop myself. Last time I did that, I ended up on the bathroom floor and if that happens again, Daisy is likely to drag my sorry ass to the emergency room, and then my parents will find out and nothing good will come from that. Speaking of Daisy, she was reading my manuscript when I fell asleep. My heart kicks into high gear and I take in the empty space beside me.

I wanted to stay awake, wanted to watch her every reaction to my written words, but the second my head hit the pillow, I was a goner. Just like she's gone right now. Christ, is she out of bed, avoiding me because she hated it, or because she liked it? Will the badly written sex scenes embarrass her? Or turn her on? Which do I want?

Fuck me sideways.

Honestly, I'm well aware of her innocence, but just because she's never had sex doesn't mean she doesn't think about it. Hell, she's always threatening to tell me about my mother's books, which means she probably has high expectations. I snort to myself. I guess I'm glad I'm not the guy who has to try to fill those expectations.

Are you though, Brandon? Are you really the guy who doesn't want to try to live up to her fantasies?

"Good morning."

I turn at the sound of her voice, and she comes toward me, a big cup of coffee in her hand. My heart beats a little faster at her presence. Did it always do that, or is that something new? "You're the best, Daise..."

"I thought we'd already established that when we were five, when none of you guys could find me when we played hide and seek." As she stands over me, looking relaxed and casual in her ripped jean shorts and tight T-shirt, hide and seek takes on a whole different meaning.

She sits beside me, her eyes narrowing as she lightly touches my forehead and threads her fingers through my hair as she pushes it back. "Did you sleep well?"

"Like a baby. How about you?" I guess most would think it's weird that we always end up in the same bed, but to us it's just as natural as breathing.

"Good. How are you feeling?"

The truth is, I'm feeling thankful that I haven't pushed my covers all the way off, otherwise she'd see my boner—again. I keep that to myself and say, "I think this is the first time in a long time that I haven't woken up with a headache."

Her smile is soft, the blue in her eyes is clear and translucent as she tucks a strand of blonde hair behind her ears. "That's good to hear. Now drink your coffee so you don't get a caffeine headache."

She really does know me well. I sit up a little straighter and take a sip of the hot coffee, made just the way I like it. I was only half joking when I told Daisy I needed a cook, a servant...someone to sponge bathe me, but man, I could get used to this kind of attention. I lift my head, and let my gaze move over her pretty face. For as long as I can remember, Daisy has been taking care of us all. Who the hell is taking care of her? My stomach takes that moment to grumble.

Her lips curl up in a grin, and my dick jumps. Dammit, that kiss we shared. I had no idea her lips would be so soft, or that she'd taste so sweet.

"I guess peanut butter and bread didn't cut it, huh?"

"What?" I ask. Shit, I need to stop fantasizing and reliving that dream. If I don't, she's going to know something is up... and yes, something is up, and it's raging between my legs.

Fuck, dude.

"The peanut butter didn't cut it," she repeats.

"Yeah, I'm hungry," I say and there is nothing, and I mean absolutely nothing I can do to keep my gaze from straying to her lush cleavage. She's so toned and tight from playing hockey, but there's a real feminine softness about her too. I guess you could say she has it all—and I want it all.

Holy shit, what is happening to me? I'd better get with a girl soon, otherwise I'm going to fuck up our relationship. I guess it's a good thing we invited everyone next weekend. Even if Naomi doesn't want to be with me, I need the distraction.

"I could probably eat that pizza now."

"I tossed it. Sorry."

"It's okay." I'm really not in the mood for pizza anyway. It's just that she went through the trouble of getting my fave last night. "Grocery run?" I ask.

She puts her hand on my leg, and the only thing separating skin from skin is a thin cotton sheet. "Yeah, but why don't we hit up our favorite pancake house for breakfast first?"

"Wow, it's almost like you know me." She laughs. I guess now, after discovering my secret, she knows more about me than anyone else. She stands, and I capture her hand and pull her back. I take a big fueling breath, and prepare for the worst when I ask, "How was it?"

Her face flushes, and her chest rises and falls quickly. "You mean your book?"

I keep my hand on her wrist, and lightly rub my thumb over her flesh. "What else would I mean?"

She shakes her head quickly and I eye her. Did something happen last night after I fell asleep? Something to make her think I'm asking something else entirely?

I'm about to ask, but she speaks first.

"It's really good, Brandon," she gushes. "Like really good. I'm shocked. Well, not shocked, you were always great in English, but this goes well beyond being good in a class. You have real talent, my friend."

I laugh as she rambles. Daisy never rambles—unless she's flustered, and I have to say, if my book flustered her, then I'm doing something right.

"Your scenes are fun, funny and vibrant. I feel like I'm right there, living them."

"How far did you get?"

"All the way."

"You finished it?"

"No, I mean...I ah, finished until the end of the sex scene... where the characters went all the way."

"That needs some work, huh?"

She stands and turns from me, as she walks out the door, she mumbles, "Not as much as you think."

"What?"

"Just some tweaks," she shoots back over her shoulder. "Get dressed. I'm starved."

I watch the door until she disappears, and take another sip of my coffee, which I nearly choke on as last night's dream flashes through my brain. Man, I have to get my mind off Daisy and all the things I suddenly want to do to her. What is going on with my subconscious?

Damn you, concussion.

I push the sheet off, get my boner under control and sip my coffee as I make a quick trip to the bathroom for a cold shower. By the time I finish and dress, Daisy is downstairs on her phone. She glances up as I come into the room, but her smile is forced.

"What's up?" I ask.

"I just heard from Naomi. Looks like she's going to try to make it for next Friday night."

"Great news." Okay, if it's such great news, why did my stomach just sour? Oh, probably because I've been thinking about my best friend in ways that can only lead to no good.

"Sounds like you might have another chance," she says, a smile on her face, but her voice lacks conviction. Does she know something I don't know? Is Naomi coming only as a favor to Daisy?

"Good."

I walk to the counter and needing something to do with my hands, grab a glass from the cupboard and fill it with water I have no thirst for. No, the only thing I have thirst for is the girl sitting on my kitchen chair.

"Although..."

I turn back toward Daisy. "What?"

She frowns. "We might have to really step up your game."

I take a drink of the water. "Why do you say that?"

"She asked who was all going to be here, and if it was a party."

"Okay, and what are you reading into that?"

"I don't know. I just...I know you like her and I need this to work out."

"Need?"

Her body stiffens and she frowns. "Want," she blurts out. "I meant to say want. I want you to be happy, B?"

I step up behind her and put my hand on her shoulder, rubbing her muscles like I always do, except this time...I don't know, but there's something different between us. I can feel it in my core, and when I say core, I mean dick, because yes, massaging her shoulders, and the way it moves her T-shirt around and exposes her cleavage, is messing with my dick.

I tug my hand back like it's on fire. "We should get going."

I step back and Daisy jumps from her seat. "I'll get us an Uber."

Ten minutes later, we're at our favorite pancake restaurant, and as we sip coffee and wait for our order, in walks Sebastian Wilson and some guy I don't know. I like the guy well enough. Except for the night he let Daisy drink too much at his party. Okay, I have to be real here. He had no control over her consumption of alcohol. I'm just very overprotective when it comes to her, and honestly, he seemed concerned for her well-being after she called me to come rescue her. I like that I can be there for her. It's just that she's a strong, independent woman, who likes to do things on her own. Wednesday however, when she finds out if she was accepted to Med school, I plan to be right there beside her.

"Hey Brandon, Daisy," he begins. "I saw action at your place last night. I was wondering if it was you or your folks." He holds his hand out and I grasp it.

"Back for the week."

"Daisy," he says and slides into the booth beside her, and it's weird, but I suddenly want to punch Sebastian in the face.

"What's up, Sebastian. How's Penn?"

"Penn's great. How's the Academy?"

"Good."

He gestures toward his friend who is still standing and we exchange a nod as Sebastian introduces him. "This is my buddy, Nick. He's on the rowing team with me at Penn. Nick, this is Brandon, and Daisy...wait, should I say Dr. Reed?

"Not yet," she corrects a little nervous flutter in her voice. "I don't find out until Wednesday."

"She'll get in," I say, and she gives me a warm smile before turning her attention to Nick. I make mental notes of all the things I need to put in place before Wednesday.

Her smile widens, and just like that, Nick is under her spell. "Hi Nick."

I grin. I don't really think she knows the power she has over men. I think it's her easygoing, carefree attitude. While she shows that to the world, I see the other side of her. The side that works hard and worries about everyone.

"Daisy," Nick begins. "Are you and your boyfriend Brandon going to the year-end blowout next weekend?"

Really subtle, Nick. Real subtle.

"Brandon and I are friends," Daisy clarifies, and for a second it feels like a hit to the gut. Didn't we say we were going to pretend, and do real couple things? I guess she doesn't want to fake date around these guys. Wait, I did ask her if she was packing sexy panties for someone in Seattle. Was she hoping to run into Sebastian? No, that can't be right. She likes someone from the hockey team. "And yes, we'll both be at the party."

Nick's face lights up. "Great."

"Should be fun," Sebastian says, and I really don't like the way his eyes just flickered to Daisy's breasts. "You guys heard about the break-ins in the area?"

That's when my brain kicks into gear. "Yeah, that's right. My parents said something about that last night when I called."

"Keep the place locked," he warns and stands. "Security is pretty sure it's a bunch of kids. They're not stealing anything; they're just ransacking and causing mischief. Anyway, stop by tonight if you guys are free. I'm having a few friends over for drinks and a fire."

I'm about to tell him I'm not sure if we'll make it, when Daisy nods quickly. "Okay, sounds great. I'll bring the marshmallows. See you then." Sebastian grins as the hostess leads them to a table away from us.

"You really want to go to his place tonight?" I ask when he's no longer within hearing distance.

"Sure, you don't?"

"I don't know. I thought maybe we could hang out."

"We can, at Sebastian's." The server comes and sets our food in front of us, and Daisy takes the syrup and makes a happy face on her pancake, like she's been doing since we were kids. I do the same and then stare at her for a second. She's not interested in Sebastian, is she? Nah, she can't be and maybe after my inappropriate kiss—and dream—she's reluctant to be alone with me and that's fair.

She cuts into her pancake and eats what's supposed to be the eyeball. "Always the eyeball first," I tease.

"Delicious."

"And yet eyeballs on fish freak you out."

She glares at me, as she chews, one brow arched. "Not quite the same, B."

Honestly, I love all her little idiosyncrasies and all her superstitions. My thoughts go back to Sebastian. Would he love all those little things about her? Would any guy? A headache begins at the base of my neck, and I reach around and rub it. I'm just not certain it's from my concussion. Daisy's head lifts, her fork inches from her mouth. "Are you okay?"

"Yeah, just thinking about the break-ins." Not true. I'm thinking about her hooking up with Sebastian and I don't like it one little bit. She's my friend, and I want her with a guy who is going to treat her right. Not that I think Sebastian wouldn't, he's not a bad guy. It's just that he goes to school in the States, and she goes to school in Canada and how can they be there for each other if they're so far apart?

Is that what's really bothering you, Brandon?

Yes, yes it is. Daisy needs to date someone at the Academy, a guy who's going to listen to her, adore her and put her first. There's only one guy I know of like that and it's me.

Dear God, what am I fucking saying?

9

DAISY

I stand before the mirror and turn left and right, checking myself out in my new dress. We decided after unloading our groceries at home, to head back out for a walk, and I stopped at one of the boutique shops on the way to get something to wear for tonight. In my haste to pack, I brought mostly fall clothes. It's much cooler in Halifax than here at the cottage, and most of my summer things were put away. Not to mention the fact that Brandon had me so flustered I wasn't even sure what I'd thrown in my suitcase.

The pretty blue dress swishes and I catch a flash in the mirror. I turn to find Brandon looking good enough to eat as he comes up behind me, finger combing his hair. I turn to him and help him.

"You need a haircut." I touch the scruff on his chin, loving the way it feels on my fingertips. "And a shave."

"Nope. Movember is coming up and I'm growing my hair and beard along with the usual mustache." He leans into me, looking over my shoulder to check his beard out in the mirror, and my entire body reacts to his closeness. My heart picks up pace, and warmth travels through my body, settling between my legs. "You don't like it?"

"I like it," I admit. "I bet Naomi will like it too," I say, a reminder to myself that he likes another girl, and I need to stop holding out hope that he'll see me as more. Heck, maybe tonight I'll spend time getting to know Sebastian better. In the past he was always asking me to hang out, but I always turned him down. I always turned everyone down. Maybe I'll flirt with him—not that I'm very good at it—and show him I could be open to hanging out. I honestly want to be open to it.

A loud noise reverberates up the steps and we both go stiff. "What was that?" I whisper.

He frowns. "You stay here, I'll go look."

He turns, and I stay tight on his heels as he reaches the open bedroom door. "I'm not staying here by myself."

"I'm sure it's nothing."

I grip the back of his shirt. "You heard what Sebastian said. Someone is breaking into the cottages. What if someone is down there?"

"People are breaking in when no one is home. It's very easy to tell this one is occupied."

"How? There are no cars outside."

He scrubs his chin, knowing I'm right. "You've watched too many scary shows, Daise..."

"Thanks to you."

He turns, and my hands fall from his shirt. "Just stay here."

"Wait." I run to the closet, and pull out his brother's old baseball bat. "I'm coming."

He takes the bat. "No, you're not. Stay here."

I grab my phone ready to dial 911 at the first sign of trouble. I work to keep my breathing calm, and listen as he goes down the stairs quietly. A moment later he calls up. "It's okay, Daisy. We left the kitchen window open, and the breeze blew over the vase."

I hurry down the stairs, relieved. "Did it break?" In the kitchen, I find Brandon picking up the little white pieces from the sink. "Shoot."

"Maybe we can glue it back together," he says as he puzzles the pieces back together.

"We'll hit up the store tomorrow for some glue." Another warm breeze blows in off the water and he shuts the window. He turns to me, and runs his hands up and down my arm.

"Are you okay now?"

I steal a glance around. "Yeah, I'm still a little freaked out."

"I'll go home tomorrow and borrow one of the cars. That way no one will mistake this place for empty."

I look him over, take in his eyes. "You're ready to see your parents?"

"I'm feeling pretty good today."

"You don't have to go tonight if you don't want to, B."

"No, if you want to go, I'll go."

"I...we can stay in, watch a movie."

His brows pull together, and I'm pretty sure he likes that idea, but he says, "Hey maybe I'll get good fodder for my book tonight and..." He wags his brows, in a sexually playful manner. "I want you to do more than just take care of me while you're here."

I laugh, sure he's kidding. He doesn't mean sexually, right? "Okay, let's go and see what plays out."

I snatch the bag of marshmallows off the table, and Brandon checks all the windows and locks up tight. The sun is low on the horizon as we walk along the beach, and a sense of warmth and contentment falls over me. I exhale, and a happy sigh rumbles in my throat.

"When you finish medical school, where do you want to live?" he asks. "Do you think you'll come back to the States?" He waves his hand around. "I know you love it here."

"I'm still thinking about it. What about you, B? Where do you think you'll end up?" He shrugs. "Do you even want to play hockey?"

"Yeah, I mean sure." He gives a humorless laugh, as we walk the beach, my flats sinking into the wet sand. "It's not like I could make it as a romance author."

"Why not?"

He throws his arm around me. "You can't be serious."

As we get closer to Sebastian's house, music pours from his open windows and reaches our ears. No burglar will mistake his place for empty. "I think you can do anything you put your mind to. Your mom could help. She has an agent and has lots of connections."

"That means I'd have to tell her." He gulps. "Or worse, let her read what I wrote."

As his hand dangles over my shoulder, I thread my fingers through his. "I think she'd be stoked, B." He stares straight ahead. "You don't believe me."

"I'm just...I'm a hockey player."

"You can be more than that." The last rays of sun sink into the ocean, and darkness falls over us. "All of us kids feel the pressure."

"You felt pressured?"

"Of course. My dad wanted me to play professionally. Why is it that we all have to follow in our father's footsteps?"

"You're not."

"Nope, I'm not. As you know, my mom is a speech pathologist, and I sort of went that route myself. But I think there was more pressure on you guys."

He pulls me closer. "I think you're right, and there's nothing wrong with following in your mother's footsteps."

"Exactly." I breathe in the salty air. "I never knew what my biological mom did, or does, for a living."

"Yeah..." is all he says, and we both fall quiet. A moment later he breaks the silence. "You're nothing like her."

"What makes you say that?"

"Because you're always helping others, and would never use anyone to get what you want. You're the least selfish person I know. But you know what they say..."

I eye him. "What do they say?"

"That people who are always helping others are running away from something themselves."

I stare straight ahead, my stomach tightening. "No one says that, Brandon." It's a lie. People do say that. I help others to avoid my own issues, and my biggest issue is abandonment. If I don't get emotionally involved, I don't get hurt when I'm eventually dumped. Others with my issues would leave the relationship first before getting hurt. I take it one step further and never get involved in the first place. Besides, there's only one guy I want, and I can't have him.

He shrugs, not wanting to argue. There is however, part of me that knows if I focus on others, I don't have to focus on myself, or think about how I was used by my birth mother, and then abandoned. I fall quiet, and my steps slow.

"Ignore me," Brandon says and lets his arm fall from my shoulder when he realizes he might have hit a nerve with me. "We're here to have fun, so let's have fun."

"Yeah, fun," I agree and smile, even though my insides are tight. We reach the fire pit in front of Sebastian's house and I recognize some of the people seated around it. But there are plenty of unfamiliar faces, too.

"You guys made it," Sebastian yells and jumps up. He reaches into his cooler and pulls out two cans of beer and hands them to us. He takes the marshmallows from me and shakes the bag. "Let me cook you one." I nod and he leads me to the chair beside him. I glance at Brandon, not wanting to just walk away from him when I'm supposed to be watching over him, but he's not alone. Nope, not alone at all. A bunch of girls surround him, some we know, some we don't, but every one of them are fawning all over him.

I drop into the chair next to Sebastian as the girls pull Brandon down on a log. Soon enough he's lost in conversation, and I can't help but wonder if this is too much for a guy with a concussion. And yes, it's true. I'm jealous.

Sebastian rips into the bag, loads up a stick with marshmallows and passes the bag around. "I'm glad you came." He stares at me, his voice low and husky as he holds the gooey treats over the fire. The flames flare higher.

I reach out and put my hand over his. "Careful."

He smiles at me, and for some reason, my gaze flies to Brandon, and I find him watching our exchange. I guess if I decide to go with plan B and tell Brandon it's Sebastian I like, now is a good opportunity to flirt. "Burnt marshmallows are carcinogenic," I tell him.

He laughs. "Look at you, you're already a doctor."

I laugh with him, probably too hard, but I've seen enough puck bunnies in action to know how to do at least that much.

"Talk more doctor to me, it's hot." God, is he for real. "Wait, do you have a white coat? Those things are hot too."

"Not yet. I'm not even sure if I've been accepted yet."

Once the marshmallow is brown, I tug on the stick, my hand still on his. I peel the marshmallow off, and plop it into my mouth. I moan as the flavor bursts on my tongue.

"That good, huh?" Sebastian asks, his voice dropping an octave like watching me eat a marshmallow is the biggest turn on of his life. I can't quite imagine it, but who knows. I think at this age, guys can get turned on by just about anything, even a cool ocean breeze. I take another one off the stick and hold it out to him. He takes it into his mouth, and

I'm about to pull my fingers back, but he holds my hand to his mouth, and licks the sticky goo from my fingers.

All righty then.

Did Brandon just growl?

I cast a fast glance his way and he's putting his own marshmallow on a stick, and I turn as Nick sits down beside me. "I'm glad you came," he says, and I decide I like his smile.

"What are you taking at Penn?" I ask, making light conversation.

"Engineering."

I nod, not knowing much about the field, but maybe this would be a good time to ask questions and learn. This new Daisy needs to take an interest in guys besides Brandon. Sebastian hands the stick over. Only problem is Nick grabs it, where it's still hot from the fire.

"Fuck," he yells, and jumps to his feet as the stick falls.

Sebastian winces. "Shit, sorry man."

Nick shakes his hand, and curses. "You need to run it under some cold water right away. Here," I say thinking fast and opening the cooler, so he can shove his hand into the ice. As he moans, I look at Sebastian. "Do you have anything for burns?"

"Probably inside. Bathroom medicine cabinet."

"Do you mind if I go get it?"

"Nope. I'll help." He stands, and as Nick keeps his hand cooling, we head into the house and it's strange, I don't need to turn to know Brandon's eyes are burning into my back. Does he not like Sebastian, or is he jealous? That last thought makes me chuckle, because while Brandon is protective of me and all his friends, he can't be jealous. Heck, he wants to set me up with the player I'm crushing on.

Sebastian puts his hand on my lower back as we go to the bathroom, and I rifle through the medicine cabinet and gather what I need. I close the mirrored door and find him sitting on the bathroom sink, grinning at me.

"What?" I ask.

He nudges me with his shoulder, and unlike when Brandon touches me, it does not do weird things to me, but he's being nice, and maybe I should really give this a shot. What do I have to lose?

"Why did you have to go to college in Canada?" he asks, a genuine curiosity on his face. He's handsome, and nice, and I'm sure the girls love him and if I knew what was good for me, I'd stop comparing every guy I met to Brandon.

"Because I like the program." They do have a good program and Brandon really sold it to me when he went to check it out, and let's face it, the city is amazing.

"You should be at Penn, with me. I think you'd liven the place right up. Remember you used to talk about going there years ago."

I nod. It's true, I did, but then Brandon decided to go to the Academy and like a big stupid loser, I followed him. Don't get me wrong, I love the Academy, but in hindsight, I should have gone to Penn where I wouldn't be tortured every single day.

"Yeah, it might have been a better choice," I say, mostly to myself.

"Hey."

I turn at the sound of Brandon's voice and find his body eating up the door frame. My gaze jerks to his and it's strange really, because I feel like I've been doing something I shouldn't have been doing. But all Sebastian and I are doing is talking and I can talk to whoever I want. Heck, I can hang out and date Sebastian too if I wanted. Why then is Brandon looking at me like I'd just wounded him? Maybe that drink went straight to my head.

"I came to find the bathroom," he tells us.

His body is tight and for the briefest of seconds, I'm not sure he's telling me the truth, and we're always honest with each other right. Well mostly. "We'll get out of your way," I tell him, keeping my voice light as Sebastian jumps from the sink. I brush past Brandon, and close the door on my way out.

Back at the fire, we all sip on our beer, and Sebastian starts telling ghost stories after Brandon joins us, except this time he takes Nick's seat. It's empty because a bunch of the girls pulled him to the log after I bandaged him. It's cute how he's sucking up all the attention.

Brandon leans into me, and I take a fast sip of my drink as his warm scent overwhelms my senses. He laughs quietly and teases, "You should probably plug your ears, or you'll end up in my bed again."

"It was you who slept in mine last night, remember?"

His throat makes a sound as he says, "I remember."

Jeez, was it that bad?

"And just so you know, I wasn't afraid earlier." I lift my chin and hold my arms like I'm ready to swing a bat. "I was going to put that guy on his knees."

He swallows. Was it something I said?

"I have no doubt about that, Duke."

"Good," I respond, my lungs deflating—because yeah, I'd like for him to see me as a girl, just once, instead of the tomboy I used to be and maybe still am. I grew up swinging a bat and hitting a puck with the best of them. I guess he knows I can take care of myself. I have to say though, it was kind of nice how he wanted to take care of me in the moment. Sure, I'm independent, but there's just something about Brandon when he goes all alpha.

Everyone listens intently as Sebastian tells a story, and a dog barks in the distance. I nearly jump out of my seat, and quickly turn to find Brandon watching me. His lids flicker and I narrow my eyes.

"How are you feeling?"

"Not bad, actually. Just tired."

I put my hands on my chair, about to push myself up. "Why don't we get going?"

"No, you want to be here."

"I think I'm ready for bed, too."

We wait a second until Sebastian finishes his spooky story, and it ends with a funny punch line and everyone laughs. I lean into him. "Thanks for the invite. We're going to take off. I'll see you around though."

"Yeah, can't wait. You're still coming to the blowout, right?"

"Yup."

Brandon and I stand, and say goodbye before we make our way down the beach and back to his cottage. We're both a bit quiet, lost in our thoughts, and he breaks it with, "Do you regret going to the Academy?"

I guess he overhead me talking to Sebastian. "You didn't go because I went there, did you?" He nudges me playfully. "Thinking I couldn't cut it on my own."

"Wow, that's some ego, Brandon." He's half right. I went there because he was going there, but I knew he'd be just fine without me. I wish the reverse was true.

He captures my arm and holds me still. "Did you hear that?"

I go quiet, and in the distance, a banging sound reaches my ears and curls through my blood. "Do you think it's coming from your cottage, or mine?" I ask, and struggle to keep my voice even. That bang earlier today scared me. So did Sebastian's story.

"I don't know." He peers into the dark. "Let's go check."

I'd just told him I was brave, so instead of running and hiding under the covers like I want to, I nod and stay close as we follow the banging noise.

His long legs eat up the beach and suddenly slow as we reach my cottage. "I think it's coming from the Conrads."

The place is dark, no vehicles in the driveway. They're a young couple, late twenties or early thirties, with no kids, and they always pack up the end of August. During the summer months, they have lots of parties at their place. Not that we've ever been to any. They're older than us, and younger than our parents age group. We usually just wave from a distance, but they've always been nice when I ran into them, so I'd hate for their place to get ransacked or robbed.

I swallow. "Do you think…"

"Wait here."

I grip his shirt. "No, you're not going over there alone."

He stares at me and I pinch my lips tight. "Fine. We'll walk the perimeter and if we see anything out of the ordinary, we'll call security."

I reach for his hand and his palm swallows mine whole as we keep to the shadows and walk around the house. In the back, we find the screen door banging in the wind. I relax and let out a breath. "It's just the door."

"I'll shut it." I let go of his hand, and now that my eyes are adjusted, I watch his form as he hurries to the door. "Shit," he mumbles.

"What?" My heart jumps into my throat and I grab my phone.

"The back door, it's unlocked." The sound of the door creaking open trickles down my spine and elicits a hard shiver.

"I'm calling security."

"Wait. It's good."

"Is everything okay, nothing out of the ordinary?"

"Everything is okay, and lots out of the ordinary."

I glance over my shoulder, sure the boogeyman is standing there ready to pounce but I'm all alone behind the Conrad's cottage. "Then I should call?"

"No, you should come see this."

I hurry inside and the door bangs shut behind me. I step up to Brandon and come to a complete stop when my gaze races over the room, lit by his flashlight up. What the hell am I looking at? I'm not sure, but judging by the toys, props and equipment, I'd have to say it was some kind of sexual playground, fit for a masochist.

Haven't I already called myself that a few times? What a coincidence, even though I don't really believe in them. I snort. Honestly though, here I am in Washington, standing in a playground designed to fulfill fantasies, with my crush—a guy who will only ever see me as a tomboy—and yes everything about this is painful, and no I will not be deriving any pleasure from it.

Maybe you should, Daisy.

10

BRANDON

I flick on a lamp in the windowless room. "Holy. Shit," Daisy says, as her gaze races around the room, like she can't take it all in quick enough. I can't either. There are far too many things calling my name.

As my dick jumps, I give a long slow whistle. "Holy shit, is right."

She jerks her thumb over her shoulder, but the door is no longer banging. Great, now I have the word banging on my brain, as I stand in a room full of sex toys with a girl I totally want to...yeah...bang. If I believed in fate, that everything happens for a reason, I'd think the noise from the unhinged door lured us here for a reason. Wait, I do believe in fate. Well, fuck me sideways.

"Do you think they just forgot to lock their door?" she asks.

I nod. "Yeah, there's no sign of forced entry or anything."

We stand side by side, in a room we shouldn't be in, staring at sex toys and equipment that I've never had the privilege of trying on any girl before. Beside me, Daisy makes a noise in her throat, and I step away from her to run my hands over numerous ropes, handcuffs, whips and feathers all arranged on hooks along the back wall of the room.

"Unreal," Daisy whispers, as my heart crashes in my chest as I pick up one of the feather ticklers that looks unopened in a package. Of course, my heart isn't banging around inside my chest because we're technically breaking and entering, but because we're in some kind of kinky playroom and I'm totally digging it.

"What do you think this is used for?" I ask Daisy as I pull the tickler from the box, and run my fingers over the soft feathers.

"Dusting," she says, her cheeks the prettiest shade of pink I've ever seen. My dick thickens a little more, and I resist the urge to reach into my pants and take a hold of it. That'll have to wait until I'm alone in bed later, fantasizing about using this piece of equipment on sweet little Daisy, who is staring at me wide-eyed and full of innocence. But there's something else there, just below the surface, something I want to tease, and tempt...to introduce to a world of untamed pleasure.

I chuckle at her response, and it comes out low, deep... aroused. "I don't think so." Her chest rises and falls fast, and I kind of like everything in the way she's reacting. "I think it's for sex."

"We should go," she whispers, but steps further into the room to stand before what looks like a bench or table, although it's not like any bench or table I've ever seen before. She touches the plush leather, and takes a fast breath. "What do you think this is for?"

I abandon the tickler, crouch, and take the shackles into my hands, and my cock is pretty much screaming for release as I think about restraining Daisy and having my way with her. "I think it's a bondage table, Daise..."

"Oh, okay."

Her voice sounds just as foreign to my ears as my own does. I scrub my chin, and watch Daisy. If she notices the dilation in my eyes, will she think it's from my concussion, or from my arousal?

"Hey," she begins, her voice a little higher, and I get it, she's uncomfortable and trying to make light of the situation. "Maybe all this will give you some fun ideas for your sex scenes."

"Sex scenes?" I ask, my voice going down a path it has no right to go. "You think I need to work on my sex?"

"For your book," she adds quickly. "Fun scenes for your book."

"Right." I fasten and unfasten one of the shackles. "Do you think it's too kinky for the book I'm working on?"

She takes a small tentative step forward and I'm pretty sure she takes a quick breath every time I tug on the shackles. Is this something innocent little Daisy might like to try. "Maybe, but I've read lots of romances with fun stuff like this."

"Fun?" Her face turns every shade of red as my eyes meet hers. "This is fun to you?"

"I don't know." She gives a hard shake of her head, leaving her hair a tangled mess around her flushed cheeks. "I guess it's fun to read about it. I've never tried it. Have you?"

"No." Metal grinds against metal as I drop the shackles. "Yeah, maybe you're right and I could incorporate this into a book someday."

"I guess...you'd have to know how to use this stuff, first though right?" she asks, her breathing completely ragged and off the charts now.

"How do you think I could go about learning that?"

She shrugs, and her body visibly quivers. "I don't know."

Oh, but I do. I really do.

Walk away, Brandon. Do not say the words lingering on your tongue.

I stand and face her, and my dick is well aware that our bodies are mere inches apart and she's practically vibrating before me. "I'm not sure I can quite get the visual or the details. Nothing without seeing someone use it."

Goddammit, I've said the words.

She moves around me, and runs her hands along the table. Her fingers linger on the leather as she angles her head and lifts her eyes to mine. "No?"

"Do you think you could uh...just uh...maybe stretch out on this, to give me a better idea."

She goes deadly quiet, and my throat tightens. What the fuck am I doing? This is my best friend Daisy, and I shouldn't be using my book as an excuse to lay her over a table, just to see how sweet she'd look with her ass in the air, mine to admire... touch even, if I played my cards right. Shit, that's just wrong. I can't play any cards here, and I'm about to yell abort, tell her I'm sorry and get the fuck out of this playroom when she speaks.

"I did say I'd help you, B." She runs her pretty pink tongue over her dry bottom lip, and that's when I realize my throat is so dry I can barely swallow. "You know, with your book."

Oh my... fuck. What the hell are we doing?

"Yeah, you did," I say, my cock taking full control of my brain, giving me little choice as to what comes out of my mouth next. "But what exactly are you saying?'

"Maybe I was wrong." She continues to run her finger over the table and I want her to run it down the length of my dick, just like that. I also want to run my tongue over her entire body, but one thing at a time here. "We talked about discovering dating together to help you get Naomi. Maybe we have to discover sex together, just to make sure we get the book right."

I gulp, one working brain cell firing and reminding me this is a bad idea. "You want to do this...for my book?"

Her smile falters. "If you don't—"

"No, I do. I do," I blurt out, my cock taking charge. *Way to sound eager, dick.* Yes, I'm talking to the throbbing appendage between my legs.

"I mean, maybe in order for us to nail the sex scenes..." She goes quiet like she's remembering something from my book. "There's this scene you have. I wasn't sure you had the details right."

"Really?"

"Yeah, we can talk about that later, but right now, I'm thinking we'll just have to discover how this table works. Not just in theory, but with a real-life experience. You know, for the book."

My stomach tightens a bit. I want her to want this, and not for the damn book. Heck maybe she does, and is using it as an excuse, much like I am.

She stands beside the board, which is like an upside-down V. How it works, is you place your hips at one end of the padded board on top, putting your backside on display. Then you lay down on the board. There is a soft pad on the sides of the V toward the bottom, where your arms and knees rest. These bottom board have the shackles attached to them. As she stands there, her brow furrowed, I step up behind her, put my hands on her hips and position her against the resting pad.

With my mouth close to her ear, I whisper, "Bend over it."

"Okay," she squeaks out and that one word wraps around my dick like a hot mouth. What would Daisy's mouth feel like on my dick? Dammed if I don't want to find out.

She bends and settles her knees and arms on the lower padded boards. Her dress lifts high on the back of her legs. She shifts, and a little gasp catches in her throat. "How is this?"

A little grumbling growl catches in my throat. "Fucking perfect."

She falls quiet, and my heart jumps. Jesus, I don't want to fuck things up between us. Her friendship is the most important thing in the world to me, and I don't want her doing something she doesn't want to do. She already does so much for me, all the time, I don't want her doing this just to help me out.

Oh, but she wants this, Brandon. She really wants this, and maybe now, I can finally do something for her. Something like give her a mind-blowing orgasm. Except she's so quiet, I'm begin-ning to question the intelligence of all this.

"Daisy?" I ask.

"Can you...see my panties?"

I back up an inch, and take in her long, gorgeous, toned legs. She's a fucking virgin and likely saving herself for someone special, and while I don't plan on taking her virginity, there are so many other things I can do. "Do you want me to see them?" I ask.

A long beat of silence, and then, "Yes."

The room closes in on me. Sweet, innocent Daisy Reed wants me to see her panties, and fuck me sideways because I'm sure I've died and gone to heaven. I blink once, then twice, posi-tive I'm having another one of my sex dreams, even though none of them have been this vivid, and when I open my eyes wide, she's still bent over the board, her gorgeous, lush ass high in the air, and inches from my fingertips.

"Take mental notes, B. For the book."

"Yeah? This is about the book," I say quietly, dazed, my mind on other things and there's no way I'll have to take notes. The sight of her is now burned into my brain, and I will not forget one second of this. I move in behind her, take the soft hem of her dress into my hands and ever so slowly lift it until I see her panties. The white lace I've played with before hugs her lush ass to perfection, and as she wiggles, they ride up a little, exposing the bottom curve of her cheeks—right where I'd like to sink my teeth.

"Are you getting a visual?" she asks, her voice low and breathless.

"I am, and it's helping immensely." With my erection that is. "Would it be okay with you, if I used the feathers? Later on, maybe you can describe the sensations, so I can get them right in the book."

"Yes, please..."

Okay, it's all I can do to stay standing and not tug those panties to the side and plunge into her. What is it about hearing those two words on her tongue that turns me into a caveman, with one thing on the brain—raw fucking.

"B?" She's about to lift herself up, no doubt to figure out what the hell is wrong with me, considering I just went silent, but I put my hand on her back, and hold her down, loving everything about her laid out like this. "Oh," she sighs, her voice barely a whisper. Would she like being restrained? Let's find out.

I clear my throat and step to her side. She angles her head to see me, and in my best serious, 'author' voice, I begin, "To really understand how this works, and how the female protagonist in my book might react, I think I should shackle your hands and legs."

Two quick breaths and then admits, "Yes."

I bite back a grin. I expected her to think on it, mull over what it might be like to be restrained, but maybe she already has, and my guess is she likes it.

I walk to where her hands are dangling and pick up one of the shackles. It's plush inside so I know it won't chafe her. Her head lifts, and her eyes are swimming with heat when they meet mine.

"This is going to be really helpful, Duke."

"Yeah," is all she says in response.

I lightly run my thumb over the inside of her wrist and she wiggles as a little whimper catches in her throat. I wrap the shackle around her, testing to make sure it's not too tight. "What do you think?"

She tugs on it. "I think I'm secure."

"How does it make you feel?"

She goes quiet. Is she nervous, embarrassed by her arousal? My guess is yes. Changing tactics, I say, "Can you do something for me, Daisy?"

"Yes," she squeaks out.

"Can you put yourself in my protagonist's shoes, and tell me how all of this would make her feel?" She nods eagerly, her eyes coming alive as I give her a means to let go, because maybe, just maybe this isn't all for the book. And if it's not, it's a good way for her to shed inhibitions and really give herself over to enjoying every moment and letting herself go as far as she needs to.

"I think she'd be really turned on by this." I secure her other hand and a keening cry catches in her throat as she tugs. "There's something really arousing in giving yourself—or rather your protagonist giving herself over—to a guy. I don't know how to explain it really, but it's freeing somehow."

"My heroine is always doing things for others. I guess she likes the idea of someone else being in charge for a change."

"Yeah, I think that's it. I knew you'd be able to explain it better than me." I walk around her, and lightly run my fingers down her spine, stopping to drop to my knees when I reach the shackles at her feet. I quickly secure her legs and more keening cries catch in her throat.

"I might not have been able to figure that out if you didn't tell me it was freeing. What I need you to do, Daisy, is tell me everything my protagonist might or might not like."

"She'd probably like to spread her legs."

Holy fuck.

I put my hands on the back of her legs, and step between them as I spread her wide. Once the shackles prevent me from widening her more, I lean over her back. "How's that?"

"Good, really good."

Wanting to take charge and let her enjoy this, I toy with the band on her panties. "Since my protagonist wants her guy to take charge, why don't I go ahead and do that and later you can tell me all about it...for the book."

"Yes, please."

"Can I do what I want to you, Daisy?" I ask, my voice taking on a serious note. I need her to want this as Daisy, and need to hear her full consent.

"Whatever you want," she murmurs, and I don't miss the sheer excitement in her voice.

"What I want is for you to stay just like this. Your ass in the air, your hot wet cunt wide open and waiting for my mouth and fingers."

"Holy God, yes. That's what I...I mean she...your heroine... would want."

I chuckle at her broken speech. I have never seen Daisy come apart and I love everything about it. "Yeah, she would want that."

I tug her panties down a bit to expose the lush top of her ass. Leaning into her, I lightly sink my teeth into the fleshy part of her ass, and she wiggles.

"Oh, God."

I grin, loving her response. Hell, I love my own too, and if I don't get my pants undone, I'm going to rupture something. I release my pants, and her moan curls around me as the zipper hisses open. I take my dick in my hands and give it a stroke as I knead her sweet ass.

But now I need both hands on her, so I let my dick go, slide my hands up her inner thighs until I'm touching her soaked panties, and I tug them to the side to expose her gorgeous, soaked pussy. I exhale quickly, hardly able to believe I get to touch and taste her beautiful pink clit.

"Daise..." I murmur, my heart clenching tight, honored and humbled that she's shackled, and spread wide open, mine to do with as I please, and I damn well please. "The first thing my hero would do is take a taste," I say, and she writhes and cries, in sweet anticipation.

I lean down and run my tongue all over her exposed sex, tasting every delicious drop of her arousal, and with each long stroke, I run my tongue around her swollen clit. I have never, ever in my life tasted anything so pure and delicious. I eat at her, barely able to believe this is happening and so goddamn happy that it is. I slurp like a man dying of thirst unable to get enough of her, and honest to God, nothing like this has ever happened to me before, and no it has nothing to do with too many hits to the head.

"Like that," she cries out. "Oh, God, just like that."

As she grows slicker, I push my finger into her. She so hot and tight it's a struggle to get my thick finger all the way in. Her body spasms as I muscle my way in, until I find that sweet bundle of nerves deep inside my woman. I lightly brush them as her breathing becomes rough and labored, and somewhere in the back of my addled brain I register that she's tugging on the shackles, and loving every second of being held down while I do dirty things to her.

My dick throbs aching to feel her hot tight muscles around it, but that can wait. She's close, so freaking close and my mind is blown at how much she likes my finger in her, my mouth on her hot flesh. I suck at her and fuck her with my finger, until she's a hot roiling mess of need.

"That's it, you just lay there and let me take care of you," I murmur as I put my mouth all over her, and a second later her cry cuts through the quiet, and she breaks beneath my ministrations, her body shaking and gyrating as she revels in the pleasure and soaks my hand and face. I stay between her legs until she rides out every glorious pulse, and when her body collapses into a heap of satisfaction, I wipe my face and inch back to remove the shackles on her ankles.

She remains quiet, her breathing ragged, her limbs limp and dangling as I move around the bench and release her wrists. I rub them gently and bring each hand to my mouth for a gentle kiss. Her head lifts, the blue in her eyes darker than I'd ever seen it before.

"Hey," I say quietly suddenly worried that I've gone too far, taken too much, crossed a line and...ruined *us*.

"Your book is going to be a best seller," she responds a smile tugging at her lips and in an instant, I know we're okay. A laugh bubbles out of my throat.

"You think so?"

"I know so."

I help her to her feet, and the look of satisfaction on her face wraps around my dick and tugs, but it tugs at something else, something in my chest, right around the vicinity of my heart.

"Daise," I croak out, my pounding heart doing some weird flip-flopping thing in my chest. Daisy and I are close, best friends, but the intimacy in what we'd just done...that broke through barriers I didn't even know existed, and while she always felt like a part of me, there's something new going on here, something so deep and profound, it touched me on another level. What the hell is going on with me? I've had sex before.

But you never had sex with Daisy before.

Her eyes go wide and she backs up a bit. "B," she murmurs, as I put my arm around her back and tug her against my body. She goes stiff—much like my dick. "Do you hear that?" she whispers.

The sound of cock screaming for release? Oh, yeah, I hear that.

"Sirens," she yelps, her eyes going wide and that's when I realize that the back door is banging again and we're about to get caught with our pants—and panties—down. Great, breaking into the neighbors' playroom is one thing, but coming face to face with security while sporting the boner of all boners, that's something else entirely.

11

DAISY

I stand on rubbery legs, and know the exact moment when Brandon registers that sirens are approaching. His eyes go wide and he reaches between my legs, tugging my panties back up and I appreciate that he's worried about me. My hand closes over his and I help him adjust the thin cotton.

"Your pants," I say, and a strange inappropriate giggle rises up in my throat. He laughs too, and it's deep and rich and curls through my blood as he tucks his cock away and fastens his pants. I can't seem to stop laughing, and neither can he. Honest to God, this is so unlike us, and I can't remember the last time we laughed liked this

"We need to get it together," he says grabbing our phones. "And get our stories straight."

I adjust my panties again. "How can we get our stories straight when I can't even get my panties straight."

"Jesus, Daisy," he groans and starts helping me again.

Once we get them fixed, I smooth my dress out and he stands back to look me over. "Good?" I ask.

"Yeah, what about me."

I point to his crotch. "I'm not sure he can hear the sirens?"

"Shit." He shifts his pants, and then captures my hand. "Come on."

"Are we making a run for it?"

"I think it's too late for that."

"Yeah," I agree. It's too late for a lot of things, like not accompanying Brandon to Seattle, not agreeing to help him get Naomi, and not reading his work and agreeing to help him with the sex scenes. But boy oh boy, it was fun, and after four years at the academy and studying all summer for my medical school entrance exams I can't remember the last time I had fun. Maybe that's what I'll do. Keep emotions out of it, and just have fun helping Brandon this week. I'll deal with real life when Naomi shows up and we head back to Nova Scotia. As my brain settles on that, we hurry to the back door, just as a flashlight shines in our eyes.

Busted.

"Hey there," Brandon says to the security guard who patrols the cottages here at Wautauga Beach. He lifts his hand to block the light from his eyes, as the security guy waves his flashlight back and forth between the two of us.

"Is this your place?" he asks in a serious tone.

"Ah, no we're just a few cottages down. We heard a noise, and came to make sure the place was secure. We heard about the recent break-ins."

"The neighbors called. They heard banging."

Brandon puts his arm around my waist, and pinches me playfully when the officer says, *banging*. I bite my bottom lip to keep myself from giggling.

"You heard the banging?" the guard asks.

Brandon pinches me again, and a high pitch noise catches in my throat. "Yeah, lots of banging going on."

The flashlight lands back on me. "Are you okay?"

"Yeah, I was afraid when I heard all the banging." Another pinch, and now this has become a game.

"Wait, aren't you Daisy Reed?" I nod but he can't see me, not when he turns the flashlight back on Brandon. "And you're Brandon Cannon." He laughs and his shoulders relax as he lets the light fall to the floor.

"That's us," Brandon responds. "We're just here for reading week, and we heard about the break-ins."

"If you heard banging..." Pinch. "You should have called security. It's not wise to walk into a place that might be compromised. You never know what you might come up against, especially if there are weapons involved."

Brandon scrubs his face. "Come up against, right."

This time I pinch Brandon, and he flinches.

The guard shines the light past us. "Did you take a look around?"

"Yeah, everything is good. I think the storm door isn't latching right, or the owners might have forgotten to lock the door."

"I'll take care of that." We give him a nod. "Say hello to your parents for me."

"Will do," Brandon agrees and we hurry outside and practically run back to his cottage. We're laughing and breathless, as we cut through the backyards, and since my legs are still weak, I stop at the treehouse. I lean against the wooden ladder to catch my breath, and the second I can fill my lungs again, I climb the rungs until I'm inside. Brandon comes up behind me, and we both lean against the rail and look past the cottage to the ocean in the distance.

"It was right here, in this tree house, the first time we played together." I glance around the floor and find candy wrappers and comic books. I guess someone has been making good use of the old place.

He smiles as he kicks at a piece of crumpled paper. "I remember it like it was yesterday."

"Me too." I'm pretty sure that was the day I fell in love with him. The side of his body presses against mine, big and strong and protective. That's Brandon in a nutshell. "Oh, am I still allowed in here?" I ask, teasing that I was the only girl the guys would let in.

"I think we might have to take another look at the contract."

I laugh. "Oh?"

He licks his bottom lip, like he's savoring the taste of me on his tongue. "You see, I just tasted you. Just had my mouth all over your hot pussy, and I think you're far too sweet to be playing in a dirty old fort like this."

Oh God, who knew dirty talk could be so arousing. "You think?" I manage to get out as I grip the wooden rail harder.

"I know."

Is he saying he sees me as more than a tomboy?

As we stand here beneath the stars, memories of his mouth on my body sends heat to the apex of my legs as sexual tension sizzles between us. "Should we have told the guard there were weapons involved?" I tease.

"You mean this?"

I lift my head, and beneath the moonlight, Brandon pulls the feather tickler out from under the back of his shirt. "Oh, my God, you did not."

"Apparently I did.".

"We have to take that back."

"Do you think they'll notice it's missing?" He slaps the feathers against his palm. "I was actually thinking this could be our reward for our bravery in trying to stop their place from being burglarized."

I back up and press against the other wall, the tingle between my legs a lovely reminder that less than five minutes ago, Brandon had his fingers in me and his mouth all over my sex. "Call it whatever you want, it doesn't change the fact that you stole a sex toy."

He runs the feathers through is fingers, and my entire body quivers. "Yeah, you're right," he agrees.

He steps closer, and I watch as he plays with the feathers. "Why did you do it?" I ask.

His head lifts, and eyes full of heat and mischief meet mine. "No one wants it after we opened it, and it seemed like a waste so I thought we could use it."

I take a fast breath, positive we're not. "For the book."

"Of course."

He puts the tickler between my knees and slowly moves it up my thighs until he reaches my wet, panty covered pussy. "Brandon..." I reach out and put my hand on his chest, desperate to touch him, to take his cock into my hands, and mouth, even though I've never done anything like that before and he's well aware of it.

But earlier, I decided to simply have fun this week with the man I've been in love with for as long as I can remember. His breath catches as I drop to my knees, and reach for the button on his pants.

"Daisy," I lift my head until our eyes meet.

"Yes."

"You don't have—"

"I want to...for the book." It's a lie of course. I'm doing this for me. I've dreamt about Brandon, of touching and tasting him and I may never be presented with this opportunity again and I'm going to take advantage of it.

His chest rises and falls quickly. "This treehouse...it's dirty."

"Maybe I like dirty, Brandon."

He curses under his breath as I unbuckle his pants, lower the zipper, and free his cock. He grows thicker beneath my visual inspection, and my lust-addled brain takes a quick moment to register that I'm on my knees in front of my best friend, and he's as wide as the blade of my hockey stick, waiting for me to touch him.

Just remember this is about sex, Daisy, and you'll be just fine.

I run my hand along the long length of him, reveling in the softness of his skin spread tight over his hardness. I take my time as I introduce my hands to his cock, and he grips my hair.

"You're killing me, Daise..."

I grin. I probably should be worried about doing something wrong, but from the heat in his eyes and the tortured sounds he's making, I'm pretty sure there is nothing I can do wrong, and I sort of love that. Love the way he's responding.

Pre-cum spurts from his tip, and acting on instinct, I lean into him and slowly slide my tongue over his crown. His cock jumps and hits my eye, and he begins to apologize profusely.

"Sorry, Daise...sorry. It's just...fuck, you've got me so hard." He groans and tilts his head back and a thrill goes through me as he becomes unhinged right before my eyes. I've seen many sides of Brandon before—all of them really, except this one— and I think this might be my favorite.

I grip the base of his cock with my hand, to tame the appendage he currently has no control over, and I open my mouth. He goes completely still and I'm not even sure he's breathing as I glance up at him. His eyes meet mine, and that's when he gets it. I want to kneel here while he feeds me his cock. I want him to control me.

"Holy shit," he groans, and moves his hips forward, and tortured noises fill the silence around us as he watches his hard length stretch my mouth open and disappear inside. "So fucking hot."

I like making this hot for him. Hell, it's hot for me too, judging by how much damper my panties have become. He grips my head with both hands and holds me still as he moves back and forth, and I offer him the heat of my mouth as he controls the pace and rhythm. He fucks my mouth, and when his thrust becomes harder, I grip his hips to stop him, and move my head back and forth, taking control so he can simply enjoy the pleasure, much like he'd taken control of me in the playroom.

I moan around his big fat cock, and he throbs inside my mouth. "Is it good, babe? Do you like doing that?"

Since I can't talk with a mouthful of cock, I nod and as I tug his dick downward, his groan deepens. I guess he likes that. But if he keeps making loud noises, someone is going to call security on us, and the guard will stumble upon a very different kind of banging. That thought makes me giggle.

"Something funny?" Brandon asks, his voice deep and tortured.

I inch back, and his cock falls from my mouth. I use my hand, and slide it up and down the slick length of him. "I was just thinking about banging."

"You want to bang, Daise? You want me to bend you over the rail and fuck you right here in this filthy treehouse?"

Holy shit, I love it when he's blunt and dirty like that, and while I've never had sex before, I want that with Brandon.

"You mean for the book?"

"Yeah, sure."

With my brain racing and my body on hyperdrive, I don't answer. Instead, I take him back into my mouth and suck until he's grunting and growling. "I think you like that idea, don't you?"

I moan and he continues with, "You like the idea of bending over for me so I can push your lacey panties to the side and put my cock inside you? Right here, in this filthy treehouse."

Oh God, if he keeps talking like that, I'm sure I'm going to orgasm without needing to be touched, and dammit, I want to be touched by him again. I mumble around his fat cock, something about this being for his book, even though it's not —and not that he can hear me anyway. Still, it seems to encourage him.

"Maybe I'll tie you up and have my—"

I take him deeper into my throat, and he groans and tugs on my hair, and I revel in the way he suddenly can't talk. He grows thicker in my mouth, and I slide my hand beneath his balls and massage lightly.

"Daise..." His voice is thick and rusty and tortured and I love everything about this. He tugs on my hair, and I get what he's trying to do, but I want him to come in my mouth. I want everything.

I shake my head no, and his groan curls around me. A second later, he's as hard as granite, and he stops moving his hips and lets his body go, filling my mouth with his cum. I swallow, and swallow and swallow some more, but it's too much. He spills from my mouth, and drips onto my chest, making a lovely mess on my new dress. When he's done spasming, I lick him clean with my tongue, and suddenly notice that he's gone very still...and very quiet.

I glance up at him and beneath the moonlight, I catch the twist of his lips, the worry radiating in his eyes. But I'm not having any of that. I can't—won't—let this come between us. I realize we have no romantic future, but right now, we have this.

"I needed you to come in my mouth," I tell him and he lightly runs his fingers under my jaw.

"Yeah?"

I lean into his touch, and he might as well be stroking my heart. Is this wrong? Should I not be messing around with the man I love because I'm in the middle of setting him up with a friend? The way I see it is they went on one bad date and they're not a couple. They're both free to be with whoever they want. Right now, he wants to be with me, and it's going to take a jab from a skilled anesthesiologist to knock me unconscious and get me to stop. As long as I'm awake and breathing, nothing is going to keep me from wanting Brandon. "For the book."

His soft laugh cuts through the silence. "Right, for the book," he agrees.

"I think if we want to get the book right, we're going to have to do a lot of things like this, a lot of experimenting." I stare at him, and my heart races. Is he having second thoughts? Hell, I don't want to ruin our relationship either, but I want this man, just for a little while.

He swallows, hard, and the sound vibrates around me. "But what if—"

"No regrets," I say quickly, before he can finish, and he doesn't need to finish for me to know what he's thinking. He's worried about us, and there's no better time than now for us to address it.

"No regrets," he agrees quietly.

"At the end of the week, things go back to the way they were." Once again, the worried look shines in his eyes.

"Okay," he answers softly as he sweeps his big, callused thumb over my cheek.

"One more thing," I say and he frowns. I stand, and his big body crowds mine, doing deliriously delicious things to my throbbing sex. I snatch the tickler from him, and smack it against my palm. "There might be one other thing we might need to experiment with, for the book."

"Yeah?"

"Something I think I..." His brow arches and I clear my throat and try again, "I mean your protagonist, might like."

He dips his head, his breath hot on my face as he growls, "Tell me exactly what she'd like..."

12

BRANDON

I wake to the sound of seagulls outside the window, and I peel one eye open, waiting for my pain sensors to go on high alert, as they have almost every morning for the last couple of weeks, compliments of my concussion. This morning, there's only a faint dull ache behind my eyes, and as the room comes into view, it doesn't spin and churn my stomach.

What is churning my stomach, however, are memories of last night. Not that I didn't enjoy every second of what we did. Hell, enjoying can't even begin to describe what it was like to play with Daisy, to touch her curvy body and put my mouth on her. Fuck, did I really do that? Yeah, I did and in turn she took my cock into her warm, wet mouth and took me on a ride unlike any I've ever been on before. Does that sound corny? Probably but it's the truth, and I'm not going to pretend otherwise.

She makes a noise in her sleep and I slowly turn my head, my heart jumping into my throat as I take in her body, the blankets twisted around her legs, and her upper body contorted in ways that look painful. She moans again. Is she too having sex dreams about us?

My stomach churns a little more. Even though last night was amazing, maybe it shouldn't have happened. Maybe my concussion really is messing with me, and Daisy acted on impulse after we stumbled across that playroom. Combine that with almost getting caught by security and she simply could have been riding out an adrenaline rush in the tree-house. What if she wakes up and we can't keep our no regrets deal? I can't let anything come between us. I need her in my life.

I shift and turn her way, and she rolls so fast, her fist hitting my mouth. I curse under my breath. Her lids fly open, and she zeroes in on my mouth.

"B." Alarm fills her voice and her eyes. "Are you okay?"

"You punched me in the mouth."

"Sorry. I was dreaming."

"No kidding." I lick my lip and taste blood. "I'd hate to be the guy you were fighting."

She smiles, and taking me by surprise, she pulls my hand from my mouth, winches as she visibly inspects me, before dropping a very tender kiss onto my swelling lip. "I'm sorry, and for the record, you were the guy."

"You were fighting me in your sleep."

"I wouldn't exactly call it fighting."

I forget all about the pain. "A sex dream?"

"Maybe I have a concussion too," she teases.

Ignoring that, I probe. "Tell me what we were doing to make you fling around like that." Last night she teased me, and never did tell me the one other thing we might need to experiment with. Was she dreaming about it? If so, and judging by her moans and the way her body was twisted up, I can't wait to find out. Worry leaves my gut and it stops churning as her face turns a million shades of red.

"We're okay, Daise?"

"We're okay," she responds and I avert my gaze as she works to disentangle herself from the sheets. Fear grips my throat, a warning that things might not be as they seem.

I touch her arm and bring her attention back to me. "Hey."

She turns my way, and her smile is soft and sincere. Why then is my gut tightening again. "Waffles?" she asks and I stare at her for a quick moment before my worry ebbs. It's Monday, and she finds out about medical school on Wednesday. It's possible she's tied up in knots about that, so I let it go.

"If there's syrup involved, you know I'm in."

Her smile widens and the last of my anxiety fades. She finishes untangling herself and I can't help but admire her sweet, sexy body, all snug in a pair of pajama shorts and a T-shirt.

Her eyes turn back to me, and they narrow as she gives me an assessment. "How are you feeling?"

"Good, actually."

In a very serious voice she asks, "You think the oral sex helped?"

My head jerks back and I nearly bite my tongue off. "What?"

"The oral sex?" She's having a hell of a time biting back a grin. "Do you think it helped?"

Jesus, who is this version of Daisy? I'm not sure, but I like her. Hell, we've always been open and honest, but we never delved into sex. Which sucks, because I like this side of her.

"Yeah, and while I know we were doing it for the book," I say. "Putting my mouth on you probably really helped with my concussion. I'll have to do it more often."

Her chest rises and falls slowly. Oh yeah, she likes the idea of that. "And me putting my mouth on you. That helped?"

This time I nearly swallow my tongue. I snatch her arm and pull her to me. "Fuck yeah, that helped."

"Good, then I'll have to do it more often, too."

I slide my hand around her head, fist her hair and bring her mouth to mine for a good morning kiss. Ignoring the cut on my lip, I ravage her mouth and she sinks into my kisses, her small moans registering in the back of my brain.

I'm kissing Daisy.

That thought nearly makes me erupt in laughter, considering last night I buried my mouth in her sweet pussy, and she took my cock deep into her throat. Speaking of my cock. It jumps to life, aching to find a nice soft place to burrow. But that can't happen. Daisy is a virgin and I'm not the guy to take that from her. No, the guy for that is the one she's crushing on back home and it's insane how much that bugs me. It can only be because I'm used to having her for myself, and I'm nothing but a selfish bastard.

I break the kiss and her stomach grumbles. "What was that about waffles?" she asks.

"I'll make them." I jump up, and adjust my boxers over my bulge, and I glance up in time to see the grin on her face.

"I guess I wasn't the only one dreaming."

I wink at her and tease, "At least I can blame it on the concussion. You on the other hand, were hot for my dick."

"Hey!" She grabs a pillow and tosses it at me. I laugh as I catch it, but I know she likes when I talk like that, and I like this sexy side of Daisy. "Okay yeah, it's true." She sighs. "I guess the rumors are true. One touch by Cannon and it's...." She puts her hand by her head, and widens her fingers as she pulls them away, making an explosion sound. "Blast off."

I laugh at that, but I love her honesty and how she's not at all embarrassed by what happened between us. I guess if she's embracing it, I'm going to embrace it too, for the next week, that is. After that, it's back to normal.

"It's called a Cannon Blast, Duke. And it's actually a drink."

"Don't drink the Kool-Aid," she murmurs under her breath, like she's mentally berating herself. "I was always warned not to drink the Cannon Kool-Aid. Once you do, there's no going back."

Chuckling, she heads to the door, and I catch up to her, putting my arms around her waist, and she yelps as I tug her to me. I put my mouth to her ear. "Admit it, you liked it."

"Wrong."

I go still and she spins in my arms, a smile on her mouth. "I loved it, but there's a problem."

"Yeah."

"It hasn't quite quenched my thirst."

Holy fuck. I shake my head and laugh. I love this coy, sexy side to her. I'm about to pick her up and toss her onto the bed, and eat at her until she screaming my name and so damn sated she won't be able to walk for the rest of the day. I make a move to lift her and go still when her phone rings.

"My parents," she explains, all teasing gone from her voice. I nod and she puts her hand on my shoulder. "Don't worry, I won't say anything about your concussion."

"I know." I trust Daisy implicitly and I have to say, I love how supportive she is with my writing. It's a ridiculous pipe dream, but hey, we can entertain the idea while we're here having fun. When it's back to reality I'll dabble a bit, but that's it. My future is at the rink, not in front of my laptop creating new worlds. Oddly enough, with Daisy's support, that bothers me just a little bit more.

She darts back into the room, grabs her phone from the nightstand and jumps on the bed. "Hey Mom, how's Mexico?"

I stand in the doorway for a second, and Daisy smiles at me and relaxes back on her pillow. I nod, and grab my jeans, knowing she'll be a while. I mouth the word, shower, and leave the room to give her privacy. I head to the bathroom, shower quickly, tug on my boxers and jeans, and make my way downstairs.

Out the front window, I spot Sebastian walking into the water. I thought Daisy might have been interested in him last night, but it was my bed she ended up in. Of course, that doesn't mean she's interested in me. Not in a long-term way anyway. Hell, she's setting me up with one of her friends, which seems all kinds of strange right now.

I walk into the kitchen, put a coffee pod into the machine and get that going before I grab the waffle maker and the boxed batter we bought yesterday. I turn fast, and for a split second I'm dizzy, but fortunately, it passes quickly.

At the sink, I look at the broken vase, and remember we have to pick up some glue. I grin as my gaze goes to the feather tickler. I should probably pick up a new one, break back into the neighbors' cottage and replace it. Not that I think they'd notice it was gone. There were a ton of them, but I'm not a thief. Maybe Daisy will help me return it and we can see what other kind of trouble we can get ourselves into. Upstairs I hear the shower turn on, and guess she's finished the call with her folks.

A short time later, footsteps echo behind me and I spin. Daisy comes bouncing into the kitchen, her gorgeous breasts covered only by a thin cotton dress, and those legs of hers—when did they get so long and sleek? Okay, I knew Daisy had grown into a beautiful woman, but why the hell hadn't I noticed it before now? I guess a part of me always knew she was hands off, and blocked out the fact that she was a gorgeous, desirable woman —who I knew better than to corrupt.

"Coffee," she says and steps up to me, glancing over my shoulder. I put my hand around her waist and breathe in the scent of my soap on her skin. We always touched, a lot, but the touch is different now. In fact, it sends electrical pulses straight to my dick.

"Everything good?"

"Yup. My parents aren't upset and they're glad you're with me for when I get the results."

I gesture over my shoulder. "First cup is yours."

"You're the best."

Nah, she's the best.

She moves to the side and takes the first mug of coffee. She holds it out for me to take a sip before snatching the milk from the fridge and adding it. I turn my attention to the waffles as she tosses in another pod for me.

"What time are we going to see your parents?" she asks as my coffee percolates.

"Right after we eat, if that's okay with you."

"It's fine with me. I'm here for you, B. I have nothing to do but be at your beck and call."

I grin at that and as she checks her phone for messages, I consider our plans for Wednesday. I want to do something extra special for her, because I know she's going to get accepted to med school, and all her dreams are going to come true.

My dream was to find a nice girl I could bring home to Mom and Dad. Wait, am I suddenly wavering on that, suddenly wondering if asking Daisy to set me up with Naomi was a big mistake?

Fuck me twice.

"You okay, B?"

"What?" I take in her concerned expression. "Oh, yeah, just thinking about my folks and hoping they don't think anything is out of the ordinary." Hell, there's a lot out of the ordinary and I'm not just talking about my concussion.

"It'll be okay."

I turn the waffle maker over when it beeps, and at the same time, my coffee is done. I take a big sip and Daisy jumps up and grabs the plates.

"I wish I could have read some of your other books," she says, and puts the plates in front of me.

"Why?"

"I don't know. Maybe to see where you struggled."

"I struggle with the happily ever after in the end, and maybe with a few of the sex scenes."

"Turgid manhood, I know," she teases with a smirk. "Why do you think you have trouble with the endings?"

I shrug. "Maybe because I've only ever had happy endings, and never a happily ever after."

She laughs at that, and that's what I was hoping for, then her smile falls. "After we fake date and learn a thing or two, you can find that happily ever after, maybe even with Naomi."

"Yeah, maybe."

She leans toward me. "So what should we do first? Where should we go for our 'real date'?" She does air quotes around the last two words.

I put a big waffle on a plate and slide it in front of her. She opens the syrup and does her cute little happy face with it. "What do you think Naomi would like to do?"

"She told me she's never been to Seattle, so I say you hit up all the hot spots."

I pour more batter into the waffle maker. "Like the gum wall?"

She cuts into her waffle, going for the big dollop of syrup representing the eyeball of the happy face. "That is so gross, B." But that's all forgotten as she takes a big bite and moans as she slides the fork from her mouth.

Okay, never in my life did I think that was sexy—until now. My cock twitches. "Right now I'm thinking the market and a hike, and a nice restaurant to end the night. Oh, maybe even a bike ride or a ride on the boat."

"But no fishing and no touching eyeballs," she warns.

I wag my brows, insinuating I might not be able to heed her last warning. "Those are all the things we always do. We never considered them dating before."

"Because it was us, and we're friends. We hang out but those things could be considered dating."

"All this time I was dating you and I had no idea."

She rolls her eyes at me, stabs her fork into a piece of waffle and waves it at me. "I'd toss a piece of waffle at you, but it's too good to waste." She shoves it into her mouth and moans.

"Do you think Naomi will like those things?"

She shrugs. "I'm only just getting to know her, but I can't see why she wouldn't. You could also take her to the typical touristy places like the Space Needle." She chews and goes quiet for a moment, and I can't help but wonder what's going through her mind. "Tonight though, instead of us fake dating, I think we should work on your book. There are fun things we can add."

"From last night?"

"Uh huh," she says and moans as she slides another piece of waffle into her mouth.

I lean against the counter, and there is nothing I can do to convince my dick now is neither the time nor place to get hard. "Did you always moan like that when you ate waffles?"

"Yes, why?"

I point downward. "That's why?"

Her eyes go big and her lips curl. "Brandon!" she shrieks.

"It's not my fault."

"Can't you control that thing?"

I angle my head, like she must be out of her mind, and a change comes over her. "I was thinking..." She pushes from the table, and her steps are slow as she comes toward me, licking syrup from her finger and I swear to God, I'm seconds from ejaculating in my pants.

"About?" I croak out, and my broken voice brings a grin to her face.

"Your book."

"What about it?"

"I think it might need a kitchen sex scene."

I gulp. Is she fucking serious? "You want...you want to have sex in the kitchen."

"If by sex you mean me putting your cock in my mouth, then yes, I want to have sex in the kitchen."

13

DAISY

I love the hungry yet dumbfounded look taking over Brandon's face as I blatantly tell him what I want to do. And why wouldn't he be shocked at my behavior? It's totally out of character for me, but hey, I'm not playing myself. I'm playing a character in his book and that makes taking what I want so much easier. Yeah, without all the pretending, I might not have the guts to act on the things I want—have always wanted. Talk about a perfect excuse. Although, maybe, just maybe, with Brandon, this is who I really am deep inside.

And who exactly is that, Daisy?

Oh, just a girl who wants to give her body to the guy she's been in love with forever, and take pleasure in what all the other girls on campus have been enjoying for years. I drop to my knees and shimmy close, glancing up to take in his gaping jaw.

"Also we can't have you going out like this. Two birds, one stone and all." I lightly touch his cock, trace the length of it as it swells against his pants. "Although I would never stand for anyone throwing a stone at a bird." I unbutton his pants, and say, "Two birds, and—"

"One scone," he murmurs, knowing me so well he knew exactly what I was going to say. I grin up at him.

"With a scone you can feed the birds instead of killing them."

"Daise..."

I tug his zipper down, and the hiss curls around me and seeps under my skin to tease my arousal. "Actually, you can probably feed more than two birds with one scone."

"Daise..."

Tugging his gorgeous, hard cock free, I glance up at him as he keeps chanting my name. I love how tortured he looks, how he's standing there his lids half-mast, his hand gripping the counter behind him like he doesn't know what to make of it all. Hell, I don't really, either.

"Speaking of feeding..."

I go quiet and his eyes refocus on me. "What?" he asks, his head rolling a little.

"Are you going to feed me your cock?"

He grabs a fistful of his hair. "Sweet mother of Jesus."

I bite back a smirk as he grips his cock by the base and takes a step closer. I open my mouth for him and moan as the scent of his soapy skin reaches my nostrils. I breathe him in, and the back of my jaw tingles as his tang hits my tongue.

Brandon asked me if I wanted to have sex in the kitchen, and while I realize this isn't really his version of sex, it has me fantasizing about things...things like him bending me over and fucking me. Here, or in the treehouse. That thought sends a rush of moist heat to my sex, and I lean into him to take him deeper, so damn aroused I don't even care that his cock is cutting off my air supply. I love everything about this.

Do I want Brandon to be my first?

"Just like that," he murmurs, his voice a low, growling whisper. His body moves, his hips pistoning forward as I rock into him. He swells in my mouth, and I'm sure his orgasm is fast approaching. But catching me completely by surprise, he pulls his cock out and I stare up at him, my mouth open, wet and hungry.

Intense brown eyes full of heat and hunger latch onto mine, and he tugs me to my feet. His big warm hands drop to my sides and slide under my loose dress. A shiver goes through me and I lift my arms as he peels it from my body. He groans as he takes my naked breasts into his hands, bending to suck each nipple until they are hard enough to score the ice on a rink.

"Daise..."

"Yeah?"

He backs me up, holding me carefully so I don't fall, and nudges me into a chair until my mouth is poised in front of his cock. Oh, is this how he wants it. I'm about to take him back into my mouth when he puts his leg on either side of the chair, to straddle me. Oh, fun.

"I was thinking, my heroine might like taking my cock like this?"

"Oh, yeah, I'm sure she would," I agree even though I'm not exactly sure what he has in mind, but I'm game. I'm game for anything with Brandon.

"I thought you might agree. As you know, the heroine asked the hero to teach her things, so she doesn't finish her college years an inexperienced virgin."

I chuckle slightly and a little jolt goes through me. "You could almost be writing about us."

His face blanks for a second, like he hadn't put that together, and then he smiles. "Yeah, maybe. I guess I never thought about it that way."

"All the more reason I can help you with the story." I'd be foolish really, to think on some subconscious level that he was writing about us. It does make me wonder about the other tropes he's used in his other books.

"Open your mouth."

I love the soft command in his voice. I do as he says and instead of putting his cock between my lips, he tugs on it, until pre-cum spills between my breasts. I make a little gasping sound and he takes my hands and puts them on my breasts, and as he encourages me to squeeze them together, I get exactly what he wants to do.

He eyes me for a second, like he's checking in to make sure I'm okay with this. I nod, and run my tongue over my bottom lip in encouragement. He pushes his cock between the tight channel I'm making with my breasts and he takes my thumbs and puts them over my nipples. I rub my nipples and add that sensation to the one of him fucking my breasts, his cock stroking long and deep and reaching my mouth. Each thrust has to be the most erotic thing I've ever done. Not that I've done a lot, and hopefully that will be rectified this week.

"B," I moan as his cock reaches my lips and slides into my mouth. His gaze stays on mine, and this animalistic intensity about him is like a hot caress over my clit. I've never orgasmed without touching myself, but this—holy hell, I think it might be the first. Then again, isn't this whole week about firsts—that are going to leave me craving seconds and possibly thirds. Yeah, most definitely thirds. What I'm really hoping is it sates my need for him and helps me move on, but with each touch, each stroke, I fear it's having the opposite effect. FML.

He powers forward and back, taking full control of his body and mine, and I love the need on his face, not to mention the intensity about him. He puts a hand on my shoulder and hangs on as his grunts grow louder, and faster until it's one long tortured sound that I'm bound to play out in my brain on repeat when this is long over. I lick his crown and suck on him with every upward thrust, and I'm so damp between my legs I'm practically soaking the chair.

"Babe," he growls, and slides into my mouth, going perfectly still as his cock jumps and he pumps his release into my mouth. He's never called me babe before. Duke yes, but never babe. I swallow him, and moan with sheer pleasure as his cock spasms beneath my tongue. Has he grown sensitive? I circle his crown, taking care not to touch his overstimulated slit, and when he's clean, he exhales a harsh breath and sinks to his knees in front of me. He places his head on my lap and takes deep gulping breaths and I run my fingers through his damp hair, never wanting this new deeper intimacy between us to end. Honestly, I've always felt close to him, but now, it's weird, it's like he's a part of my soul.

"Daise..." he moans quietly as he lifts his head, his eyes still half lidded. He reaches up and swipes his thumb over my mouth as my entire body quivers, buzzing, my brain on an endorphin high simply from the way he just fucked my breasts and mouth. His gaze is soft and sated, and this time I'm the one taking deep gulping breaths as he buries his mouth in the apex of my legs, his breath hot on my core, through the thin fabric of my panties. He nips at the lace, tugs them from my body.

"I need to touch you. I need to see your sweet pussy, and see if fucking me with your mouth made you wet." I could simply tell him it did, but I want him to see for himself. Want to see what it does to him. He slides his hand up my quivering legs, spreading me just a little bit until he can work his fingers between my inner thigh and the lacy band of my panties. Everything about sex in his kitchen—where anyone could walk in on us—feels naughty and titillating. Who knew there was a budding voyeur inside of me? I'd say Brandon knows me better than I know myself, but I'm the one who initiated this.

He bends and licks me through my panties as his deft finger finds my swollen clit. "Fuck, I like tasting you."

I gulp. "I like you tasting me too." His low chuckle reverberates through me and the vibrations stimulate my clit.

"Good, because I plan to do it a lot." He tugs on my panties to expose more of my wet sex and I grab the chair and lift my hips as he swipes the soft blade of his tongue over my wet flesh and growls with hunger. "Sweet peach," he mumbles, or at least that's what I think he said.

"That's why we get along so well." I try to keep my voice from shaking but it's futile, so I continue with, "We like the same things." He chuckles again and I honestly have no idea what I'm saying or why I'm even talking.

Shut up, Daisy, and enjoy. You only get one week of this.

I clamp my mouth shut, and a groan of pleasure squeaks through my clenched lips, but I can no longer keep silent, not when he's sliding a thick finger inside me and touching all the places that drive me crazy. How does he know my body so well? Okay, fine, I know why he's experienced, and I don't want to think about that, because for a little while longer, I don't have to share him with anyone.

He slides a second finger into me, filling me completely and I can't even imagine what it would be like to have his cock spreading me open. But I want that. God, I really want that. Would he?

I put my hands on his shoulders, touching his muscles as they bunch and relax as he fucks me with his fingers. I almost laugh at that thought. This is Brandon Cannon—and his face is between my legs.

"Oh," I squeak out as he nibbles my clit, a new kind of desperation about me. I want—need—this more than I've ever needed anything. Moisture breaks out on my entire body and I almost forget how to breathe as pleasure gathers in a big ball between my legs. "Please," I moan, even though I'm not sure what I'm begging for. I rock against him, trying to drive his fingers in deeper. He changes the pace and rhythm, slowing down. Does he not want me to orgasm?

"B..." I cry his name and I don't care if I sound desperate. I am desperate.

"Don't worry, babe. I've got you. I'm going to give you exactly what you need. Now you just sit there and let me make you feel good."

"Oh, yes..." I try to control my breathing, to stop writhing like bacon in a hot pan and just relax and let him take care of me. I'm not used to it really. Usually I'm the one taking care of others and a girl could definitely get used to this kind of attention—from a guy like Brandon. Yeah, I'm not sure I'd want this from any other guy, but I need to find a way to change that, unless I want to spend forever alone, and I don't want that. I need to somehow get past my feelings for my best friend and find a way to move on when the week is over.

He puts another finger in me, and I'm sure it's not enough. The room closes in on me, and I work to keep my eyes open. I want to see everything he's doing to me. His head moves between my legs, and I writhe against the chair, rubbing my pussy all over his face. Judging from the growls coming from his throat, I think he likes it.

"More," I cry out again, and his head lifts, his dark eyes on mine.

"You want me to fuck you, Daise…"

He continues to work his fingers in me and I open my mouth to scream, yes, but I lose the ability to speak as my orgasm breaks from my body and I come all over his fingers and hand.

"Oh, God."

He grins and dives back between my legs, lapping and slurping and just plain drinking me in. I gasp and grip his hair and hold on for dear life as I go limp enough to slide off the chair. His tongue is like magic, licking and probing, and wait…am I supposed to be getting aroused again?

His head lifts, and his face is soaked with my cum as he licks his lips. "Sex in the kitchen, best thing ever. Definitely going in my book."

I grin. "Sometimes I have good ideas." He goes back on his heels, and the closeness between us prompts me to say, "It wasn't really sex, though."

He leans into me, brushes my hair from my shoulder. "Of course, it was. It was oral sex." I nod and go quiet and he angles his head. "Daise..."

"Yeah?"

"What's on your mind?"

I chicken out and roll one shoulder. "Nothing."

"Nothing, or would you like me to put my cock in you?"

I nearly choke on my tongue. Dammit, I should have known he'd be able to read me. I'm like an open book to him— mostly. I turn it around and ask, "Is that something you'd like to do?"

He snorts. "Do you really have to ask that?" A thrill goes through me. Brandon wants to fuck me. He cups my face and his voice is low when he continues with, "I just need to be sure it's what you want to do," he asks, his demeanor changing, becoming serious. "You're a—"

"Virgin, I know, and you know I'd do anything to help with the book. I mean, if I'm taking on the part of the heroine, also a virgin in the book, we'd be able to really get the details and you know, the...specifics."

He goes quiet, a measure of worry in his eyes at my lame reasoning. "You're not holding out for someone special?" Oh, God if he only knew how special he was to me, how special this would be—that I've been holding out for him my whole life. "I don't want you to regret—"

"No, I'm not and no regrets, remember?"

He leans in, and presses his lips to mine. "I want to fuck you, Daisy. I want to put my cock deep inside your sweet pussy, and fuck you well into next week, but your reasoning...I just can't."

Well hell. That totally backfired.

14

BRANDON

Do I want to sleep with Daisy?

Hell yeah, I do.

Is it smart?

Hell no, it's not?

Fuck, she's setting me up with her friend, but there's more going on here. I know Daisy well, better than any other woman, and while I know she's enjoying the sex and stepping out of character, I can't have her going all the way with me for my book. I want her to go all the way because it's what she wants.

I WANT HER TO GO ALL THE WAY BECAUSE IT'S WHAT SHE WANTS.

So, if I break that down, what exactly is the reasoning behind it? Oh, maybe that I want Daisy to like me, as in want me. As in more than friends. But if we went down that path, and it didn't work out, then what? Hell, we've already started down a path we never should have ventured, and I have to make sure it doesn't fuck with 'us'. Oh right, and I can't fucking forget she likes some guy on the team.

I glance at her in the seat next to me as we Uber to my parents' place. After sex in the kitchen, when I told her I wouldn't fuck her for my book, she didn't answer. She might have wanted to, but my brother Casey called asking when we'd be coming by—it's reading week for him too, but he and his friends have a coding competition this afternoon. I put my conversation with Daisy on hold, leaving the ball in her court, where it's going to stay until she brings it up. I want her but taking her virginity... that's a big fucking deal. This is Daisy here, not some random chick looking for a quick hookup with a hockey player.

"Everything okay?" I ask when she frowns at her phone.

She lifts her head and smiles. "Yup, just catching up on messages." She tucks her phone into her pocket and gazes out the window, and my stomach knots. Shit, I'm really hoping things aren't already messed up between us.

"Nothing from med school yet?"

She exhales and shakes her head. "I don't know how I'm going to make it through the next two days."

Wanting things normal between us, and wanting to keep her mind off school, I say, "By keeping busy. How about we hit the market later, grab some snacks and go for a hike up Mount Rainier?" She smiles and I relax. I'm glad I know what she likes to do. "It's what we always used to do when we were stressed. Remember when you were waiting to see if you made the women's team at the Academy?"

"Hike."

"And when I was waiting to hear if I was accepted to the Academy," I add.

"Hike."

"When—"

"Hike," she says before I can continue. "It sounds like the perfect afternoon, B. Maybe we can get some of those gigantic peaches from the market." She holds her hand out, making a circle the size of her head.

I laugh. "They're not that big." Reaching out, I put my hand on her thigh and give it a squeeze. I've done it a million times before, but it's never elicited a small intake of air from Daisy. I don't think.

"We also need to get glue to fix your mom's vase. Let's not forget about that." I nod, and I'm about to tell her we can do that anytime, but she says, "I think we should do that before the hike. I don't want to leave it until later and risk the store closing. I do feel responsible. I think I'm the one who opened the window."

"Okay," I agree, even though I'm pretty sure she wasn't responsible for leaving the window open. But if it's important to her, it's important to me. Wait, maybe there's something else she wants to pick up at the store? She never did tell me what other things my protagonist might like to experiment with. Curiosity causes my dick to jump but I marshal him into submission as the driver pulls up in front of my parents' home and I climb out. Daisy exits on the other side, and she smooths her hair down as she circles the front of the vehicle to meet me.

"Do you think they'll know?" she asks. "Your mom is pretty observant."

"No, it's fine. You look great, Duke."

Her smile falters for a second. Was it something I said? I'm about to ask when the front door bursts open and Casey comes running out.

"Brandon, my man," he says and holds his fist out for a bump.

"Get in here, asshole." I pull him too me and hug him.

"Easy, bro?"

"What, are you too big for hugs now?"

He turns to Daisy, and something comes over his face. His shoulders straighten as he pulls himself up to his full height, and his eyes narrow, oozing all kinds of dirty suggestions. What the fuck? I know those moves. I've used the moves. Hell, I think I taught those moves to him but why the hell is he putting on the charm with Daisy.

"No," he says his voice deep and thick. "Never too big to be hugged." He opens his arms to Daisy, and she walks into him.

Little bastard.

"Back up, little brother," I order and practically peel him off Daisy. But I get it, she's a gorgeous woman with a killer body. Was I the only one who hadn't seen it up until a week ago?

"Brandon," Mom says as she comes out on the steps, her hair pinned on the top of her head, a good sign she's elbow deep into her next book and I have to say I'm a bit envious that she gets to follow her passion and is supported by all those around her. She holds her arms out, and I'm still trying to drag Casey off Daisy as I step up to her and give her a hug. Her warm, familiar scent wraps around me.

"Let me look at you." She cups my face, and her gaze moves over me.

"Hey Nina," Daisy calls out, dragging Mom's attention away from me and I'm grateful for her interruption.

"Daisy." Mom smiles holding her arms out. "I'm so happy to see you." Daisy hugs her. "I was talking to your mom and she told me the results come in Wednesday."

"Trying not to think about it," Daisy says with a wince.

"Oh, honey, I have all the faith in the world in you. Come on, would coffee and your favorite pastry from Freeman's help?"

"Uh, yeah," she says, and I fling my arm over Casey's shoulder as he watches them step into the house.

"Stop fucking staring."

"What," he snorts. "She's hot."

"She's like...your sister."

"No, she's fucking not."

I slap the back of his head. "Language."

Ignoring me he gives a low, slow whistle. "She might be your best friend, dude, but she's not mine." He makes two fists and taps them together. "I'd like to be tap—"

"Casey," Dad growls, clearing his throat as he joins us on the stoop. "Do you want to think about what you're going to say before saying it?"

"Uh, I was just asking Brandon here if he's been ah...tap... taping his games. You know, so we can all watch them together later?"

Nice save, little brother. Knowing full well that's not what he was going to say, Dad jerks his thumb over his shoulder. Like Casey could pull a fast one on him. Back in the day, Dad had a reputation, and this apple—me—didn't fall far from that tree. While Casey is into coding, he's a chip off the old block too. "Don't you have a coding competition to prepare for?"

"Yeah, sure. Catch up with you later, bro."

"Actually Casey, there's something I want to talk to you about. I need a favor."

He smirks. "Yeah, you do," he needles, like I'm asking *him* to tap Daisy or something. God, was I ever that bad?

"I'll catch up with you before you go."

Dad shakes his head as Casey bolts upstairs. "That kid is going to be the death of me."

"I thought that was my job," I tease.

"Believe it or not, you're the one I don't have to worry about. You got your head on your shoulders and are well on your way to the NHL. Casey... He's like a loose cannon sometimes. If I get him through high school in one piece it will be an achievement."

I laugh at that. Casey is a good kid; he just gets sidetracked by the first shiny thing he sees. But he's going to kick ass at Stanford, and we all know it. A strange wave of nausea hits, and it might be because it's unusually hot in Seattle for October. I wobble a bit.

"You okay, son?"

"Yeah." I square my shoulders. "It's just so hot here."

He puts his arm around me and I'm grateful for the guidance as he leads me inside. "There's a big box of pastries from your favorite café."

My heart squeezes. "That was nice of Mom."

"Hey what makes you think it was your mother?"

"Are you saying you did it?"

"No." His big bark of laughter cuts through the quiet of the foyer, and we head to the kitchen, where I find Daisy and Mom deep into conversation about Mom's latest book. My chest constricts for a brief second, but Daisy isn't about to spill my deepest secret.

"What are you working on now?" Daisy asks.

Mom opens a box and takes out our favorite pastries and puts them on a plate. "I'm actually working on a romantic comedy."

"Ah, so you're writing about my love life, are you?" Daisy teases. "If you need any help with that."

Mom laughs and grabs four mugs from the cupboard. "Come on Daisy, the guys must be fighting to date you. Look at you. You're smart, athletic, and gorgeous."

She smiles, but it's forced. "I haven't had time to date."

That's the story she tells everyone, but now I realize it's because she's hung up on some guy on my team—a guy who clearly is an idiot if he doesn't know she exists. Yes, I'm an idiot, too, because I failed to see the incredible woman right under my nose. Maybe that's not entirely true. I always knew she was one of a kind, but I couldn't make a move and risk messing up our relationship.

I wink at Daisy, and I'm pretty sure that pink hue suddenly painting her cheeks isn't from the heat. "She's breaking hearts all over town, Mom."

She chuckles and brushes me off. "The only thing I'm breaking is hockey sticks with my killer shot."

"Well," Mom begins. "If she does break hearts, at least she'll be able to put them back together again when she's a doctor." Mom fills a cup of coffee from the carafe. "Have you decided if you want to specialize?"

"I was actually thinking about sports medicine."

"Really? I didn't know that." Then again, I didn't ask. Probably because I'm a selfish bastard, caught up in my own life.

Her gaze jerks to me. "I haven't completely decided." Daisy adds a splash of milk to her coffee and takes a sip.

"I hear the Seattle Shooters are looking for a new doctor," Dad informs her. It's his old team and he follows them very closely.

Daisy sets her mug down. "That would get me back to Seattle, and I do miss home, but the East Coast is growing on me. I'll probably end up choosing Halifax."

My gaze jerks to hers. "I thought you said you weren't sure yet."

Fuck, if I'm in Seattle and she's in Halifax, we'll never see each other.

"I can ask around if you change your mind," Dad informs her. "As you know, we're still holding out hope that Brandon plays for the Shooters. I have no doubt he'll be the next greatest."

"How could he not be when he's following in your footsteps?" Mom says, and as they smile at each other, my throat tightens, and my shoulders droop as pressure weighs heavily on them.

"Then you two can stay close," Dad adds, like he has our futures all figured out and I'm guessing he thinks he does. "I know what your friendship means to each of you."

Or...I could play hockey as a hobby, and become a full-time writer, instead of the other way around, and stay in Halifax with Daisy.

What the fuck are you saying, dude?

"What do you guys plan to do while you're home?" Mom asks, changing the subject.

"Hang out, swim. Oh, I need to grab a suit from upstairs. The one at the cottage is stretched out or something."

Daisy snatches up her mug, and nearly spills the coffee as she brings it to her mouth, and I can't help but think she's remembering how my old suit couldn't contain my turgid manhood. I bite back a laugh and add, "Probably hit the market, maybe go on a hike later today." I turn to my father. "You're still okay with me borrowing your car for a few days?"

"Not a problem at all," he replies and takes a big bite of pastry. He chews and rubs his very fit body. "Good thing you're not home more often," he jokes. "Otherwise, I'd be in trouble."

I laugh with him. He's in great shape and he knows it. He might not be in the NHL anymore, but he's working with the high school students and is always on the go. This week he's off for reading week like the rest of us.

"Oh," Mom says. "Wanda Jenkins called. She said there was a commotion at the Conrads cottage. Did you guys hear anything about that?"

"Ah, yeah." I reach over my shoulder and rub the muscles on my back. "We heard some banging."

This time Daisy practically snorts coffee through her nose.

"Are you okay?" Mom asks, passing over a handful of napkins.

"Yup, good. Just forgot how to drink for a second there." She dabs her face with the napkin and doesn't dare make eye contact with me. "Stress," she tells my Mom. Mom taps Daisy's arm and reassures her she'll get into med school.

I turn the conversation back to our week off and let Mom and Dad know I'll be having some friends join us come next weekend for the year end blowout and to celebrate Daisy and Naomi getting into med school. But the thoughts of Naomi coming to give me a second chance feels wrong. Should I tell Daisy? I mean, I'm the one who asked her to set us up, and if I tell Daisy I might be seeing her as more than the tomboy we allowed in the treehouse—that bending her over that bench and wanting her has nothing to do with my book—would it ruin us?

With those dark thoughts racing around my brain, we sit around the table a little longer, and I have to say, I'm glad the room isn't spinning. Maybe the sex with Daisy is helping. My cock jumps. Shit, can't think about that right now. Mom and Daisy break off into conversation about medical school and Mom's writing, and Dad and I finish our pastries and talk about hockey, as per usual.

Casey pokes his head into the kitchen. "I have to take off. See you around later, bro?"

"Yeah, wait up, I need to talk to you."

Daisy's attention turns to me as I step from the table throw my arm around my little bro and walk into the living room. "What are you doing Wednesday?"

"Probably busy?" He holds his hand out and I slap his palm, but what he's looking for is money for a favor. I don't mind helping him out. I dig into my wallet and hand him a couple hundred dollars.

"Are you kidding me?"

"No, I need you to do something for me and you'll need money. When you're done, you get to keep the change, but don't be cheap."

"What makes you think I'm going to do you a favor for a few lousy bucks?"

"Because it's for Daisy."

He stands tall again, his chest out as he peacocks.

Really, dude?

"What is it?" he asks, a new deepness to his voice.

I lower my voice and give him very clear details on what I want from him on Wednesday, and he listens eagerly. Just as I'm finishing up, Daisy and Mom walk down the hall. Daisy peeks in and glances at Casey.

"Hey Case, if I don't see you before I go back—"

Cutting her off, he puts his hand on his chest and says, "You'll break my heart."

"Told you she was a heartbreaker," I pipe in and shake my head at my brother's antics. I'm sure the girls at his school are all fighting over him.

Daisy laughs. "Your mom is hooking me up with a few books." She winks at me before she follows Mom down the hall, and I'm hoping Casey doesn't read anything into it, but it's hard to get anything by the kid. He's too bright for his own good.

When they disappear, and I continue to stare at the spot Daisy had just vacated, my heart pounds a little harder against my ribs as I reach out and grab the windowsill to stabilize myself. I'm a bit lightheaded again, but I can't blame it on the concussion this time. Nope, I can only blame it on Daisy and how she makes my blood burn hot, in a way it's never burned before.

"Holy shit," Casey blurts out and my gaze wanders back to find him blatantly examining me. "Wait, are you..." His eyes narrow in on me and for a second I think he's going to notice I'm not up to par—that the room is spinning before my eyes — but unfortunately, he's far more observant than that.

His jaw gapes open. "What the fuck are you doing, dude, she's your best friend..."

15

DAISY

"Everything okay?" I ask Brandon as he slides into the driver's seat of his dad's car and adjusts the seat.

"Yeah."

"You're not dizzy or nauseous?"

"Nope, why?" He tosses his bathing suit into the back seat and starts the SUV.

I take in his handsome profile and as his folks stand at the door to wave us off, I resist the urge to touch the scruff on his face. "You seemed to be in a very deep conversation with Casey. I thought something might be wrong, or that you told him about your concussion."

"I'm actually feeling a lot better." He grins at me. "Big brother stuff."

"Keeping him on the straight and narrow, are you? Or giving him tips on how to charm the ladies?" I laugh, but Brandon doesn't seem to find humor in what I'm saying. He didn't seem to like it when I told his parents I was probably going to stay in Halifax either, but honestly, the more I think about it, the more I realize I can't keep following him around. It's pathetic, really.

Maybe distance is what it's going to take for me to get over him, and Lord knows seeing him with Naomi every day might just be my undoing. But this week I decided to have fun with Brandon, which means I need to keep my emotions in check. There'll be plenty of time for heartbreak when we return to the Academy and Naomi is on his arm. "I don't remember Casey being so flirty before," I add, keeping the conversation light. "What was up with that?"

"He knows a beautiful woman when he sees one." His compliment curls around me like a comfy blanket, but I notice the stiffness in his body. I can't help but think Casey said something to upset Brandon. Could it have been about me?

"Are you sure you're okay?"

He tilts his neck to the side, stretching out his tight muscles, and shoots me a quick glance. "I pray for the girls at Stanford," he says, shifting the conversation and adding playfulness back to his tone. I stare at him for a second and he looks straight ahead. "Head to get some glue before our hike?"

I turn over one of the books his mom gave me and scan the back. "Yup." I read the blurb. "You know, with a little practice, you could be as good as your mom."

His fingers tighten around the steering wheel, but I'm not entirely sure not being able to follow his passion is what's bothering him. "I like your faith in me, but you heard my father. He's holding out hope that I play for the Shooters."

I reach across the seat and give his arm a squeeze. His muscles flinch, and once again I wonder what's going on with him. "I know, I heard. I'm sorry."

"Don't be sorry."

I stare straight ahead and try to think of a way for him to follow in his mother's footsteps, instead of what everyone else wants for him. Maybe I could look into publishing for him. In today's climate, he doesn't need an agent or a publishing house. Heck, he can do it himself and slowly build up a name.

"I have a friend in the English department who could probably edit for you, and we can find cover designers anywhere. I was asking your mom a few questions." His gaze jerks my way and I hold my hand up. "Don't worry, I didn't say anything."

"I'm not worried. You'd never do that. But did she wonder why you were asking?" He shifts looking a bit uncomfortable and it sucks, really. I wish he felt more comfortable writing romance.

"Nope, just told her I was curious about the process. She's a wealth of information."

"Yeah, I know," he responds almost absentmindedly, and I can feel the pressure on his shoulders as if it were my own. I drop the subject. He's here recovering from a concussion and the last thing I want to do is give him more to stress about. I want to make this a nice relaxing—stress free—week for him, and help him with his book. I change the subject. "Are you looking forward to everyone coming for the blowout?"

He nods and smiles but it doesn't reach his eyes. "I am. It will be fun. How about you? Did I happen to invite the guy you've been crushing on?"

My stomach tightens. I'm really going to have to deal with this. "Maybe," I say, the plan to use Sebastian as my crush still at the back of my mind. I sit back in my seat as he drives us to the store, not wanting to think about the weekend, or how I'll be handing him over to a friend—if she still wants to give him a chance, that is. It might take work on my part, but I have to convince her Brandon is one of the good guys. I want him to be happy, and if it's with Naomi, then so be it.

I also think about how we left things after I had his cock in my mouth and he brought me to a glorious orgasm with his fingers and mouth. He told me he wanted to fuck me. Okay, sure, I get that. He's a guy and guys like sex. But he doesn't want me doing it for the wrong reasons. I understand he doesn't want me to have regrets, giving him something that I've been hanging on to for a while now. What he doesn't know is that I've been holding on to my virginity because there was no one other than him I wanted to give it to. But the ball is in my court now, and I've been very carefully planning my next move.

He eases the SUV into a parking spot and reaches for his buckle. I put my hand on his to stop him and his eyes hold confusion as his head lifts. "No, you wait here," I say quickly. "I'll just be a second."

"Yeah?"

"In and out, real quick. You'll just slow me down."

He laughs at that and I'm happy to see his playfulness is back. "When have I ever slowed you down?"

I want to say this morning when I was anxious for him to bring me to orgasm, and he changed the pace and rhythm of his fingers inside me, drawing out and prolonging my pleasure and for that I'm grateful.

"What are you up to Daisy?"

"Me?" I ask all innocently. "Just getting glue to piece together the vase that broke."

"Okay." He shakes his head, disbelief all over his face.

I leave the car and a warm breeze blows over my face, ruffling my dress as I hurry into the store. I dart through the aisles until I find what I need, and hurry back to the car. I tap the back of the SUV, wanting to put my purchases in the trunk area, away from probing eyes.

After I slide back into the passenger seat, Brandon eyes me. "Get everything?"

"Yup."

His glance goes over my body. "You'll need to change before we go hiking."

"I have stuff at my cottage." He nods, and pulls out of the parking lot and a short while later, he's pulling into my driveway. I step from the car and wave to Sebastian as he comes from the water.

"I'll just get your things in the back," Brandon says with a smirk.

"No, it's okay. I'll get them." I gather my bags, pull my key from my purse and say, "Come on."

Brandon follows me up the path to my cottage, and I open the door. It creaks and I glance around, just to make sure nothing has been ransacked. "I'll be right back."

He nods. "I'll just take a look around to make sure everything is okay."

I head up the stairs, and Brandon's footsteps reverberate downstairs. I hurry to my room and shove my purchases into my backpack. Once done, and they're well hidden, I tug the drawer open on my dresser and pull out a pair of cut-off jean shorts and a T-shirt, perfect for a hike up Mount Rainier. While I love Nova Scotia, I do miss things about Seattle. I pull my hair into a ponytail and clip it at the top of my head, and grip the hem of my dress to tug it off. Deciding on a bra that has more support than the lacy one I'm in, I unhook it, and drop it onto my bed.

"Everything okay?"

I spin at the sound of Brandon's voice, and my hands instantly go to cover my breasts when I find him standing in my doorway. As he leans against my doorjamb looking drop dead sexy, his gaze latched on me with hunger and need, my nipples take that moment to harden.

"Brandon! What are you doing?"

"Checking to see if everything is okay." His wolfish grin teases the needy spot between my legs. "Actually, everything is better than okay. Everything is perfect." His tongue snakes out and wets his bottom lip as his gaze leaves my face, tracking downward to my hands, which are doing a pretty crappy job of covering my chest. Wait, is he talking about me when he said everything is perfect?

A growl crawls out of his throat and his eyes track back to mine. He tilts his head, like a wild animal with its prey in target. "Why are you covering yourself, Duke?"

"Because...because..."

He pushes off the doorjamb and takes a small step toward me. His big body overwhelms the room and my senses. Honestly, he's been in this very bedroom a million times, but he's never ever looked at me the way he's looking at me right now. "I've had my mouth all over those beauties and my cock between them."

Oh, God, when he says things like that. "You...surprised me, is all."

"You don't like surprises?"

"You know I don't." I really hope he's not planning some sort of surprise for Wednesday. Ever since that Halloween where he and Chase and a few of the other guys hid in the treehouse and scared the hell out of me, I'm not much into surprises. Then again, maybe he'll surprise me with a white coat so we can play doctor.

"You can't just walk into my bedroom, B." Okay, my voice lacks conviction and we both know it.

He stands there, looking like it's exactly where he belongs and that he's not in a hurry to move when he jerks his finger over his shoulder and asks, "Do you want me to leave?"

No, I want him to stay and do dirty, delicious things to my body. "It's a little late for that, isn't it?" I shoot back, my fingers slipping to expose my nipple. I struggle to get it hidden, but his eyes tell me I'm not doing a very good job of it, and let's face it, maybe I'm not trying to. "I thought you were downstairs."

"Did you think there was a stranger up here watching you?"

"I don't know...I thought...you could have been an axe murderer or something?" Lord knows they've made me watch enough scary movies to believe it could be true.

"Yeah, that's true." His grin is teasing and playful. "There are a lot of axe murders here at Wautauga Beach."

Heat crawls up my neck, not because I just said something foolish, but because he's now circling me, his hard body close but not touching. Heat radiates off every inch of his torso and sears my blood.

I square my shoulders. "You know burglars are breaking into the cottages and making a mess of things. You could have been one of them."

One callused finger touches the small of my back and I gasp. "I'm not a burglar," he says, his mouth close to my ear.

"I know."

"I'm not a thief, either."

"Yeah, you are. You stole that feather tickler," I point out as it becomes harder and harder to remain standing. God, the way he's looking at my near naked body, like he wants to eat me alive, is messing with my brain. Why is this so exciting?

"Borrowed," he corrected, his voice a low deep whisper that curls over my skin and teases my arousal until I can barely think. "I'm going to make a trip to the store and replace it."

Touch me already.

"You know I don't take things that don't belong to me— things that weren't meant for me."

I swallow, and read more into his words than he's saying. "You only take things that are given to you?"

"That's right," he answers, and stops circling me. He stands in front of me, takes my hands from my breasts, and puts them by my sides. "I might not be a burglar or a thief, but I do like making a mess of things...especially you."

"You like making a mess of me." The man really has no idea just how messed up I am when it comes to him.

He grins and backs up. I instantly miss his warmth as he sits on my bed. My God, how many times have I laid in that bed and imagined him in this room with me. I angle my head and eye him. "I love your tits, Daisy. I love making a mess on them with my cum."

I gulp as my body burns hot. Jesus, does he have any idea how much I like when he talks like that. Probably not, because he's never talked to me like this before and I only recently discovered how much I love it myself.

"I...had no idea," I moan and hope I don't sound as needy as I feel. Is this some kind of torturous foreplay? If so, it's working and if he doesn't soon touch me, I'm damn well going to touch myself. Yeah, if he likes it messy, let's see how that messes with him.

"If I were a thief," he says, and I pull a bra from my drawer and struggle to put it around my ribcage. "And I came upon you like this, I'd have a hard time not taking what I wanted."

I gulp. "What...do you want?"

"I'd probably want to tie you to this bed, and put my mouth and hands all over you." He stands, cups my chin and lifts my head until my eyes meet his. "But I'm not sure I'd have to be a thief to get what I wanted."

"You wouldn't," I croak out.

"You'd let me have my way with you?"

"Uh huh."

"What would you want me to do, Daisy?" He stands there, a challenge in his eyes.

"I'd want you to touch me."

He puts his hands on my hips and moves me around like I'm nothing but a tiny, moveable doll in his arms. "Why don't you show me?"

He positions me on the bed, puts his feet between my legs and nudges them until they're open. My eyes never leave his as he backs up, pulls a chair from my small makeup table, and lowers himself into it, looking like he has all the patience in the world, but he doesn't. I see the urgency in his eyes, his need to see my body, to watch me touch myself.

I widen my legs a little more and slide my hand inside my panties. His chest rises and falls with his fast intake of breath, and I bite back a smile.

"That's how you do it when you're alone, Daise..." he asks, his voice low and deep.

"Yeah," I murmur, and my head rolls to the side as I slick my finger over my clit. His moan mingles with mine as I apply pressure. Over the years, my mind has played out a lot of scenarios where Brandon is concerned, but never in my fantasies did I pleasure myself in front of him while he watched on in sheer fascination. There's something so deliciously naughty about this.

I fall back on the bed, and stroke myself until I'm writhing and moaning, and so close to breaking under his watchful eye, it's crazy.

"While I like watching," he says, as he crawls onto the bed beside me and slides his hand into my panties, "For the rest of the week, it's going to be me taking care of you." I lift my hips as his finger dips inside me. God, the way this man touches me is amazing. His head dips, his eyes dark and serious, when he adds, "Anything you need, Daise...anything at all."

My heart misses a beat, because what I need is for him to love me the way I love him, and I'm not sure that's ever going to happen in this lifetime.

16

BRANDON

I love the pure delight on Daisy's face as she breathes in the scent of peaches. The littlest things make her happy and I love that she's not high maintenance. "Where do you think they get them this time of year?" she asks, looking very much like a child on Christmas morning. Not that we've spent Christmas morning together, ever, but maybe that's something we ought to do. Actually, I want to spend every waking moment with her, and every sleeping one too. But that's not going to happen, especially if she's in Halifax and I'm in Seattle. Why again did she suddenly decide she was going to stay in Halifax?

"They're probably not local, right?"

Her words pull me back and I smile at her as her eyes dim, much the same way they had hours earlier when I brought her to orgasm on her bed. Honestly, after hearing my brother's warning, it reminded me that I could lose my very best friend by fucking around with her. I vowed to keep my distance after we left my parents' place. That was pretty fucking short-lived, obviously. Christ, when I saw her in her room, her gorgeous, lush body exposed, so ripe, and so ready for the picking, I didn't have enough blood left in my brain to stop me from acting on my urges.

Dumbass.

Yeah, that's me, Brandon Cannon the dumbass who's fucking around with his very best friend, and possibly risking the relationship. But right now, as we stand at Pike's Place Market, Daisy looking over the gigantic peaches like she's done with me a million times before, things seem good between us. Great even.

"Idaho," I inform her and point to the label on the box.

She laughs. "Oh, I thought it would be somewhere exotic like Costa Rica or Peru."

"That's pretty random, Duke." I lean in and smell the box of peaches and my mouth waters. "Are those places you consider exotic?"

"Hey," she continues, her eyes wide, her face fully animated, and still flushed from earlier "Maybe I could plant a peach tree back in the city."

"We can look into it if you want." I lean into her and her eyes widen as I lightly brush my lips over hers, and moan in appreciation. "But as far as I'm concerned, the sweetest peaches are here in Seattle." She shakes her head at my cheesiness. "You're really thinking of staying in Halifax?" I ask.

She quickly runs her tongue over her lips, like she's tasting me in return, and I like that. "You say that like it's a bad thing."

Hell, I just...shit, if I do end up playing for the Shooters, she'll be so far away and I hate that. "Nope, it's not. You know I love it there too."

She puts one hand on her hip and her face twists. "I also know you told Chase that Halifax has the hottest women on the planet."

I arch a brow, and give her a dubious look. I'm guessing she overheard me tell my buddy that. "He told you that?"

Her chin lifts, playfully indignant. "I'll have you know that Chase and I don't keep secrets."

Is she suggesting I do? That she might know I'm a hot mess of unfamiliar feelings inside, but maybe they're simply not so unfamiliar and it's more that I've been burying them. "It wasn't exactly a secret." I wink at her. "Do you have a secret? Something you've never shared with me."

Her face falls fast, but then she pulls herself together so quickly it's impressive. It does, however, make me think about her secrets, and the fact that there's someone on my team she likes. Shit, I fucking hate that, and why did she keep that from me?

You kept your writing a secret, dude, but that's nothing compared to what you're keeping from her now.

Yeah, I know, I'm keeping a big secret, but it's to make sure I don't fuck up our relationship.

"No, of course not. You know everything." She turns from me, and I take in her bouncing blonde curls and the sweet curve of her face.

"I was wrong, though. Seattle has the hottest women."

"Oh sure." She rolls her eyes so hard it almost gives me a headache. "You're only saying that because...well, we've been, you know...working on your book."

Oh, yeah, I know.

But wanting her has nothing to do with my book. "Nope, it's the truth. All I had to do was look in my own backyard to see the prettiest girl on the planet." Why the hell am I saying this? Testing her to see if it's possible that she has feelings for me to? God, I don't fucking know. Clearly, I'm losing my shit.

"Sure." She laughs and fake punches my gut as the vendor steps up to us, and Daisy asks for two big peaches and two big nectarines. I stand back and watch her. I've been to this market a million times, and it's always fun with Daisy. In fact, I'm always happiest when Daisy and I are simply hanging out and doing nothing in particular. We never lack for conversation, and when conversation does drift off, we're simply happy being in our own heads as long as we have each other's company. I never really gave that much thought before, but I'm sure as hell thinking about it now.

She pays for the fruit and carefully slides them into her backpack. I uncap my water bottle, take a big drink and hand it to her. "Thanks." She takes a long pull and adjusts her ballcap, and as I look at her, dressed in an old T-shirt and those frayed jean shorts, my dick twitches.

"Are you ready to go to Paradise?" I ask her as she hands the bottle back. Paradise is one of the stops on Mount Rainier's trail and it's Daisy's favorite place to rest and take in the scenery.

She grins and leans into me. "I think I was just there."

I laugh, a new lightness about me, because things aren't weird between us. If they were, she wouldn't be joking about me bringing her to climax on her bed. "Yeah, I was just there too and the scenery was much better." I nudge her, simply because I want to touch her. "But you know that's not what I was talking about."

"Unfortunately," she exhales with a sigh.

"Come on, let's go for a hike."

We walk back to the SUV and I pull out of the downtown core. She sings along with the radio, horribly. Unlike our very good friend Kennedy, Daisy does not have a singing voice, but I love that she doesn't care and always sings her heart out. Does she just do that with me, or does she do it with everyone? I kind of like the idea of her being comfortable enough with me, belting out lyrics that aren't even in the song, and could quite possibly send every animal within earshot into hiding.

"What?" she asks as a stupid grin crosses my face.

I nod toward the radio. "Don't you hate it when the artist gets the words wrong?" She laughs and whacks me. "Did you bring sunscreen?"

She gives and exaggerated exhaled. "Oh, Brandon, you would be so lost without me."

"No shit," I say, knowing that it's true.

"It's in my bag, we'll put it on when we get there. Can you drive faster? I really want that peach."

"Just eat it."

"Nope, I want to save it for Paradise."

I laugh at all her funny little idiosyncrasies. She starts singing again, and I actually do pick up the speed a bit. It's early afternoon by the time I pull into the parking lot, and glance around to see that it's not too busy on this Monday afternoon.

We hop from the car, and Daisy squirts a generous amount of lotion in my hand. As I coat myself, I keep my eyes on her and the way she rubs the lotion on her body.

"Shit," I mumble under my breath.

"What's up?"

I laugh at that. "You don't want to know."

She shakes her head but it's easy to tell from the grin she's fighting that she likes how much she turns me on, without even having to do anything. "Honestly, B. I don't know how you walk around with that things."

I laugh and look at the gobs of lotion on her face. "You're a mess." I step closer and run my hand over her nose to rub the lotion in and I don't miss her fast intake of air. My body bumps hers and little electrical charges arc between us.

"I'm a mess now," she mumbles, and she lightly touches my abs as I finish rubbing her lotion in. Jesus, now all I can think about is stripping her off, bending her over the hood of the car, and making a real mess of her, right here in the parking lot. But that's not going to happen. Daisy and I aren't going to have sex—unless of course it's not for the book and she wants to.

Fuck me twice.

I adjust my backpack and we start up the trail. We walk for a bit in silence and move to the side when a family of four come down the hill. The dad is carrying his little girl and the mom is holding hands with a boy who looks to be around four.

The father slows as he sees us and I can almost hear his brain spinning, trying to place us. I just smile and nod and Daisy does the same. Once they pass, I walk beside Daisy again.

She's quiet, pensive, and I say, "Cute family."

"Yeah," she answers absently, as she stares straight ahead, taking in the views that are coming into view as we climb higher.

"Do you want kids?" I ask. A long time ago, Daisy told me she didn't want kids. Maybe she's changed her mind.

"Nope," she says, but there's something in her voice, something I've never heard before. Is it longing? Does Daisy secretly want a family of her own? "You still do, right?"

"Yeah."

We fall silent again, and a knot tightens in my throat because while I want to start thinking about the future, about life and family after college, the only person I can see at my side is Daisy. Should I tell her? Should I just open up and announce that I'm feeling more? What if she isn't, and what if I fuck us up? What if I never say anything though. I open my mouth and swallow my words fast when she speaks.

"Naomi told me she wants to do pediatrics. I'm guessing, like you, she wants a family."

I nod and I'm glad she's walking in front of me so she can't see what a mess I am at the moment. Fuck, Naomi is coming here at the end of the week—for me. Should I bury what I'm feeling for Daisy and see if the two of us can work it out?

"I think you two will be good together," she says over her shoulder as she hikes her backpack up and struts up the path.

"Yeah," is all I say. We climb higher, and I spot movement just off the beaten path. "Daise..." I put my hand on her waist, and with my mouth near her ear, I whisper, "Look." She turns to me, and follows my gaze into the woods where a gorgeous deer is standing just a few feet away.

She gasps and very slowly pulls her phone from her back pocket. I stand very close to her, and keep my hand on her body as she snaps a few pictures. "She's beautiful," she whispers. "I'm so glad you spotted her. "Look," she murmurs. "She has a young one by her side."

"Bambi," I say, and she grins. My God, Daisy cried for days after we watched that show as kids. I back up an inch, and a twig snaps under my hiking boots. The deer lifts its head and she takes off, running deeper into the woods, turning back for a second to make sure her baby is right on her heels.

"So sweet," she murmurs.

My heart beats a little faster as I take in Daisy's smile, and catching me by surprise, she leans into me and kisses my cheek.

"What was that for?" I ask.

"For spotting the deer and for never hunting them."

I chuckle at that. "You'd kill me if I ever tried." She gives me a look that suggests death would be too easy for me, and instead she'd go for a good neutering. I playfully put my hands over my balls. "No worries, never going to hunt."

She stares at me for a second, and I can almost hear her brain spinning. "Why did you pick the friends to lovers trope?"

Okay, talk about a complete change of subject. "I don't know." Truthfully, it's just a trope I like. I wouldn't have thought it was based on Daisy and me, but now, I think maybe my subconscious was trying to tell me something.

"What other tropes have you used?" she asks.

"My first book was brother's best friend. I think I did that because it was familiar. You know, my mom started dating Dad—her brother's best friend—after he was down and out with a concussion."

"I do love their story," she responds quietly. "I'd like to read that one."

"I think that one will stay buried forever. It's pretty shitty."

"I'll be the judge of that."

"No, you won't."

"Come on. I want to read it."

"Nope," I say, loving our easy back and forth banter. It's always been like this for us. I think I've just taken it for granted over the years. But my God, I'd be lost without her.

"How about this, if I make it to the clearing before you, you have to let me read it."

I stare at her. "Okay, but what's in it for me?"

She puckers her lips. "What do you want?"

"To bite into a big, juicy peach." My gaze drops to her mouth and my heart beats a little faster. How did I get to a place where I can't stop thinking about her, can't stop wanting her? What the hell am I going to do about this raw need inside me? I'm pretty sure if I don't soon have her—don't soon bury my cock inside her—I'm going to lose my goddamn mind. Then again maybe I've already lost it because I crossed a line with my best friend that never should have been crossed.

"That's it?" She angles her head like she doesn't believe me. "That's all you want?"

"Uh huh?"

She steps up to me, all seductive like, and puts her hands on my shoulders. For a second, I think she's going to kiss me, but then she slides my backpack off my shoulders, turns and laughs as she darts up the hill.

"That's cheating."

"Nope, that's being clever," she shoots back. I laugh and shake my head as I snatch up my backpack and chase after her. She's fast, but I'm faster, and of course I'm not laughing my ass off the way she is, thinking she got the better of me.

I grab her to stop her and she whacks at me as I run past her. "Cheater."

"Don't you mean, clever?"

"B!" she yells. "Get back here!"

I reach the clearing and hold my hands up in the air. "I have no equal."

"Okay, so you win." She's breathless and still laughing as she drops her bag, and produces a big peach. "Here you go. You were going to get it anyway, so you should have asked for something else."

Everything in my brain urges me to put a stop to this, to walk away from Daisy and go back to being just friends before it's too late.

Walk away, dude.

I step up to her, put my hand around her waist and tug her to me. "Not the peach I was talking about, babe."

I am in so much fucking trouble here...

My lips are still tingling from today's rough and raw—possessive—kiss on Mount Rainier. I'd reached Paradise in so many ways the second his mouth closed over mine and he pulled me against his throbbing—manhood. I'm convinced he would have laid me right out on the side of the path and buried his mouth between my legs if hikers hadn't come upon us. Tonight though, I plan to give him his winnings from that race, and then some. My entire body burns thinking about it, but I'm also as nervous as hell. What if he doesn't want to take my virginity because he thinks I'm saving it for someone special, or that I'll have regrets? I can't admit the truth. It's too risky.

I glance at Brandon sitting on the sofa beside me, a very serious expression on his face. "You really hate commas, don't you?" I laugh as I add a comma to his manuscript, in the scene I'm sure he set in the female bathroom at Tandoor's restaurant.

"No, I don't hate them, and you don't put a comma there." He snatches the laptop off my lap, and hits delete.

I hold my hands up, palms out. "Okay, fine, we'll let whoever edits this decide." He scrubs his face, and I like this serious side to him. In my heart, I know if he gave this a chance, he could really make a career out of it, but the decision has to be his, not mine, and I do understand the pressures. "Do you want to get started on the scene...you know, from the other night."

A new kind of hunger comes over him. "Yeah, that sounds good."

"Did you make mental notes?"

"If I said no, can we go back and do it again?"

I laugh at that, but my body isn't laughing. Nope, it's not laughing at all. It's screaming at me to get my ass back over there and try a few new toys. "We still have to return that tickler, you know."

"I know."

"Because you're not a thief."

His head lifts, heat blazing in his eyes as they look at me. "That's right, I don't take things that don't belong to me— things that weren't meant for me."

It's not the first time he said those exact words to me, which makes me certain, like one-hundred percent positive, that he's not talking about the tickler at all.

"How are we going to do that?"

"We'll have to break back in."

"Sounds risky, and I've never known you as a guy to take risks."

His smile flatlines for a second. "No, you're right, but we can't keep it. I'll find a way to return it."

I turn my mind back to his story. "Have you thought about how you're going to end it?" Ugh, just thinking about the end —of this week, and possibly Brandon and me—turns my stomach.

"I'm not sure yet. Like I said I have a hard time with endings, possibly because I haven't had a happily ever after."

"You know," I say, my mind racing through all the romance books I've read. "What I see done a lot is tying the beginning to the end."

"Yeah?"

"Okay, so your characters here, they met at a high school dance, right? And they have been friends forever. Maybe the grand gesture could be him recreating that dance or something? You know, bring it back to the moment when she friend zoned him. Put them in the same spot, doing the same thing, but feeling differently about it."

He goes contemplative as he nods. Brandon always was a deep thinker. There's so much more to him than people realize. I knew that even before I found out he was writing romance. "Okay, that could be a fun ending. I'm going to have to think about it."

Completely proud of myself, I smile at him. "We're a good team."

He makes a fist and nudges my chin, a hard reminder that, like the heroine in his book, he friend zoned me a very long time ago. "For a girl who doesn't date, you're good at this romance stuff, Duke."

"Thanks. I read a lot." I swallow against a painful throat and remind myself that while I'm here, I'm playing a part, and tonight I plan to play the hell out of it and convince him I'm ready for the taking—for his book. "Why don't you make some notes on that. I'm going to shower. I'm still a bit sticky from our hike."

He turns back to his computer, his expression serious again as his fingers hurry across his keyboard. While I'm happy he's in the zone, I want those fingers on my body and his mouth on my hot flesh.

I hurry up the stairs and walk past my bedroom. My backpack containing a prop I'm hoping he'll use sits on the desk chair beside the bed. A little quiver goes through me as I step into the bathroom. My body isn't just hot from the hike. Nope, reading through his scenes again doused me in need, and as I peel my panties off, their dampness doesn't go unnoticed. I turn the water on, keeping it a bit cool, and step into the refreshing spray.

I wash my hair first and lather my body, and my nipples are hard as bullets as I touch myself, recalling the way I ran my hands over my flesh and put them deep inside my pussy as Brandon watched. I can't believe what we're doing here. After all these years, my dreams are finally coming true.

A noise grabs my attention and I turn to see Brandon's silhouette on the other side of the glass panel. My heart jumps into my throat.

"B," I say quickly and open the door. Everything about him is needy and intense. I take in his dilated pupils. Oh God, is he sick again? "Are you okay?"

"No." I reach for the nozzle about to turn the shower off but he captures my hand. "I'm not okay."

"I know. Let me help you."

"You don't understand." I narrow my eyes and that's when it hits me. His eyes are dilated from raw need. I suck in a fast breath. "You see, I was downstairs, making notes, but it was damn hard to concentrate knowing you were up here, in my shower, soaping up your gorgeous body. That's when I remembered the terms of our little race this afternoon, and how I have yet to claim my reward."

As he continues to hold my wrist in his hand—who knew I'd love it when the man restrained me? Actually, I did, otherwise I wouldn't have bought a little extra something at the store today—he slides his other hand between my legs, and lightly strokes my soaked pussy, but it's not only soaked from the shower. Liquid arousal pools on his fingers.

"Were you up here touching yourself?" he asks, his voice a low, rumbling growl as he dips into my heat.

As his eyes darken with need, my body hums. I used to think it was his concussion making him weird and flirty with me. I'm not sure if I totally believe that anymore. But since there's still a chance a brain injury has changed his personality, and since I don't want to do or say anything to mess with our friendship, I answer with, "I was...thinking about your protagonist, and that she needed a shower scene." He goes completely still for a second, and as his hand pauses between my legs, I almost sense disappointment in him. It cuts into me. God, I never want to disappoint Brandon.

"You think I need a shower scene?" he finally asks.

I take a breath, put my hand around his head and bring his mouth close to mine. "I think it's exactly what your book is missing."

I wait for the kiss, but he stands there for a few seconds and I reach down, and place my palm over his engorged cock. I give him a gentle squeeze and finally—much to my relief—tension leaves his body in a rush and he groans.

He inches back and tears off his T-shirt. "I think you're right. A shower scene is needed."

My gaze moves over his hard body. God, I'll never get tired of the view, and I step back to make room for him as he sheds the rest of his clothes and climbs in with me. "Be sure to make mental notes." I go straight for his hard cock, taking it in both of my hands and he sucks in a breath.

"Wow, okay, I guess you're a girl who always knew what she wanted." He grins. "I guess I just never knew it was my dick."

"Looks like we're both learning," I respond, talking about his protagonist, who is loving the sex lessons from her very best friend. I guess in a way I'm getting lessons too, lessons I can carry with me for when I start dating for real, and while I hate the thought of it, it has to happen, preferably sooner rather than later. Knowing he wants to be in a serious relationship and move forward in life—with me still being his buddy—means I need to get over him and fast. Is all this helping me with that though?

Uh no. More like it's doing the opposite.

"Babe, that is so good," he moans as he rocks his hips, into my soapy hands and I revel in the clenching of his hard abs. Those same abs I'd love to taste.

"As good as the real thing?" His eyes fly open. Shit, why did I say that? A segue into talking about us finally doing it? Maybe, but it wasn't a very good one. I can't be too hard on myself. I'm pretty inexperienced.

"The real thing, meaning as good as putting my cock in your pussy?" he asks.

I snort out a laugh at his bluntness. "Okay way to straight up say it."

He laughs. "Babe, this feels incredible, and I'm sure it's just as good as putting my cock inside you, but you know we don't have to do that."

"I know," I agree and love the way he trembles as I stroke him from base to crown. "I was just curious. I don't believe you, though."

"Why would I lie to you?" He holds his finger up to stop me from reminding him about the concussion. "That wasn't a lie, it was just an omission."

Don't I know all about omission. I have a whopper of one that will never pass my lips. "Yeah, but you're lying, saying this hand job is as good as sex."

"Anything with you is as good as sex, Daisy." Seriousness tinges the arousal in his voice.

"I like everything we're doing too, B."

He grins, and leans into me, pressing his soft lips to mine as I continue to stroke him and he grows impossibly thicker in my palms. I am so ready to feel him inside me. A little squeal of nervousness and excitement spills from my lips and a second later, his fingers are between my legs, stroking deep and threatening my ability to keep my emotions on lockdown. If with his probing fingers he can turn me into a bumbling mess of a woman ready to confess her deepest darkest secret, what will he do to me with his cock?

I guess it's time to find out.

"Let's go to my bedroom."

"Okay," he agrees quickly as he lightly strokes my sex. "That way I can finally take a bite of my sweet prize."

I quickly turn the shower off, wanting that too. He wraps me in a big warm towel, ties another around his waist, and my heart crashes with all the things I'm feeling for him as he puts his hand on my waist and leads me to my bedroom. We've been close, always, but nothing could prepare my heart for the way it's swelling. I know giving myself to him, putting my entire body in his hands, his to do with as he pleases, is the right thing to do. Honestly, it's time and I am so ready I'm afraid I might spontaneously combust if he doesn't soon put his cock in me.

I sit on the bed, and the first thing he does is give me a little nudge until I'm flat on my back. I tuck my hair around my face and he drops to his knees, grips my thighs and widens my legs, completely exposing my sex to him. He stares at me like I'm a prize, something to be cherished and treasured, and stupid tears prick my eyes. I'm not sad, not at all, but no guy has ever looked at me like I was worthy of love.

"B," I whisper and go up on my elbows to see him. My heart lodges in my throat as he smiles a soft, sexy, even tender smile at me. I realize there's no goddamn way I'll be able to walk away with my heart intact.

"This," he murmurs his warm breath hot against my skin as he licks his lips, like he's about to devour his favorite dessert. My sex flutters, and I'm sure, just watching the hunger grow in his eyes as he gently spreads me, could bring me to orgasm. "This is the peach I've been craving all fucking day."

"Come take a bite," I say, and his eyes briefly dim, his chest expanding as he runs his nose along my inner thighs and breathes me in. "B," I cry out, and my words seem to do something to him. He slides his hands under my legs, grips my ass, and lifts my hot sex to his mouth, diving straight in, licking and sucking and slurping like a man who's been denied the juiciest fruit on the planet.

"Oh, God!" I fall back onto the bed, and the knot securing the towel to my body lets go and it falls to my sides as I grip the sheets to hold on. Brandon moans as he devours me, my juices dripping down his chin, and that's when I understand why he's compared my sex to a peach. One bite and I'm making a hot mess out of his face. I love it, actually. He likes making a mess of me, and I like making a mess of him, too.

He takes his time with me, despite the way I'm wiggling, desperate for so much more. I moan and cry and grip fistfuls of his hair and hold him to me, like a sex-starved woman— which clearly, I am. His teeth find my engorged clit and he nibbles as one hand leaves my ass, so he can slide a thick finger inside me.

"Holy..." I cry out as a fierce orgasm catches me by surprise and rips through me, my body opening like a dam and soaking his face, his fingers, my thighs and the sheets. I'm not certain I've ever come so hard.

He licks me, staying deep between my legs and holding me to him as I struggle to breathe—to recover. I chant his name, over and over and toss my head from side to side. "I need..." I beg, and swallow against a dry throat.

Tell him what you need, Daisy.

"I need," I begin again and he climbs out from between my legs, standing next to the bed, his cock tenting his towel, rock hard and ready for what I need.

"What do you need, Daisy?"

"You," I tell him. "I need you, B."

He seems to stumble a bit, and worry zings through me. Am I asking for too much from a man who's recovering from a concussion? I sit up fast, and my body hits his. He stumbles again, and knocks my backpack from the chair, spilling my purchases onto the wood floor.

The second he sets eyes on the bottle of glue for the vase, and the hemp rope for...tying me up, a confused look crosses his face, but it quickly morphs into understanding.

He drops down and picks up the hemp. "This...this is what you had in mind when you talked about my heroine experimenting, isn't it?" he asks quietly, a strange kind of heaviness clouding him.

A burst of heat warms my cheeks and I swallow hard. "I thought you could...you know, show me the ropes."

His face changes, becomes harder as I sense a complete shift in him. What the hell? He stares at the rope like it might be a poisonous snake. I inch back on the bed, worry gnawing at my gut. Feeling exposed in more ways than one, I pull the blankets up to cover my naked body, and his head lifts, his dark eyes back on mine.

"You know," I add quickly, hating the change coming over him and wanting to get us back on track. "I thought your protagonist might like it." He doesn't speak, instead he just stares at me. Oh God, what is going on here? Does he not want to go all the way with me? He's been with a lot of women. Am I simply not worthy or loveable? I shake my head. No, that can't be it. He told me he wanted to fuck me, right? Or was that just something I thought I heard because I wanted to hear it. I try to get my brain to work, as something niggles close to the surface. But old fears and securities that I'm not good enough dominate my thoughts. He continues to stay quiet, too quiet so in a softer voice, I blurt out, "I thought this might be something she'd like to experiment with."

"You want me to..."

I thought the ropes would show him that we can indeed have no regret sex for his book, and it's true, I want to do it for his book, but I want it for me too. I'm just not sure I can admit that. I take a fueling breath and blurt out, "Tie me up...take me."

"No, Daisy. Not a goddamn fucking chance."

18

BRANDON

My heart beats so hard against my rib cage, I can barely think, let alone see what's right in front of me. As the room blurs, I pinch my eyes shut to clear them, but things are still fuzzy as I focus back in on Daisy. The world crashes in around me as she sits there, the sweet, delicate taste of her hot release still on my tongue, the blankets clutched to her chest, looking fragile and destroyed. Want, need and worry flare inside me. I have never, ever seen her look so vulnerable or lost before. I need to make this right somehow. I reach for her and as she flinches, a tortured sound gurgles in her throat as she struggles to hold back her emotions.

My God, what have I done?

Yes, I want to fuck her. Yes, I want to put my cock in her more than I want anything in the world. But I can't—won't—let her do it because she wants to help me with my book. Fuck that shit. I want her to want me for me, and this has to be about her and what she needs, too. I take a measured step back that brings a frown to her forehead, but I won't put another finger on her until I know for sure that this is what *she* wants. Only then will I give her everything—all of me.

Jesus Christ, I never should have started anything with her. This whole thing—whatever it is we're doing here—is spiraling out of control. Looking at her sitting on my brother's bed, shivering beneath the covers on this warm fall evening, it's clear I could have already fucked things up by not agreeing to fuck her.

"I'm sorry," she says and makes a move to scramble off the bed, and no doubt out of my life.

"Daisy, no." My voice comes out harsher than I intended, but it accomplishes exactly what I wanted.

She stops moving, her gaze slowly turning to me and my lungs constrict at the way she's trying to put on a brave face. Daisy is brave, one of the bravest girls I know. She's dealt with a lot, being abandoned when she was merely a few months old fucks with a person. The last thing I want to do is hurt her more, or have her think I don't want her.

"I know. I heard you. You said no. I thought before, I thought...you said you wanted to fuck me. I must have misunderstood." She shakes her head. "If that's not something you want to do with me, I—"

"You don't understand."

Tell her, dude. Tell her how you really feel.

I open my mouth, but fear that I'd really mess things up grips my gut and I chicken out.

"I...I want to be inside you," I tell her, and step closer to put my hand on her leg, the blanket keeping my shaky palm from her flesh, but it does nothing to dampen the little electrical impulses zapping back and forth between the two of us.

She takes in a breath and for a second I think she's going to scamper away again, but she doesn't. Instead she holds her chin high, but it's the little quiver in her lips that hints at her vulnerability. She might be able to hide it from others, but she can't hide it from me. "You just said absolutely not and that's okay—"

"Daisy, I...the truth is..." I take a deep breath and let it out slowly as I try to quiet my brain and figure out how to explain. "...You're my best friend, and I don't want to do something we'll regret later." She nods in understanding and I continue with, "And I definitely don't want you to have sex because of my book. If you've been saving—"

"B," she says quietly, her face softening around the edges— like she just remembered something— despite the seriousness still radiating in her eyes and her voice.

"You don't understand. I'm struggling with this, Daisy." I reach up and rub the back of my neck. "I'm really fucking struggling." Not just because I'm worried about taking her virginity, but because I'm falling hard for my best friend, who is crushing on another guy. I mean, this sex might mean nothing to her, but for the first time in my life, sex means something to me, something fucking enormous and beautiful, something that could ruin us and take us down a path there's no coming back from.

Christ, I need to tell her all this, but right now, as she looks at me with utter hope and fierce need, the first thing I need to do is show her what she means to me. I understand her demons—hell, I can see them all over her face—and right now, I need to show her just how much I want her, just how desirable and worthy she really is and that nothing is ever going to make me walk away from her.

When it comes right down to it, I'm the one that isn't worthy of her, but maybe if I spend the rest of the week showing her how much she means to me before we go back home, she'll forget all about that guy on the team, and see how good *we* are together. Yeah, maybe that's what I'll do. We're supposed to be acting like a couple and go on dates this week, so she can show me the ropes, to help me get a girl I thought I wanted—when all along the one I needed was right under my nose. Maybe the way to her heart is showing *her* the ropes too, and proving to her that we're good together in and out of the bedroom.

"B," she says quietly. "I want this. I want you. No regrets, remember?"

"This isn't for the book?" I ask, needing to hear the words on her tongue. "I told you I didn't want to go all the way because of my book." She swallows hard, and for a quick second I can see a deep debate going on behind her eyes. "Answer me." I demand softly. "The truth."

She lets loose a breath. "No."

I study her face. I believe her. It's not about the book. What is it about though? Why now does she suddenly want to go all the way. Does she want the experience for another guy, like the heroine in my book wants? I swallow the lump in my throat. "What about the guy back home, on the team?"

"I'm here with you, B, and you're the only guy who matters to me right now." Liking that I matter to her, I press my lips to hers. Is it possible that she's feeling everything I'm feeling or is she saying when she goes back, the guy on the team will once again matter to her, and she'll have experience?

"You're the only girl who matters to me," I tell her, leaving off the *right now*. I brush her hair from her face, take in her pulse beating in her throat. I exhale and ask one more time. "Are you sure?"

She grins at me, and holds up her right hand, palm forward. "I, Daisy Reed, of sound mind and memory, want Brandon Cannon to take my virginity—and not for his book."

"Daise..."

"Look, if you help me with sex, it only benefits me. I don't want to be a bumbling virgin if I do hook up—"

My heart sinks. "With the guy on the team?"

"Yeah."

"So basically, you're helping me with things, and this is helping you?"

"Yeah, it's helping me." I stiffen, not sure I can do this, until she puts her hand on my face, her voice low and soft and says, "Take me, B."

I nod, willing to do anything for her, and absolutely fucking not wanting to think she's learning moves for another guy—I have to block that from my mind—I kiss her, every ounce of need inside me rushing to the surface, but I force myself to slow down. If I only get this night with her, and I fucking pray this isn't the only time, it has to be a night to remember for both of us. Maybe it will help her see things differently.

I inch my hand between her damp legs, and slide a finger into her. My cock jumps, knowing his turn is coming and I'm just as excited as he is. I fall over her, and move her to the middle of the bed to give me the room I'll need to prepare her.

I go back on my knees between her spread legs. I love having her naked like this, her wet pussy wide open and on display as warm, familiar comfort, combined with sheer need cocoons us. Being with her is right. I know it in my head and in my heart—and between my legs. I know once I'm past her barriers and her body opens to me, we're going to fit perfectly.

"I don't want to hurt you." I swallow against a suddenly too dry throat. "Ever," I add, but I'm not just talking about physically. I'm talking about emotionally and mentally, too. She's my world. I've always known that, but the fact that she's the one girl in the world who dropped everything to take care of me really drove the point home. Now, I want to spend the rest of my days taking care of all her needs.

"I'm already hurting," she responds and it brings a light laugh to my throat and eases some of the tension inside me. My sweet, funny Daisy is back and I'm going to take her virginity. I stroke her damp pussy, determined to make tonight special for her. "Poor girl," I murmur as my gaze races over her trembling body. "You really are hurting."

She eyes my cock as it tents the towel, and arches a brow. "I don't think you have any room to laugh."

I shake my head. "No, you're right. I'm a hot mess."

She grins, and takes my cock into her hands. "Did I tell you I like it when you're a mess?"

I throw my head back and clench my teeth as she wraps her small warm hands around my hard length.

"Turgid," she teases, and I chuckle as she sits up and spreads my towel to examine my swollen crown. I grip the back of her head. "Take me in your mouth, babe. Let me watch you suck it deep." A quiver goes through her as she widens her lips, granting me entry. "Fuck, I love when you take me like that." She mumbles something about liking it too, and I believe her. She likes pleasuring me as much as I like pleasuring her. "I'm going to take you too, Daisy." She breathes a little faster. "I'm going to tie you to this bed, and take such good fucking care of you, you'll never want to leave."

With any luck, she won't.

She whimpers, and I cup her breasts, kneading them as I brush my thumbs over her nipples. "Turgid, I like that," I tease. She grins and as some needy part of me wants to hear her say it, I ask, "You want me to take care of you, babe?" She nods, and my cock moves up and down with the movement of her head. "Good, because I plan to put my mouth on you and taste every inch of your body, then I'm going to put my cock in you, burying myself so fucking deep, it might ruin you." She mumbles again, and I continue. "Do you want me to ruin you with my cock, babe?"

Goddammit I do want to ruin her—for any other man. I really am a selfish bastard, aren't I?

My cock slips from her mouth and her eyes meet mine. My heart nearly stops at the intensity in her gaze, the blatant, unchecked need staring back. She's desperate for this—desperate for me, and I fucking love it. I work to still my heart as I place my lips on hers and push back until she's flat on the bed.

"Hands above your head," I order as I go back on my heels, and her little intake of breath doesn't go unnoticed. I lightly stroke her face and let my hand trail down until it's sitting between her breasts as they rise and fall quickly.

"Tonight, I'm going to put my cock in you, but I'm not going to tie you up." The truth is, I get it, the rope was a prop, her way to tell me what she wanted and to pass it off as research if I was opposed to the idea. I guess we're both worried in our own way, pulling out all the stops and using whatever means necessary to ask for what we want while trying to protect our relationship. But I have to take a chance, a risk on us, which means from now until the big blowout, I plan to show her, in every way possible, what she means to me and how I'd like to shape our future.

Confusion twists her lips. "You don't want—"

"Oh, I want, Daisy." I release the knot holding the towel to my waist, and toss it away to show her my throbbing cock. Yeah, there's no denying I want her. "I want a lot of things, like experimenting with the rope and lots of other things, but right now, tonight, I need you to trust that I know what you need." She goes quiet. "You do trust me, right?"

"Of course, I do." Pretty blue eyes full of sincerity and warmth move over my face. "More than anything in the world. You know that B. And..." she adds. "I guess I can understand why you didn't tell me about the concussion. I'm not happy, but I understand, and I think you can find ways to make that up to me."

As she gives me a playful wink, my heart pinches tight, because I do know that she trusts me, and I damn well should have been honest about the concussion, among other things. But I think the plan to show her how much we belong together is a good one, so for the time being, I'll keep my mouth shut.

"I trust you too, Daisy, and tonight, I want something a little softer and gentler for you."

"Is that how you treat all your virgins?" There's a hitch in her voice, one that wasn't there a second ago, I can't tell whether she's teasing or there's actually pain and jealousy in her voice.

"That's how I treat you," I say, and with the utmost tenderness, run my lips over hers. "Of course," I explain. "I've never been with a virgin, and if I was, I'd treat her right, but you're not just any virgin, or any girl, Daisy, and the fact that you want me to be your first..." I take a deep breath and let it out ever so slowly as I shake my head in wonderment and honor. "I don't take that lightly." She puts her hand on my chest, and my heart pounds hard against her palm. "Which means we'll save the rope play, and the experimenting for another time, okay?"

"Thank you, B."

My heart swells inside my chest, making it difficult to draw in air as I position myself between her legs. By rights I should be the one thanking her for giving me something so precious, and I will thank her, with my mouth. "Shit." Her body stiffens, and her eyes go wide. "No, nothing is wrong," I assure her quickly. "I just can't believe I didn't think to get a condom." She smiles at me, and I get the sense she likes the way this is rattling me. Christ, she has no idea. "I don't have sex without a condom."

"Neither do I," she teases.

"I'll be right—"

"Brandon, wait."

I go still. "Yeah, babe?"

"I'm not sure I want my first time with a condom." She watches me, and I sense she's trying to gauge where I am on the condom stance. "I'm on the pill to regulate my periods."

I nod, because I do know that. "I'm clean," she adds, and I simply laugh. "I know you are too."

"I am," I say, even though I don't have to.

"So I was thinking, if you want—"

"I want," I blurt out quickly, and she grins.

"I kind of like the idea of you and I doing a first."

I brush her hair from her forehead. "We've done a hell of a lot of firsts, babe."

She nods, and she looks down for a second, and I wonder if she's reliving all the things we've tried together over the years.

"Yeah," she responds quietly. "We have."

"I'd like for us to have this too." Her smile widens, and she nods, and my heart jumps. Jesus, I like making her happy.

With that settled, I lean into her and the second my lips touch hers and she moans and opens so willingly to me, the entire world fades away. I'm seriously losing myself in her, and I haven't even been *in* her yet. She wraps her legs around me, and my cock probes her opening. This is right. This is so right, I know it.

But what if it isn't, dude? What if you want her so badly you just think this is right, but what you're really doing is messing with the one girl you shouldn't be messing with?

19

DAISY

I gulp and prepare myself for pain as the crown of his cock presses against my opening. I've had his tongue and fingers in me, but his cock is something else altogether. Although, I don't have anything to worry about. He's going to take good care of me, just like I knew he would.

His chest presses against mine, and my nipples are so hard, I'm sure I'm scoring his skin, but he doesn't seem to mind. He kisses my mouth, long, deep, mind-numbing kisses that raise my need for him to new levels. His big hands touch my throat gently, as he shifts lower to kiss a path downward, his lips pressing against my collar bone. My lust-imbued mind reminds me I'm about to give myself to Brandon, and my body quivers happily in response.

I want this.

I want him.

"Babe," he whispers, bringing my attention back to his face.

"Yeah?"

He smiles and drops a kiss onto my forehead, and another on my nose before moving back to my mouth. "Are you nervous?"

"No," I say. "I trust you." I cup his cheeks, and hold his face as he lightly brushes his lips over mine. "Can you please put your cock in me now?"

He growls. "Jesus, Daisy. When you say things like that…"

"It makes your manhood turgid?"

He laughs and I love how comfortable we are with one another. "I wish I'd never let you read my book." He inches his hips forward, and the pressure centers on my core. "Are you ever going to let it go?"

He's distracting me, I think. Talking to me so I don't focus on the potential pain. "Never, and when you're a famous author, I plan to tell that story at every book signing."

"You think I'm inviting you to a book signing?" he asks, his cock penetrating an inch deeper. I take a breath and he goes completely still, giving me time to adjust to his girth. I really love the way this man can read me so well.

I lightly run my hands over his back. "If you don't, I'll just crash them."

He groans a bit, and his breath is heavy in my ear as he kisses my neck. "Maybe I'll have you arrested."

"Are you going to have me handcuffed and escorted out?"

He moves slightly and a keening cry catches in my throat as he goes deeper. His head lifts, and worried eyes search my face. I smile at him, because the pleasure in what he's doing outweighs the pain a million times over. I lift my hips, telling him without words that I'm okay and I want him to continue.

"I probably wouldn't use handcuffs," he says, bringing us back to our teasing conversation as he penetrates me.

"Afraid I'll break out of them."

"No, it's not that. I'd just rather use rope." I chuckle, and when I do, he powers forward until he's deep inside of me, his crown hitting my cervix in ways that bring on waves of pleasure. Small ripples begin in my core, and ohmigod, I'm having a mini orgasm. Or at least I think that's what it's called. Heck, I've never had my cervix stimulated before.

Brandon goes up on one elbow, and lightly runs his thumb over my cheek. "I'm in," he says quietly, and smiles at me.

"Yeah, you're in."

"I think you might have just—"

"You felt that?" I ask quickly.

"I felt you flutter around me."

I shake my head, partly because I just had a mini orgasm from penetration, and partly because my best friend's cock is deep inside me and we're laying here having a conversation.

"Feel good?" he asks.

"Incredible."

"Good." He leans down and kisses me. "I want to start fucking you now, if you're ready."

I've been ready for years! I don't tell him that, instead I say, "I'm ready, B."

He shifts his body, putting both arms on either side of my head, and his eyes remain latched on mine as he inches out, and I gasp a little at the friction. "You feel incredible, Daisy."

My entire body warms at the softness in his voice, and I hug him tighter as he slides back inside. God, I love the glorious way he fills me.

"Brandon," I begin, everything in what we're doing so open and honest it prompts me to asks, "Is this normal?"

He stills inside me. "Does something feel wrong?"

"No, I guess I just mean, when people have sex do they usually make jokes, and just you know, talk so honestly."

"I can't speak for others," he answers, and drops a soft kiss onto my nose. "But for me, it's usually just in and out and done, you know."

"Actually, I don't, which is why I asked."

He laughs. "Of course, you don't. "Okay, so no, normally I just focus on the pleasure. With you it's different."

Panic invades my gut. "It's not pleasurable?"

He laughs again. "Let's just say I've been doing a lot of mental math."

"Mental math?"

"The pleasure is so intense, if I don't solve equations, this is going to be over before it starts."

I frown. "Oh."

"Babe, *babe*." He puts one hand on my face. "Because it's so fucking good. Jesus girl, it's so damn incredible, I'm afraid if I move the wrong way I'm going to come, and then this won't be good for you." He kisses my mouth. "The most important thing to me is making this good for you."

"I want it to be good for you, too."

He snorts like I just said the most ridiculous thing in the world. "That's a given."

"Okay." He grunts as he starts moving again. Warm heat fills my veins and races to every part of my quaking body. As I concentrate on the fierce pleasure, my orgasm building, and since I want this to last forever, I distract myself and ask, "What's the area of a triangle?"

"You think this is funny!" he practically shouts as the muscles in his jaw ripple like he's in excruciating pain. "You know how hard math is for me, right?" He pulls almost all the way out and pleasure shoots through my core as he powers in, and hits my cervix again. "Daisy, I'm a hockey player. Math isn't my thing."

I want to tell him he's a writer too, although that doesn't matter. Excelling at math doesn't help with either career, really. "I'm pretty good in math." I scratch my fingers along his back.

"Then you solve the equation, and I'll work on something simpler like one plus one."

I laugh, joy and happiness and every good feeling in the world invading my chest. "One plus one equals two, Brandon." I look between our bodies and a quiver goes through me as I revel in the way he pulls out, only to bury himself back inside me again. My God, that feels incredible. "Although right now, the two of us are making us one." He lifts his head and his dark eyes meet mine. "I like that, Brandon."

"I like that too."

In this moment, as I look into his eyes, I can't help but wonder if our hearts are connecting in much the same way as our bodies, but I'll have to ruminate on that later, when he's not changing the pace and rhythm between my legs.

"Oh."

He grins. "Like that?"

"That's a given," I tease, as my breathing changes, becomes a little faster, matching his. He grips my hands, laces his fingers through mine and holds them over my head. I moan as he subdues me and I do love this take-charge Brandon who is currently powering in and out of me, taking me higher and higher to a place I've never been before.

"If I'd have known how good this was, I'd have been doing it a long time ago," I tease.

Despite the softness in his eyes as he holds my gaze, a line creases his forehead. What does he not like that idea? Hell, who is he to judge? He's slept his way around campus for years.

"Maybe it's only this good because it's with me."

"Wow, ego much," I say, and a keening moan falls off my tongue as he shifts his body, to release one of my hands so he can wiggle it in between us.

"Not ego at all. I just think we fit together."

"We should have known we'd be good at this. We're good at everything together."

He smiles, and it does make me wonder. Will it be this good with anyone else? Will I compare every encounter to this one? Yeah, I probably will and that's going to suck. I gasp as he applies the perfect amount of pressure to my clit, and pleasure overtakes every cell in my body.

"Brandon," I cry out, and put my free hand on his chest as he pushes me over the precipice. "My God."

"I know, Daisy. I know." His face contorts as I tumble into orgasm, clenching and squeezing his cock as he fills me with every beautiful inch and gives my muscles something to grip on to.

He groans and thickens even more inside me as he too releases. We gasp together, our bodies vibrating as we give and take. After a long moment, when we can both catch our breath, he pulls out.

"That was the best sex I've ever had," I admit.

He laughs and brushes my hair from my face. "That was the only sex you've ever had."

He puts his hand between my legs and pets me gently. "Sore?"

"It's a good sore."

He takes his hand away. "There's a bit of blood."

I swear if he was any other guy, I'd be embarrassed, but with Brandon, I'm not. "I should get cleaned up."

"You stay here for a minute. I'll run you a warm bath."

My heart clenches. "Thank you."

He gives me a tender kiss, like it's the most natural thing in the world, and rolls off the bed. I stare at his cute butt until he disappears out the door. I stretch my arms out, warm contentment curling through my body.

I just had the most amazing sex with my best friend.

A laugh bubbles out of my throat as Brandon comes back into the room, and my gaze instantly drops to his half erect cock.

"That's not usually the reaction I get when I walk into a room naked."

I point to his cock. "That's because that is not a laughing matter."

He smiles, clearly liking the compliment, and comes to my side of the bed and sits down. He lightly brushes my hair from my forehead. He stares at me for so long, an uneasy feeling mushrooms inside me. If his lips weren't quirked, I'd be more worried.

"We okay, Daise?"

I nod, sit up and run my hands through his mussed hair. "Yeah, we're okay, B." Satisfied, he stands and, taking me by surprise, he scoops me up. I yelp. "I can walk."

"If you can walk, then I didn't do it right," he responds with a laugh.

"Ah, there's the ego." Honestly though, I'm glad he's carrying me. My legs are weak, and I am a little sore between my thighs. He carries me to the bathroom and sets me on the edge of the cool tub, which feels glorious against my hot body.

He rummages under the sink and produces a bottle of bubble bath. "Vanilla okay?"

"Vanilla is perfect." I throw my legs over the tub and dip my toes into the hot water. "This is nice, Brandon."

He squeezes a generous amount of bubble bath under the running water and I breathe in the scent. "Get in."

I slide into the tub, close my eyes and moan. "So nice."

"Don't hog the tub," he grumbles, and I open my eyes as he puts one foot in the tub, his cock dangling right there in front of my face.

"What are you doing?"

"Trying to get in, but you're such a big hog. You've always been a hog, you know."

"What? I have not," I shoot back and move forward so he can slide in behind me. He settles and stretches his long legs out on either side of me.

"Yeah, you have." I run my hands over his hard thighs. "Remember that time at the corn boil there was one cob left and you ate it?"

"You told me you didn't want it," I shoot back and laugh.

"You could have shared."

"You told me to eat it!"

"You could have read between the lines," he responds, his voice pouty.

"The lines were, YOU EAT IT! What's to read between that?"

His chest rumbles as he laughs, and as we sit here in the tub, even after the intimacies between the sheets, I've never felt closer to Brandon.

When the tub fills, I lean forward to turn off the tap. As soon as I do, Brandon pulls me back onto his chest, and I sink into his warmth.

"What about the hot dog?" he asks. "You ate the last one at Chase's birthday barbecue when we were fourteen."

"Are you kidding me? How long have you been thinking about that, and also, you told me you didn't want it." I shake my head and splash him with water.

"The shower..." he murmurs, as he lightly cups my breasts and runs the rough pad of his thumb over my nipples.

"What about it?"

"When you were using your hands on me you asked—"

"If oral sex was as good as the real thing, I know."

"I guess we now know the answer." I shift in the tub, and turn to face him.

His grin is full of wickedness as he kisses me and says, "Yeah, not as good as the real thing." I kiss him back, and my heart soars. "Not nearly as good, Duke."

Duke?

After what we just did, he's calling me Duke. A reminder that no matter what, he still thinks of me as one of the guys.

"Hey, was it something I said?" he asks, his gaze searching my face.

I force a smile. "Not as good as the real thing," I agree as I once again face the truth that Brandon and I will never be a real thing either...

20

BRANDON

My heart pounds a little harder in my chest as I set my laptop down and walk to the window. In the distance I spot Daisy in the water, talking with Sebastian and his friend Nick. Jealousy instantly pierces the happy bubble I've been in since I made love to Daisy last night, and then again this morning when we woke up.

I'd love to go out there, scoop her up and tie her to my bed to keep any other guy from looking at her—especially in that sexy bathing suit. But I have no right to have these caveman tendencies. We haven't talked about a relationship, or the fact that I want more. Maybe I should simply tell her, instead of taking this time to show her. But I'm afraid to come right out with it. If she's not interested in pursuing this when we leave here, I don't want to put a strain on our friendship.

Her laugh carries down the beach as Sebastian picks her up and starts carrying her out deeper. She pounds against his chest, but it's easy to tell she's having fun, and I want Daisy to have fun—just not with Sebastian or any other man on the planet, but me.

Fuck.

I walk away from the window and go back to my laptop and try to pick up where I left off. Daisy and I spent hours this morning talking about the book and going over certain scenes, and she's really great at helping me get inside the head of the heroine, especially in the more intimate scenes. My cock jumps to life as I think about the detailed way Daisy described what was going on in her body as she orgasmed.

I block out all the sounds around me and get myself back into the scene. My fingers fly across the keyboard, and I have to admit, writing is fucking hard, but it's so satisfying too and I'm at my happiest when I'm creating.

A sound penetrates my concentration and I recognize it's the front door opening. I lift my head to find Daisy trying to sneak in without interrupting me. She winces. "Sorry."

"Don't be, I actually got a lot done." I check out the loose sundress she has on over her bathing suit.

Her eyes light up, and I love her support. "Really?" She claps her hands. "I can't wait to read it."

"Did you have a good swim?"

She nods, and jerks her thumb over her shoulder. "Yeah, I ran into Sebastian. He dunked me."

"I saw that."

"Oh, you were watching?"

"I was stretching, and saw you."

"Ooh, a voyeur. I had no idea."

"You have some idea," I say and wag my eyebrow, my mind drifting back to the time I asked her to touch herself.

She chuckles. "Sebastian asked if we wanted to go out on his boat. I wasn't sure if you wanted to."

"Yeah, sure." I close my laptop. "I could use the break."

She eyes me. "How's the head?"

"No headache."

She bends and kisses my forehead. "Good. I'm going to grab a sandwich before we go. Want one?"

I push to my feet. "I'll help." I follow her into the kitchen and she goes to the fridge. She pulls out the meat and when she turns to me, she has that look on her face, one that only I would know means she has something to talk about.

"What?"

She chuckles. "Sometimes I wish you couldn't read me so well."

"That wasn't an answer."

She unscrews the bottle of mayonnaise and I grab a butter knife from the drawer. "What do you think of Sebastian?"

My heart stops beating. "Why do you ask?"

"Just curious."

I shrug. "I guess he's a nice guy. He's always been fun to hang around with, and if you're curious, yes, I think he's always had a thing for you."

Fuck me in the head, twice.

"Hmm."

"Hmm what?" I ask and rip into the turkey package.

"Nothing, I was just curious."

I want to ask her if she likes him, but I shut my mouth because I'm not sure I want to hear the answer. Then suddenly, my big stupid mouth has a mind of its own and I blurt out, "You don't want to fake date around him, do you?"

She rolls one shoulder and finishes putting the mayo on the bread. "I don't think it serves a purpose." She takes the open package of turkey from me and adds a generous amount to one of the sandwiches, mine I assume.

I reluctantly agree. Maybe she's right, though. We don't want to start rumors here that might get back to our friends and family if we don't work out. "Yeah, he doesn't need to know what we're up to."

"Nope, not at all."

I run my hand through my hair, needing something to do with it, before I...Oh, fuck it. I slide my hand around her waist, and her eyes widen as she turns my way. I dip my head, and my lips clamp down on hers for a deep, passionate kiss that will likely leave her lips swollen.

What the hell are you doing, dude?

Oh, I don't know, acting like a caveman and marking what's mine. *But she's not yours, now is she and if she wants Sebastian, what's stopping her?* But this kiss, I'm hoping it stays with her this afternoon when we're on Sebastian's boat, and takes up enough space in her brain that she'll forget all about that douche bag. Okay, so technically he's not a douche bag, and would probably be a great boyfriend, despite the physical distance between their colleges.

I break the kiss and run my thumb over her lush bottom lip. "What the heck was that for?" she asks.

"For making me a sandwich."

"Wow, the women who work in the Academy's cafeteria must fight over who makes your lunch."

I laugh at that. I playfully brush my shoulder. "This guy's got skill."

"Oh, I think you must have misunderstood." She's fighting back a grin as she cuts the sandwiches and puts them on the same plate. "They must fight over who *has* to make you a sandwich." She playfully wipes her mouth with the back of her hand. "I mean, I thought I'd just hooked up with a Saint Bernard."

I fold my arms and smirk at her. "Is that right?"

She crinkles her nose in distaste and sets the plate in the middle of the table. I sit across from her, and she picks up half of her sandwich and continues with, "It's probably the first time the lunch ladies were given a sloppy joe instead of serving one." She slaps the table and laughs like she just came up with the world's funniest joke.

"You're your own biggest fan, aren't you?"

She waves her hand in a circular motion toward herself as she takes a bow. "I'll be here all week."

Chuckling at her antics, and loving everything about the woman across from me, I bite into my sandwich and listen as she moans and chews. "Oh, and you might want to put on your new swim shorts. We know how the last ones worked out for you."

She laughs again and I just shake my head at her. She's all kinds of funny today. My laugh suddenly falls off. Is she in a good mood because we've been having awesome sex or because she just spent time with a guy she might actually have a thing for?

"Worry about your own suit," I tell her and take a big bite of my sandwich. I jump up and grab us each a bottle of water. I crack hers and hand it over.

"Thank you," she mumbles, as she drinks. She picks up her phone and checks it, and she exhales a nervous sigh.

"You'll get in," I tell her, having all the faith in the world in my best friend.

She sets her phone down. "I don't know why I keep checking, it's not like the results are going to be posted early." She bites, chews and then, as if she lost her appetite, she shoves the other half of her sandwich my way. "I think I'm just going to stay in bed tomorrow, under the covers, until I get the email."

"Nope, we're going out, and I'm going to keep you distracted. I was in the shed earlier, and found my old bike."

She smiles. "How many times did we nearly die on that thing, Brandon?"

I laugh. "Too many."

"We should at least wait until I'm a doctor so I can put us back together again if we wipe out."

"We only ever wiped out on the sand." I pick up the other half of her sandwich.

"Why the heck were we riding your bike on sand?"

"Correction. I was riding it, you were on the handle bars."

She laughs and turns to stare out the kitchen window. "Oh, you fixed the vase." She stands up to examine it and my gaze follows her ass. "Procrastinating much?" she teases.

"I got a lot of writing done." Once I stopped stewing about her hanging out with Sebastian.

She begins to rinse the dishes. "You go get ready. I'll tidy up."

I dart upstairs, and while I'd prefer to have the day alone with her, I'm not going to stay here imagining all the moves Sebastian might use on her out in the boat. I change into swim shorts that fit and run back downstairs, Daisy is reapplying sunscreen in the living room, one leg on the coffee table as she bends forward to do the top of her feet.

"Instant boner," I groan, and she chuckles.

I step up behind her, and run my hands along her sexy curves. "Keep that up and we'll never get out of here," she says.

"Maybe that's my plan."

"I told Sebastian I was coming, and I'm not going to leave him hanging."

"But it's okay to leave me hanging?" I tease.

She turns, and glances down at my boner. "Nothing is hanging, Brandon. In fact, it's doing the opposite." She presses the lotion into my chest and says, "I really don't know how you walk around most days."

Chuckling, I lotion up and she shoves some things into a beach bag. "All set," she asks, as I tug my T-shirt back on. I follow her outside and we lock up, and make our way down the beach. I glance back at the house. Tomorrow I have to get Daisy out doing something to take her mind off her email, and hopefully my brother comes through for me.

We reach the end of the sand and find Sebastian and Nick waving to us from their party boat. We walk the length of the dock and I go to help Daisy in, but she jumps in without anyone's aid. That's just like Daisy. She does everything on her own. Well, at least she used to. She's been letting me do all kinds of things for her and now I'm standing on the boat looking at Sebastian with a big stupid smile on my face.

"You okay, man?" he asks.

I laugh. "Yeah, just had some work to do earlier and it's nice to get out. Thanks for the invite."

"Anytime." He pats me on the back, jumps into the driver's seat and gets the boat started. Daisy sits in the big plush bench chair and Nick sits down beside her. They start talking about the party blowout on the weekend and she tells him that a few of our friends will be coming. Which he seems rather interested in. Probably because he quickly realized he wasn't going to be hooking up with Daisy and that she might actually like Sebastian.

I notice a few fishing rods. "What do you think, Daisy? Try for a largemouth bass."

"No," she blurts out and I laugh as she goes on to tell her favorite story of me making her touch a fish's eyeball.

"Dude, that's just wrong," Nick groans.

"There are two sides to every story," I inform him.

"Yeah, Brandon's side, and then the right side," Daisy says and she stands to pull off her swimsuit cover-up. No, I don't miss the way Sebastian turns in his chair to take a look. In fact, she has six eyes on her right now, and it's shocking how oblivious she is to it all. Daisy has always had guys casting lines and while she's always nice, she's never bitten. I always had a feeling she avoided relationships because of her abandonment issues. If she runs first, no one can walk away from her. But she goes one step further and doesn't even get involved. I guess now though, I could have been wrong about that, considering she's hung up on a douche bag on our team who doesn't see what's right in front of him. But now, as she stands and walks up to Sebastian, asking him if he can teach her to drive the boat, I'm beginning to think things might have changed for her, that she's seeing him—instead of me—in a different light.

Fuck that shit...

But wait. If that's what she wants, I can't be selfish, right?

21

DAISY

I wake up in Brandon's bed, and the second my eyes open, I turn toward the nightstand and snatch up my phone. I quickly open my email and hold my breath as I scan the messages. When I don't find any acceptance or rejection letter, I groan and drop my phone onto my stomach.

"Nothing?" Brandon asks, and I turn toward his voice and find him in the doorway looking rumpled and sexy and so good I want to eat him for breakfast.

"Nothing." I groan again. "This is torturous." He comes toward me with a cup of coffee in his hand, and I push myself up. "Is that for me?"

"This?" His brow lifts as he looks from me to the mug, then back to me. When I nod, he pretends to take a drink.

"I'd throw the pillow at you, but I don't want to spill the coffee."

He laughs. "Of course, it's for you." He sits on the edge of the bed, and hands me the hot mug. I breathe in the delicious scent and take a big sip.

"Thanks." I lift my phone again, and check my email, but there's nothing new.

Brandon takes my phone from me. "You really are a masochist," he concludes.

"Technically masochists like torture, and I'm not liking this at all."

"Maybe we can find a different kind of torture that you might like?"

I arch my brow, and as my imagination takes a trip down an erotic lane, my body tingles deep between my legs. "Oh."

I take another sip of coffee and eye him as he stands. I stare at his tight backside as he walks to his dresser, pulls the drawers open and produces the rope I purchased the other day.

"Oh," I say again. Last night Brandon kissed my body all over after we returned from the boat ride, pleasuring me like I was a prized possession and he had something to prove. Then we made sweet tender love—err, I mean we had sex. Afterward we showered together and snuggled into his bed, which is why I'm still naked.

I do love that he wants to take extra care with me, but why bother. He's already ruined me. Cripes, I tried and tried and tried to find common ground with Sebastian. While he's a good-looking guy, I just couldn't muster up any attraction to him. It might very well take Naomi and Brandon getting together before I can find a way to move on.

But those thoughts are for later, not for when Brandon is snapping the rope looking at me like I'm Little Red Riding Hood and he's the Big Bad Wolf.

"Okay, this is a distraction I might just like."

He arches a brow. "Better than biking on the beach?"

"I'll let you know."

"We'll be doing that later, by the way, so you can make mental notes and let me know which you prefer."

I take a quick breath as he takes the mug from me and sets it on the nightstand. He runs his finger along the inside of my wrist before tying the rope around it. "My God, is this really happening?"

"Yes, it's happening." As soon as he speaks, I furrow my brow. He stops what he's doing. "Change of heart?"

"No, I just didn't realize I said that out loud." He laughs, and I shimmy low as he lifts my arm and secures it above my head. "Ooh," I say. He runs his finger down my arm, a slow rough caress with his callused fingers that I've always loved. Something in the ruggedness of them just gets to me.

"You're mine."

My gaze flies to his. Everything in the way he just said that seemed so real, so possessive, but this is all just part of the play, right? For a brief moment yesterday, I thought he might have been jealous as Sebastian showed me how to steer the boat, but my God, we're having sex and fun, but this ends when our friends come. He wants me to set him up with Naomi, and he's not said a single word that he's changed his mind about that.

He puts his hand on my leg, wraps his palm around it as he tugs on it. "Say it."

I gulp. "I'm yours." If he only knew how much I wanted that to be true outside the bedroom, too.

His grin is feral as he zeroes in on my face. "Good."

The rope tickles my ankles as he secures me to the bed, like a virgin laid out for a sacrificial offering. Although I'm not a virgin anymore and I've offered myself up completely to my best friend. A few times now.

He spreads my legs, his gaze leisurely dropping to my damp sex as my lips widen and welcome him. Holy, that look on his face. So intense and carnal, like he once again has something to prove. But he doesn't have to prove to me he's a God in the bedroom and if he hadn't completely ruin me before, he plans to now.

He slides a hand between my legs and I whimper as he slides a finger over my pussy. "Already so wet," he whispers, and moans as he brings his finger to his mouth to taste me. "So fucking sweet." My insides soar. No man has ever made me feel so good about myself.

"Only for you," I say, but I've only been with him so he knows that. Still, I'm pretty sure no guy could ever arouse me the way he does.

"All for me too." He circles the bed, and ties my other hand and ankle and once I'm completely restrained, he stands back, his cock pushing so hard against his jeans it must hurt.

"Look at you. All wide open and mine for the taking."

Take me already!

"I can do anything I want to you right now," he continues, and walks around the bed.

"What...what do you want to do?" I manage to push out past a dry throat.

He reaches into the nightstand and I wait—impatiently—to see what he's up to. I moan as he showcases the feather tickler he...borrowed.

"I want to torture you in the best fucking way possible, until the only name on your tongue and in your brain for the next month is mine."

The next month?

This will be all over by the end of the week, though. Or maybe he said next day. Honestly, my brain can't be trusted to hear anything correctly right now.

"Brandon," I moan.

"Yeah, that's right. Just like that."

He brushes the tickler along my inner thighs and a deep heat penetrates my body. I suck in a breath, the room growing hotter and hotter as he teases my scorching flesh. He slaps the tickler against his hand before running it up my stomach and over my breast.

"You're killing me," I cry out.

His grin is devilish. "I'm just getting started."

"Oh God," I murmur, and roll my head from side to side.

Looking ever so calm and completely in control, he rolls one shoulder and casually says, "You can pray, but it's not going to help you."

I swallow, loving this side of Brandon and loving this side of myself too. "The only thing I'm praying for right now, Brandon, is for you to put your cock in me."

His jaw ticks and I don't miss the tremble in his hands. Ah, I guess the cool and collected Brandon Cannon isn't so in control after all. My dirty words are messing with him. Maybe if I keep it up, he'll stop playing and fuck me until I'm screaming his name, and we can forget about it being the only name on my tongue or in my brain for the next month. That's a given.

His fingers graze my nipples as he runs the tickler over my quivering body, until I'm a trembling mess of need. "These mental notes you want me to take. Is it for the book?"

"Nope, this scene will totally be from my point of view. You're to take notes to see if you like this better than biking on the beach."

"If you show me your cock, that might help me decide."

I can hear his fast intake of breath and love the way this man is unraveling, without me even being able to touch him.

"You want to see my cock, Daisy?"

"More than anything." The hiss of his zipper sizzles down my back. "No, that's not entirely true. I want your cock in my mouth and in my pussy. You can see how wet I am." He briefly closes his eyes as he frees his cock and takes it into his hand. "I want that, Brandon. I want you."

"You think this is about you right now?" he practically growls.

"Yeah, actually I do."

He grins, like I'm wrong, but I know I'm not. He's just playing a part, a part he knows I'll like.

"You're the one tied to the bed, Daisy. This is all about me right now. Me taking what I want."

A hard quake wracks my body and I grip the rope and hang on as he stalks closer. "I'll put my cock in you when I want, and when I want you to suck on my cock, I'll put it in your mouth."

It's crazy how he knows exactly how I want to be talked to right now. Then again is it? I know him as well as he knows me.

He climbs over my quivering body, stops to play with my nipples and his knees are practically under my armpits as his cock dangles before my mouth. I wish I could take it in my hands and force it into my mouth. but I'm all tied up at the moment. I lift my head and he holds his crown just out of reach.

"Torturous," I grumble.

Yeah," he agrees and tugs on his cock until pre-cum beads on his slit. "Open your mouth," he commands in a soft voice. "Stick your tongue out."

Holy!

I do as he says, and he groans as he drips onto my waiting tongue. I don't move, I just let his tangy cum sit on my tongue until he tells me I can swallow. Another drop lands, and once again I try to lift my head so I can lick him.

"Swallow," he orders and I moan around the warm salty taste of him.

"More," I plead after I drink every drop and lick my lips which pulls a reaction from him.

His nostrils flare and he grips my hair.

"Jesus, girl."

I bite back a grin, loving how much I can rattle him. He moves forward and puts his cock in my mouth and I happily moan around it. His hips move and I let him fuck my mouth as I grow wetter between my legs. I swear to God, the second he touches me it's going to be game over. He rocks into my mouth and grunts and groans, and now I know he's the one being tortured.

"You've got me right there," he grumbles, like it's a bad thing and I suppose it is if he wants his cock inside my pussy as much as I want it there. He inches out on a loud groan.

I blink at him, instantly missing the intimacy in what we were doing. "You can come in my mouth."

"No," he grunts, and shimmies down my needy, achy body to kneel between my spread legs. "I want to come in here." He slides a finger all the way inside and I begin to quake around his thickness. His grin is cute and playful, and my heart does a little somersault. "Obviously I'm not the only one who needs to fuck."

"Obviously," I moan and try to sit up, only to get tugged back down by the ropes, and dammit, I love how it feels. I fall back, and take pleasure in my confinement. While touching him comes with its own gratification, so does being restrained.

He fucks me with his finger until I'm writhing and moaning like I might spontaneously combust any second now and I fear I might. I'm so wet, he slips easily in and out of me, and I lift my hips, begging him for more.

"B, please."

"You need my cock, babe?"

"You know I do."

He pulls his wet finger out and falls over my body, his cock instantly finding its home and sliding all the way inside. I gasp as he fills me, and he goes still for a moment, his gaze moving over my face. My heart swells. I honestly love how he checks in on me. That look on his face right now, full of warmth and concern. He's given it to me a million times over the years. Sturdy, caring Brandon, my protector. I guess I never really thought about that until now.

"Why are you grinning?" he asks, and pushes my hair back.

"Because I love this. I...I...cherish you." Okay, that was close. I've never told Brandon I loved him over the years and I probably shouldn't start now.

"I love this too," he responds and powers his hips forward, until he's practically balls deep. "I can't seem to get enough of you."

"I'm all yours for the taking," I tell him.

He slides his hands under my shoulders, and holds my body close as he starts to move, sliding in and out of my body. This time we both fall silent and I like it every bit as much as when we talked through sex. I focus on the warmth of his flesh, the way his fingers are pressing into my skin, like he's holding on to me like his life depends on it, and the incredible way he brings pleasure to my body...to my life.

"Yes," I murmur, and turn my head to the side. He buries his mouth in my neck and his kisses penetrate my flesh and raise my arousal to new heights.

As if knowing I'm desperate to touch him, he reaches up and unties my hands, and I wrap them around his body, holding tight, because yes, I'm sure my life does depend on it. Without a speck of space between us, we cling to one another, as we give and take pleasure. Skilled lover that he is, he uses his pelvic bone to grind against my clit.

"My God, Brandon," I cry out, as my body convulses, a hard orgasm barreling through me.

His head lifts, his dark eyes on me. "Jesus, I feel you."

I come around his thick cock, my nails scratching his back as primal need takes control of me. He winches but the heat in his eyes tells me he likes it, and I like that tomorrow my scratches will be on him, and his finger bruises will be on me.

"I'm there," he groans, and I suck in a breath and concentrate on each hard pulse inside me. Later, I'm going to love the way his seed drips out of me—a glorious reminder of what we did this morning. Although maybe we'll have done it a few more times before we fall into bed together tonight.

Once he depletes himself, he collapses on top of me, and as all the stress leaves my body, I can't help but laugh.

His head lifts and he smiles at me. "Nice," he says and drops a soft kiss onto my lips.

"Nice," I respond, simply because I have no words to describe what this really means to me and he's the writer, so I'll leave that up to him. He remains on top of me for a long time, and I lightly run my fingers up and down his damp back.

A seagull squawks outside and he slowly pulls out of me, his fingers going between my legs to lightly rub my swollen sex. I sigh, and he stands. I stare at him as he walks to the foot of the bed, unties my feet, and lightly runs his fingers over the faint marks left by the rope. My hands are loose but he looks over my wrists. His gentleness with my body wraps around my heart and tugs tight.

"Did you want to check?" he asks quietly as I sit up and look over my wrists, knowing for the next twenty-four hours or so, anytime I see them, my mind will go right back to being tied up and taken by Brandon.

With a grin still on my face, I smile up at him. "Check what?"

He chuckles. "I guess my plan worked."

"Plan?"

He cocks his head. "To distract you from your phone."

"My phone," I murmur, my body is so relaxed and content, I'm still not sure I know what he's talking about.

He grins at me, clearly proud of himself. "Med school. The most important thing in the world to you. Remember?"

My heart jumps, pushing oxygen back into my woozy brain. "Oh, shit, right."

22

BRANDON

Warmth and love seep through me as I stand back, and take in the flushed, contented look on Daisy's face. I didn't want to bring up her phone after such incredible sex, but I did want her to know that distraction is much better than sitting in bed all day stressing.

She grabs her phone, her eyes wide as she checks and then she drops it again. "Nothing," she groans, but her stress level is much lower than it was when she first checked. "I should text Naomi..."

At the mention of Naomi, my stomach sinks. Daisy can't think I still want a relationship with her friend after what we've been doing, can she? Her hand hovers over her keyboard, like she's suddenly having second thoughts on that, or maybe mentioning Naomi is a reminder that come this weekend, this will be over and she hates that idea as much as I do.

"It's early and she could still be sleeping." She drops her phone, and puts her forearm over her head.

I sit beside her, pull her arm away so I can see her face, and pick up her now cold coffee. "Are you okay?"

"I'm okay," she says quietly and takes the cup from me.

"I can heat it up."

"It's coffee. It's good hot or cold." She takes a big sip, moans in delight as she swallows, and goes for another drink.

"Jeez, that's the same sound you make when you come."

She laughs and sits up. "Ohmigod, Brandon, that nearly came out of my nose. You can't say funny things when I'm swallowing."

I lean into her and kiss her nose. "I love when you swallow."

She angles her head. "Wait, what are you talking about?"

I laugh. "I really don't know." It's the truth. Sex with Daisy is fucking with me in so many ways. "But what I do know is we're going to shower, get on my bike and head to the bakery."

"Can I ride on the handlebars?"

"You can ride on anything you want to, Daise…"

"Uh, that sounds sexual."

I stand, and hold my hand out to lift her. "I don't think I can move," she says.

I arch a brow. "Sure, you just want me to carry you again."

"You think I would trick you like that?" I slide my hands under her body. "Then you'd be right."

I laugh as I carry her to the bathroom, and get the water just right before I help her into the shower, where we take our time to clean our bodies. Once we're rinsed and towel-dried, we go back to the bedroom and get into our shorts and T-shirts.

"Is my helmet still out there?" Daisy asks as we head downstairs.

"Yup, but it hasn't been used in a while, so we'd better check for spiders."

She cringes, and I laugh. She never did like spiders much. "I'll check it for you."

"My hero," she announces, and I laugh, because there is no way on the face of this earth that I can live up to any of the guys in a romance novel.

I half roll my eyes at her, and open the shed. The smell of dried cut wood for the bonfires fill my senses and Daisy smiles as she breathes it in like that scent takes her back in time. I take her helmet off the shelf, blow off the dust and check it for bugs.

As she tugs it on, she runs her hands along the handlebars of my bike. "You're not going to crash it this time, are you?"

"That was your fault. You were wiggling."

She lifts her chin, all indignant. "There was something on my leg. I was trying to get it off."

"That's what you said, but I didn't see anything."

"Maybe if you weren't trying to see and instead focused on where you were going, we wouldn't have hit that big pile of sand."

"Well, if..." I begin and start laughing.

"What?"

"We sound like an old married couple." I might be laughing, but damn, I like the idea of that.

She snorts, and I actually love it when she does that. "Like that's ever going to happen."

I go stiff as her remark hits like a wayward puck. Okay, was that comment really necessary? She can't entertain the idea for a second? I guess if she can't, then I'm not getting through to her, and I'd better up my game before this weekend is over. Ignoring the pang in my stomach, I take my bike outside, and balance it so she can climb onto the handlebars. She might complain about that fall, but we laughed for days about it, and she loves riding on the handlebars, throwing her arms out like she's on the bow of the Titanic.

"All set, Duke?"

This time she's the one who seems to take offense at her nickname. Or maybe her thoughts strayed, as she's back to worrying about med school.

"All set." There's a hitch in her voice that's hard to miss.

"Do you want to check one more time before we go?" She nods, digs her phone out of her back pocket and scrolls. Without a word, she tucks it away, and I hold the bike as she climbs on. I carefully steer the bike down the driveway and we hit the sand. She yelps and grabs the handlebars when the bike becomes wobbly.

"I remember this being easier," I say, and she laughs.

"I guess we're not fourteen anymore, and I don't weigh eighty pounds."

No, we're not and she doesn't. "You're perfect, Daisy." So goddamn perfect, I'd be the luckiest man on earth if we find our way to a happily ever after.

She glances at me over her shoulder. Her smile is twisted, and the look in her eyes tells me she thinks I'm full of crap. But as I look at her, and take in the flush on her cheeks, the way her hair blows in the wind, I'm taken back to our teenage years. Lots of things are different now, but Daisy is just as beautiful, maybe even more so than when we were growing up.

"Save your breath. You're already in my pants, B."

I laugh at her. "I'm not blowing smoke up your skirt, Duke."

"First, I'm not wearing a skirt, and if you keep feeding me lines, the only thing you'll be blowing up tonight is a blowup doll, so take my advice and save your breath for that."

I laugh so hard, I nearly lose control of the bike as my tires dig into the sand. I head down toward the water where the sand is packed, and it's easier to pedal. Once the bike is stabilized, Daisy throws her arms out and my heart fills with everything I feel for her. Yes, that might sound like a cheesy line from a romance novel, and I've probably used it, but it's the fucking truth, so sue me.

Off in the distance, Sebastian comes from his cottage and waves to us. I try not to let the jealousy welling up inside me derail me from the bike ride, or showing Daisy how good we are together. We finally reach the end of the beach and I take the gravel path to the main road, where the small café is located. I park the bike and Daisy is grinning as I help her off.

I check the time on my phone to make sure everything is going according to schedule as Daisy pulls hers out to check for messages.

"They could have at least given us a time, you know. That way we wouldn't be glued to our phones all day."

"Torturous," I grumble and a quiver goes through her. Mission accomplished. "Come on, we need coffee and bagels."

She mumbles what sounds like curses under her breath, followed by, "I need answers."

We head inside and the smell of fresh coffee and sweet treats brings a smile to her face. Personally, I love the place with its back wall filled with books. You can pay a couple bucks for one, or leave one in its place for payment.

I nod toward the back of the room, to where our usual seats sit empty. "Grab us a seat."

Since the place is empty this Wednesday morning, she walks to the back and grabs our favorite table. She turns and pulls a few books off the shelf. I get our order and carry it to her, and she turns to me, a wicked grin on her face. "Remember when we were kids," she whispers.

I laugh, remembering it all too well as she flips through the pages of a book. "Yeah, and we would sneak peeks at the dirty scenes."

"Is that when you started thinking about writing?" She takes a sip of coffee, and pulls her bagel apart.

"I don't know. I mean I've always loved to read and I loved going to Mom's book signings."

She nods in agreement. "They were fun." She bites her bagel and chews. "I can so easily picture you doing that, Brandon."

"If I were signing, do you think anyone would even show?"

"Yeah right, a hockey player turned romance novelist," she responds her tone dripping in sarcasm. "No one would show up for that?"

"I'd be a laughing stock then."

She rolls her eyes. "Brandon, look at you. You're exactly what every girl envisions when she reads a romance. You'd have the place packed."

"I'm not sure about that." I bite into my bagel and think about it. While I'm not a guy who needs fame and glory, it really would be fun to see others take enjoyment in my writing.

She shrugs. "You won't know until you give it a try."

"Do you really think so?"

She leans into me. "Brandon, I never ever want you to spend your life saying *what if*. You should do what your heart is telling you to do."

At her statement, I lean across the table and plant my lips on hers. I pull back and her brow is screwed together. I laugh. "You just told me I should do what my heart is telling me to do."

Her face falls, her eyes narrow and serious. My heart takes that moment to thunder, because I'm sure one of two things is about to happen. She's either going to tell me her heart wants the same, or she's going to remind me we're friends. I stop breathing as I wait for her to speak, and just when she opens her mouth, my phone rings.

She goes stiff, and leans back in her chair, her gaze no longer on me. Well, fuck me twice. I want to tell her to ignore my phone, but the moment is gone, so I grab it, and slide my finger across the screen when I see it's from Casey.

"I'll be right back."

She angles her head, confusion on her face, as I hurry outside, needing privacy. "Hey, what's up?"

"Just calling to make sure the coast is clear. The car is still in the driveway."

"Shit, sorry, I should have messaged you. We're at the café. We took the bike."

"Okay, good."

"Thanks so much for helping, Casey."

"Yeah, you owe me bro."

I laugh. "This is for Daisy."

"And the only reason I'm helping. Are you forgetting about that time you sat on my head?"

"It was an accident."

"The nearly suffocating me to death was an accident, sitting on my head because I stole your controller was not."

I grin. "Why is it everyone remembers the bad things I've done?" I glance off into the distance, thinking about how Daisy loves to tell the fish eyeball story.

"Just the way it is, bro. Gotta go, shit is melting."

I hang up and head back inside. Daisy's head lifts from the book she's scanning as I enter. "Everything okay?"

"Brother stuff." I put my hand around my mug. "Now, where were we?"

"We were talking about your writing, and I'm really looking forward to helping you get your ending right."

"You mean my happy ending."

She laughs and throws a sugar packet at me. "No, you've nailed the happy ending, it's the happily ever after you have to work on."

We spend the next hour chatting, eating and drinking coffee, and Daisy checks her phone every few minutes.

As she starts to get antsy again, she asks, "It's getting warm. Want to go for a swim?"

I check my phone. Did I give Casey enough time? "No, let's have another coffee."

She purses her lips. "B, what are you up to?"

"Six foot four," I answer.

She rolls her eyes at me. "You better not be up to something. I don't like surprises."

I whistle innocently, and gesture the server for another refill. "All I'm up to is getting another cup of coffee. I wore myself out biking here, and I need the rush."

She leans in, all playful. "Take me back right now, and I'll give you a rush." She nibbles her bottom lip. "With my mouth."

"Jesus, girl." I glance around to make sure no one is within ear shot. The server is making her way over, her gaze going back and forth between the two of us. She slows, like she's worried she's interrupting something. I lift my hand and wave my hand to let her know it's okay.

Daisy and I order more coffee and we're both a bit jittery by the time we bike back to the cottage without any incidents. I slow as I approach and Casey is nowhere to be found. We hop off the bike and Daisy's phone pings.

"It's from Naomi," she says, suddenly breathless. "She told me to check my email."

She wobbles a bit and I sit her on the bench. "Do you want me to leave?"

She grabs me and pulls me down. "No, stay here." She opens her email and her face goes blank for a second as she scans. "It's here. Oh, God, B." she shoves her phone into my hand. "You read it."

Confident that she got in, I open the message, and quickly read, as soon as I see the one word I'm looking for, I smile and glance at Daisy. "Congrats, Duke. You're going to medical school." She stands and squeals and I jump up with her. She jumps into my arms and I spin her around as we kiss like two fools.

"You did it!"

"I did it," she yells flying higher than I've ever seen and I couldn't be happier or prouder of her.

I hand the phone back. "And that message came just in time."

"What do you mean?"

I take her hand and we head inside the house. It's filled with flowers, balloons, ribbons and banners, with a beautiful cake on the counter, and her favorite ice cream in the freezer.

She slaps her face. "Brandon, what did you do?"

"With a little help from my brother, I got all your favorite things."

"What if I didn't—"

"I was never worried about that."

She cups my cheeks this time. "Thank you for always believing in me." My heart swells, knowing how much she believes in me too. Maybe I really should give this writing career a chance.

"We'll stop and get champagne later tonight, after dinner."

She blinks up at me, her eyes watery, but so full of happiness. "Dinner?"

"Yeah, your favorite restaurant."

"Tandoors?"

"Of course! But now you need to call a million people to let them know you've been accepted, then we're going to take that swim and go out for a nice meal, and maybe a pit stop at the boutique so we can replace the neighbors' feather tickler."

She grins and kisses me. "You're the best."

"I know. Now go make your calls and I'll go get some writing done."

I leave Daisy to herself, and grin as I hear her screaming on the phone as she makes her calls. It's hours later, the sun setting low on the horizon by the time we make it to her favorite restaurant. After we order drinks, she excuses herself for a minute and heads to the ladies' room. As I sit and wait, my heart and soul full, so happy to see that the future she wants is within her reach, I consider my future, and the one I want with her. A few moments later, she comes running from the restroom.

"Brandon!" she says, breathless as she leans into me, trying to keep her voice low, but hardly able to contain herself. What is going on with her? "That scene...from your book." I stare at her. Wait, no? Did she figure it out? She starts waving her hands around. "You know, remember when I said something was off. I was right."

"What scene and right about what?" I ask just to clarify and make sure we're on the same page.

"The night," she begins and leans in closer, her words for my ears only. "When we discovered that playroom. I mention that one of your sex scenes might not have the details right."

Okay, so yes, we're definitely on the same page, here. "I remember."

She jerks her thumb over her shoulder. "It was set in the women's bathroom. Here at Tandoor, wasn't it?"

I scrub my face, not sure whether to be embarrassed by that or not. "Uh, yeah."

"You were in there, then?"

"Briefly."

"I knew it. Okay, you have the details wrong. There is no way the heroine can reach the stall door with her foot, when the hero is you know...banging her against the sink."

"Are you sure?" I take a sip of my beer and set it back down.

"Pretty sure."

"Well if you're sure." I stand and take her hand, giving her a tug and a look that holds all kinds of suggestion. "Then we need to go in there so we can get the details right."

23

DAISY

It's nearing dinner time and Cheddar is the first to arrive at the cottage, and I worry he's going to take one look at Brandon and me and know what we've been up to. He's not a subtle guy by any means, so I'm sure he's going to blurt out that we've been fucking. I stand back a bit as he chats with Brandon in the driveway, and I wave to the cab driver as he pulls away.

Brandon slaps him on the back, and Cheddar drops his bag and runs up the stairs when he sees me. "Daisy, congrats on med school!" He gives me a big bear hug and spins me around and I don't miss the curious look on Brandon's face. Does he think Cheddar is the guy I've been crushing on?

We head inside and Brandon gets our friend a cold beer from the fridge, and Cheddar admires the ocean from the window.

"Dude, it's about time you invited me here." He takes a big swig of beer. "This place is amazing."

"Thanks. We can take a swim later if you want, and tomorrow there are a bunch of fun activities on the water for the blowout, even some races in the sand, and a volleyball tournament."

"Sandcastle contest?"

I laugh. "Yes, as a matter of fact there is."

"It's Daisy's favorite," Brandon says. "Don't beat her or she'll bury you. Trust me, I know from experience."

Cheddar laughs. "I can't believe you two have known each other since you were kids."

"Don't forget me," Chase says as he comes in through the door. "I'm part of this hockey brat pack, too."

"Chase," I squeal and hug him as Sawyer comes in behind him. I turn to her and pull her into me for a hug. "I'm so glad you could both make it."

She smiles at me, looking so happy and relaxed and I have to say I am a little jealous at what she and Chase have. "I've been hearing about this place forever," she says as she takes off her hat. "I'm so glad we finally got here." I glance down and note they don't have their suitcases. "We already dropped our stuff off, and I checked out Chase's family cottage. Cute Halloween picture of you guys on the wall."

I laugh at that. "Great, come on in." I glance past her shoulders when she angles her head as she studies my face, like she knows something is amiss but can't figure it out.

She frowns. "Are you okay?"

"Yeah, just checking in on Naomi." I check my phone. "She's excited to celebrate our acceptance this weekend." While she is excited about that, I'm not sure how excited she is about trying another date with Brandon. I texted her a few times, and I think she's only going to give it another shot because of me. But I have to try, right? This is what Brandon wants, and I want him happy.

"Me too," Sawyer says, pulling my thoughts back, and I put my arm through hers, so happy to have such great friends. I honestly wish I could tell her everything, and even tell her that Brandon wants to write books. Heck, she's in theater and she would love that. She wants to start her own little production company someday and maybe she could turn his stories into plays. But I'm getting way ahead of myself. Brandon isn't ready to switch careers. I'm not sure he'd ever want to disappoint his family like that. He's a good guy who cares about other people's feelings, but I wish he'd start putting his own feelings first, once in a while. He has an entire future to think about.

I guide her toward the kitchen. "I'm disappointed that Matt and Kennedy can't make it. But they had a family trip planned to go back to Alberta. They're bringing Madelyn to meet Matt's family. Beckett and Piper will be arriving early tomorrow. They can stay at my cottage or Chase's. But right now, they're all with us in spirit and would want us to get started on that celebration."

"Is your roommate Alysha coming?"

"She can't. She's in the Hamptons."

She frowns again. "What?"

"I actually thought I saw her the other day. I must have been mistaken."

I nod. "Yeah, probably." There are plenty more in our circle of friends, but we only invited our closest. "We also invited

Ryan, but he's back in Prince Edward Island for the week."
His parents are potato farmers. I still wonder about those
two, and why Ryan was sleeping on Alysa's couch. I'll have to
ask about that when I get home.

"Oh, I actually thought I saw him too."

I catch Brandon's eyes as I walk past him and the guys as they
start talking about none other than hockey. In the kitchen, I
point to the chair, and head to the fridge to grab the wine I've
been chilling. Before Sawyer sits down, she glances out the
window with a strange look on her face.

I set the wine on the counter. "What?"

"Ah, there's some guy in the treehouse out back."

I spin, expecting it to be one of the kids littering up the place
—*do not think about how filthy you and Brandon were in there, girl*
—but instead it's Sebastian. I laugh, and walk to the back
door and slide it open. "What are you doing up there?"

He waves to me, and starts down the ladder. "He's cute,"
Sawyer whispers.

"Yeah, he is," I agree.

"Are you going to go for it?"

I consider my backup plan when I can't come up with a name
for my crush. "Maybe," I tease and note the movement
behind her. I lift my head and spot Brandon in the doorway.
How much did he hear?

He takes as small step toward me. "What's going on?"

"I think Sebastian started the party a bit early. He's in the
treehouse."

"Dude," Sebastian says, coming into the kitchen.

Brandon quickly closes the distance between us. "What were you doing in the treehouse?" Brandon asks, and I'm not sure I've ever seen him so territorial, and...possessive?

"I was on my way over and thought I saw someone in there. Worried it was the kids vandalizing the cottages and thought I'd check. It was just a wrapper blowing around, though. But security was at the Conrads last night. Did you hear about that?"

I gulp. Last night after Brandon and I recreated a very memorable scene from his book in the bathroom at Tandoor's, we bought a new tickler and snuck it back to the Conrads. Brandon used skills I never knew he had, jimmied the door open and replaced the sex toy. Then when we got back, he used some other skills on my body, with the tickler we still have.

"I guess there was banging going on there again."

I was sure the screen door latch didn't click when we left. "The door," I mumble without thinking. Brandon's throat makes a sound as he swallows.

"What?" Sebastian asks.

"Oh, last time the door was banging. Must be a loose latch or something," I explain. "Wind probably caught it again."

Lies. Lies. Lies.

But at least we replaced what we borrowed.

"Bonfire tonight," Sebastian announces, switching topics and I'm grateful, because now is not the time for my body to start burning with heated memories. Now that Naomi is coming here, what happened between Brandon and me is over, right?

If so, why the hell is he hovering so close, like Sebastian might want you and he's peacocking, showing that you're his prized possession?

Okay, no that has to be wishful thinking. He's waiting for Naomi to arrive. "Okay, wine," I say, needing a glass or two.

Trying to keep my hands from shaking, I pour two huge glasses and Sawyer is looking at me carefully as I plaster on a smile and hand hers over.

"This will knock me out," she says with a laugh.

"Yeah," is all I respond, hoping mine knocks out all the things I feel for Brandon.

"I'll roast an extra gooey one for you, Daisy," Sebastian promises, and curls one long strand of my hair around his finger before giving it a tug. "Oh, and I got you this." He disappears outside for a second and comes back with a gift bag. "This is for you."

"Sebastian, what did you do?" I ask.

Dimples form as he smiles. "Open it."

I open the bag and pull out a white coat. "Ohmigod," I squeal. "I love it. Thank you." I go up on my toes, to press my lips to his cheek but he shifts and I kiss him right on the mouth.

"Glad you love it." He gives me a wink. "Bring it tonight. We can try it out."

Heat moves into my face, knowing exactly what he's getting at and maybe this is a good time to play into his advances.

"Maybe I will."

Did Brandon just growl?

My phone pings, and I steal a fast glance at it, my heart jumping into my throat. "Naomi is here," I announce in my happiest voice. My friends here know me well, so I hope they can't hear the layer of disappointment lingering just below the surface.

Sawyer jumps up. "Great."

I watch for Brandon's reaction. "Yeah, great," he says and follows Sawyer to the front door. The cab opens and both Tank and Naomi climb out. I rush to meet Naomi with arms open.

She hugs me back. "We ran into each other at the airport," Naomi explains, as Tank does a fist bump with Cheddar.

"I'm here," Tanks booms, spreading his arms as his gaze seeks Brandon's. "Now the party can start. Posh place, my man." He fist-bumps Brandon.

Brandon turns to Naomi, and I've not seen this nervous side of him before as he reaches over his shoulder and scratches his back. "You're hot."

"What?" Her eyes go wide and I stare at him. Is he freaking concussing again? If not, Naomi really throws him off his game, which means, he really does like her.

"I mean, it's hot. We should get inside and get a drink and maybe all take a cold swim before we get something to eat and go to the bonfire."

"Oh that sounds lovely." She runs her fingers through her long hair. "I don't want to get my hair wet, so I'll watch from a beach towel."

"I can sit with you," I say, when Brandon frowns.

"Perfect."

We all head inside and when Cheddar runs upstairs to claim a room, I'm glad I cleared my things out earlier.

"Where should I put my things?" Tank asks.

"Just leave them here. We can figure out sleeping arrangements later." I don't miss the way Brandon glances at me.

Brandon gets everyone a beer and the cabin is full of noise and liveliness, much like it was when we were younger and all the families came for the summer. I liked it then. Now, I kind of liked it better when it was just Brandon and me, but that's over, and I need to get my head on straight.

As everyone talks, Brandon sidles up to me. "So, is it Tank or Cheddar?" he asks, his tone and stance less playful then it was on the plane.

"It's not the end of the week just yet." I push off the counter. "I'm going to get changed."

"Careful, Cheddar is still up there, and closed doors mean nothing to him."

I laugh. "Right, which is why I'm going to change at my own cottage." I look at my friends and put on a happy face. "I'll meet you all back here in a few. I'm going to get into my swimsuit." At least this way it doesn't look like I've been holed up here alone with Brandon for the week.

I snatch up the present from Sebastian and hurry outside, thankful for the reprieve as the late day sun shines down on me. Tomorrow will be full of fun activities put on by the Wautauga beach association, and that should help keep my mind off Brandon hooking up with Naomi. I snort. Who am

I kidding? Nothing short of drowning myself in the ocean is going to help.

I spot Sebastian on his deck and wave. Yeah, I think letting Brandon believe I am crushing on him might work, and if Sebastian and I didn't have a country separating us, it's possible I would give it a go. But we do and I don't want to lead him to believe anything could ever happen between us. Which means I'm not putting on the coat and playing doctor of any kind with him. But we can hang out.

I head inside my cottage, and take a deep breath as the quiet surrounds me. Half of me wants to curl up in my bed and stay there until this weekend is over. The other half knows that's not a possibility. I change into my swimsuit, tie my hair up and throw on my coverup. A half hour later, I walk to the beach and find everyone in the water—except Naomi.

I crouch down beside her, and take in her long tanned legs and gorgeous body. Why do I feel like a troll next to her? I mean, I like my body, I'm fit and athletic and strong, but she's tall, lithe and delicate—the kind of girl the hockey players go for.

Oh, but Brandon went for you this week.

But he still calls me Duke. At that reminder, I spread out a towel and sit. "I love your suit," I tell Naomi as I check out the skimp of material that barely covers her body. No, I am not jealous. Much.

"Thanks, yours is cute too," she says as I peel my coverup off.

I instantly begin to heat up. "You don't want to get in?"

"Swimming in the ocean isn't my thing. Don't let me stop you from going in, though. Everyone looks like they're having a great time."

I take a breath and begin, "About you and Brandon."

"I'm here because you asked me to come, and I'll try to give him a chance."

Wow, that was a whole lot of reluctance in her voice. I should really try harder to build Brandon up in her eyes, but I honestly can't muster the strength to do it.

Are you purposely sabotaging him, Daisy?

Battling with myself, I stare longingly at the water and just like when we were kids, Chase and Brandon set eyes on me and start my way.

"Don't," I warn, holding up my hands. "You'll be sorry if you do."

"Oh, what are you going to do, Duke?" Brandon shoots back. "Run and tell on us?"

Okay, I would never tell on them back in the day when they dunked me and I wouldn't now. "I...I...I'm on my period," I blurt out but that doesn't deter them.

"No, you're not," Brandon says, and scoops me up. I squeal and Chase takes my legs and everyone cheers them on. Everyone but Naomi, who looks completely horrified.

"It's okay," I shout to her. Honestly, I'm not upset. This is sort of our tradition, and I kind of like horsing around with my best friends like this. They carry me out and dunk me, and I rise to the surface to find them laughing. I splash them and dunk under, and we play around like we did when we were kids. Next time I surface, Chase gets Sawyer to climb on his shoulders, and I climb on Brandon's and we play our child-hood game of trying to knock each other off.

Tank calls for Naomi to jump on his shoulders but she refuses. A few minutes later, he sits on my towel beside her and as they chat. Cheddar swims around us, and we continue our game until I knock Sawyer off.

"We have no equals," Brandon belts out as I dive into the water, nearly taking in a mouthful from laughing so much. I swim out a bit, and Sawyer comes out with me.

"I can see why you guys love it here so much," she tells me with a big smile.

I nod and glance at the beach. "I don't think Naomi is having all that much fun."

She turns to look at the sand, where Naomi is swatting at something. "So her and Brandon, huh?"

"Yeah." I can't bring myself to say much more, or even to sound positive about it.

"That sucks for you."

"Why do you say that?"

She frowns, her knowing eyes slowly moving over my face. "You know why."

My heart thunders. God, she knows. Am I that easy to read? "Brandon and I are friends."

She grins when she says, "Such good friends he knows your menstrual cycle?"

Oh, my freaking god!

"We go way back." I turn to the right and spot Sebastian. "It's Sebastian I'm interested in."

She opens her mouth, no doubt about to call me on that, but Chase swims up to us and she goes quiet. "I'm going to get the barbecue started. Want to help?"

Sawyer shakes her head. "No, I think—"

"I'm ready to get out," I pipe in, cutting Sawyer off because I'm not ready to have a conversation about Brandon and me.

Chase turns so Sawyer can put her arms and legs around his back. He swims off and I slowly follow, going even slower when I see Brandon hold his hand out and help Naomi to her feet. They head up to the cottage, and Brandon looks at me over his shoulder. I hold my hand up to let him know I'm okay, but he turns and comes back toward me.

His face is twisted, like he has something very important on his mind. "Daisy, about Naomi..."

God, I'm pretty sure I can't stay here and listen to anything about how he wants her, or how I might still go about helping him. I've done all I'm going to do. Anything more would be emotional suicide.

Just then the wind picks up and Naomi squeals. Brandon glances back at her, and I swallow hard and say, "I need to go get changed, Brandon. I'll catch up with you guys later."

"Daisy..."

I stifle a yawn. "I think after the bonfire tonight, I'm going to crawl into bed at my own cottage. It's been a long week, and I'm exhausted, plus..." I lightly tap his head. "You don't need me anymore." I'm not just talking about his concussion, and he's smart enough to know that. Brandon doesn't need me. He never has. It was me who needed him.

"Daisy, I've always—"

"Brandon," Naomi squeals as the wind carries her hat down the beach. "My hat!"

"You better go. You're needed."

"Daisy, wait, I—"

"Daisy," Sebastian calls out as he waves me over. I wave to him and turn back to Brandon. "Looks like I'm needed too."

24

BRANDON

After a late night at Sebastian's bonfire, where we all hung out and chatted—mostly about hockey—I wake with a bit of a headache. I blame it on too late of a night, and too much alcohol. Why did I drink too much? Oh, probably because Daisy and Sebastian looked so cozy sitting on the log together and laughing as Daisy made them *the world's best* s'mores—according to Sebastian.

I didn't like it. One little bit. I wanted to go over there and break them up, but talk about being caught between a rock and a hard place. Naomi came all this way to give me a second chance—one I'm obviously second-guessing—and I don't want to be a douche bag and ignore her. I'm the asshole that set this all into motion, even asking my best friend to get involved.

Can you say dumbass?

When my friends were ready to call it a night, I walked them back to my cottage and found a place for everyone to sleep. The guys shared Mom and Dad's room, and Naomi took my newly emptied brother's bedroom. I have no idea what time Daisy called it a night, or even if she went back to her place. Fuck, for all I know she spent the night in Sebastian's bed. Not my business though, right?

Wrong.

Of course, it's my goddamn business. She's my best friend, and I fucking love her.

I love Daisy Reed.

But I have a huge problem. Naomi is here to get to know me, and Daisy could very well be hooking up with another guy. What the hell happened to the guy on my team she was crushing on? Could this be any more fucked up? I push my blankets off, stand and listen to the voices downstairs. A fast glance at the clock lets me know I slept in. I'm not surprised. I walk to my window and glance out and see festivities being set up on the sand below. Hopefully I'll get a chance to talk to Daisy today. How I'm going to deal with Naomi is a mystery and I feel like a goddamn asshole. She's here because I invited her, wanting to make a better impression of myself. Fucking home ice advantage was a stupid idea.

Maybe if I act like an asshole again, she'll walk away, but man, that's just not in my nature. I tug on my jeans, and make my way down the steps to find Naomi and Tank sitting on the sofa, in deep conversation. From the look on Tank's face, he's enamored with her. Although, if I put any girl in front of him, he'd be interested. He's kind of like that and hell, maybe I was too, so who am I to judge?

"Hey," I greet them, and they both look my way. They inch back a bit, like they might have been sitting too close—like they might have something to hide—and I note the warm flush on Naomi's cheeks. It's warm in here, so it could be nothing, and she's not the type of girl to go after a hockey player simply because he's a hockey player. That's why I involved Daisy in the first place.

I note the mugs of coffee in their hands. "Did you guys eat?" I nod toward the window. "There's a great pastry shop at the end of the beach. We could walk or bike there." I laugh as I remember Daisy wiggling like mad on the handlebars. Could she have been any more adorable?

With her mug inches from her lips, Naomi asks, "You have bikes for us all?"

"No, but you could ride on my handlebars though," I suggest, half kidding. I think. Or maybe I'm simply comparing her to Daisy to see if there is a possibility that we'd be a good fit.

She blinks at me, like I might have just asked her to jump from a plane without a parachute. "You're kidding right?"

"Well, I guess. I mean, maybe not. Daisy and I did it yesterday."

"Well, I'm not a daredevil like Daisy, and I don't eat carbs anyway."

Right, okay then. So much for her making happy faces on her pancakes and honestly, I never thought of my Duke as a daredevil, but maybe she is. She sure kept up with us guys. Or rather, we had to keep up to her.

I start toward the kitchen. "I think I have some eggs."

"Egg whites?"

"Yeah, I can do that."

She nods, like that will suffice, and I leave them to their conversation. The first thing....coffee. After I put the pod in the machine, and check the fridge, and shove some bread into the toaster in case Tank wants something. I check my phone, but there's nothing from Daisy. Disappointment storms through my gut like a brush fire.

"What's up, bro?" Cheddar asks, scratching his crotch as he comes into the kitchen.

"Is that necessary?"

"Got sand on my balls last night, so yeah it's necessary." He scratches more, then stretches his arms. "What's your problem this morning?"

He's right. I'm being a jerk. "Nothing, sorry." The coffee finishes and I hand him a mug. "I'm really glad you're here." I put another pod in, and lean against the counter. Before I can even stop myself I blurt out, "What do you think of Daisy?"

Dude!

His hand goes still, his mug inches from his mouth. "Why? Did she say something about me? Does she like me?" He angles his head. "Wait, do you like her?"

"Of course, I like her. She's my best friend."

He nods, and takes a sip. "Yeah, Naomi is here for you." He snorts. "If you liked Daisy, that would be seriously fucked up, man."

"Yeah, fucked up."

He pretty much nailed that.

"So does she like me?" he probes.

I shouldn't say anything. I don't want to betray Daisy's trust. "Do you think she likes someone on the team? Have you seen her with anyone, or looking at anyone, you know, like she likes them?"

"The only one I've seen her with, or looking at, is you."

My heart jumps, and the idea is so ludicrous I shouldn't entertain it, but I do anyway. Am I the guy Daisy was talking about? The one on the team she likes? How crazy would that be?

"Wait." Cheddar interrupts my thoughts. "The other night at the pub, after her game, I saw her talking to Mason."

I nod, remembering that too. But Daisy talks to all the guys. "Yeah, you think she likes him?"

"I don't know. Why all the hard questions after a night of partying? My head still isn't on right."

"Yeah, you're right. I just want to see Daisy happy, is all."

"She sure as hell seemed happy enough last night with Sebastian. He banging her or what?"

"Don't say that." Christ, no one is allowed to talk about Daisy like that, not even my teammate.

"Sorry, man," he says, not looking one bit like he is, but I let it go. He lifts his arms and pretends to be spiking a ball over a net. "Can't wait to kick ass at beach volleyball today."

The noise level goes up in the other room, and I go back to making more coffee as Chase and Sawyer come in. I hear Sawyer ask about Daisy, and my ears perk up. Deciding what the hell, I grab my phone and shoot her off a text. I know she's not a teen anymore, needing me to come to her rescue because she snuck out to a party, but I am her friend, and I want to make sure she's okay. I try not to pace or look agitated as I wait for a response. Chase comes into the kitchen, and I hand him a coffee, going back to drop another pod in.

"Morning," he says and takes a sip. Cheddar raises his mug and clinks his response.

Three dots appear and air leaves my lungs when she finally responds with, "Just getting up. Be there in a few."

"Hey," I say to Chase, dying for a cup of coffee. He notes the eggs on the counter, and the bread in the toaster. "We grabbed everyone bagels."

"Nice, but Naomi doesn't eat carbs so I'm making her egg whites."

"Look at you, all domesticated." The coffee finally finishes, and Sawyer comes in with a bag of bagels which smell amazing. So does the mug of coffee that I hand over to her.

I put another pod in as Sawyer smiles at me and puts the bagels on a plate and grabs a knife for the tub of cream cheese.

She smiles at me. "Chase tells me veggie lite is your favorite cream cheese."

"That was nice of you."

"Getting us together here finally was nice of you." She goes up on her toes and presses her lips to my cheek. "Did you and Daisy have a nice week?"

"Yeah, it was relaxing."

"I'm so glad you were with her when she found out about med school. She was kind of a mess, not making good decisions or thinking straight."

My heart stops beathing. "What do you mean, not making good decisions?"

"She was all over the place. I just mean I was worried about her."

"What kind of decisions?" I press and try not to appear too pushy or crazy—which I'm totally becoming.

She eyes me, and it's clear she's debating on telling me something—something very important. Chase puts his arm around her and pulls her close, like she already might have said too much. Just then, Naomi and Tank come into the kitchen, followed by Beck and Piper.

"Guys," I say and pull Piper in for a hug. "I didn't even hear you come in."

"We're stealthy like that," Beck teases, and fist bumps me. I smile, loving that everyone is here. Well, everyone except Daisy.

"Where's Daisy?" Piper asks.

"She's on her way." I try to explain it as casually as can be, and I really hope to fuck none of them heard the hitch in my voice. I can't help but cast a glance Sawyer's way, still wanting to hear what bad decisions Daisy was making. Maybe she thinks it was a bad decision for her to come here with me. Maybe she thinks I'm not good enough for her or something. Christ, now my stupid mind is wandering.

"Okay, coffee," I reach for the cup and naturally hand it over to Piper. Then next one goes to Beck and I finally—finally—get one for myself...almost.

"Hey," Daisy says, and I manage to get one small sip of coffee before she looks at me with hopeful eyes and I hand it over to her. It's going to be that kind of day, I guess.

Everyone talks, and digs into the bagels, and I stand back, and make another cup of coffee which I pretty much swallow in one gulp.

"Naomi," I say, and catch the glance both she and Daisy give me. "How many eggs?"

"Two please."

I go to work on cracking eggs and separating them. Someone steps close and I don't need to turn to know it's Daisy. I can feel her presence clinging to me, and I like everything about it.

"Need any help?"

I smile as I turn to her. "I'm good."

"If good means feeding Naomi eggshells, then I'd agree." She takes the bowl and uses a spoon to fish out a few shells.

"Thanks. Did you uh, have a good time last night?"

"It was fun. I think I ate too many s'mores, though."

"You seemed to be enjoying them."

She punches my arm. "Hey what's that supposed to mean? Wait, are you calling me a hog again?"

And just like that, Daisy and I are okay. God, I love her. "If the term fits, Duke."

The rest of the people in the kitchen fade away as we play-fully banter, and I have to say, I can't—won't—lose this easi-ness with her. I want her, there is no doubt, but if she wants someone else, I have to let that happen. Losing what we have between us would be the worst thing in the world to ever happen to me.

I grab the frying pan, and use an oil spray on it. "Wait, is this spray okay for someone who doesn't eat carbs?"

Daisy nods. "Yeah, it's fine."

"Are you sure?"

"No. Not sure. But come on, who doesn't eat carbs?"

We both laugh like we just told the world's funniest joke, and that's when I notice all eyes on us. "Ah, be right up with the eggs," I announce as I note the way Naomi is staring at me. Yeah, I get it, I look like the village idiot. But the truth is, I am a fucking idiot for far too many reasons.

"I'm hitting the water," Cheddar says, ending the moment of uncomfortable silence and I make a note to kiss him right on the mouth for it.

I nod in agreement. "Sounds like a plan." Daisy stays close as I finish up the eggs. She grabs me a plate.

"Don't worry, you'll get a second chance to impress Naomi at beach volleyball. Prove to her you're more than just a hockey player and when you lose, you can show her you're a good sport."

"Lose? Why would I lose?" She grins, keeping quiet as I plate the eggs and set them on the table for Naomi. "Do you want anything to go with them? I have cheese."

"I don't like dairy."

"Oh, okay." I grab a bagel, spread a generous amount of cream cheese on it—because I love dairy—and head upstairs to get changed. By the time I get back down, everyone is ready to hit the beach for the day's games, activities and barbecues.

The first thing we all do is head for the beach volleyball, and I naturally assume Daisy will be on my team. She always is, but she surprises me and walks to the other side to hang out with Sebastian. My throat grows tight.

"You okay, man?" Chase asks as he slaps me on the back.

"Yeah good."

"What's going on with Daisy and Sebastian?"

"Ask her."

He holds his hands up palms out. "Wow. It was just a question."

Shit, yeah, that came out harsher than I intended.

"I've never played this," Naomi says as she ties her hair back.

I let my bad mood go as Chase jerks his head my way. "No worries. Brandon will teach you all the moves."

The only one I want to use my moves on is Daisy, but she's with Sebastian. "Okay, this is how we play," I begin, and spend the next few minutes explaining the rules of the game.

She crinkles her nose when I'm done. "I'm not very athletic. Maybe I'll just watch."

"It's not that hard. You can stand beside me. I'll help."

She looks completely unsure of herself, and I'm about to tell her she can sit it out if she wants, when she says, "Okay, I guess I'll give it a try." My mood lightens. I like a girl who is a good sport—like Daisy.

Stop comparing her to Daisy.

A few people who are back for the blowout join us on the sand, and I say hello and introduce my friends. Once the teams are set, we begin to play and everyone is having a great time, until the ball heads straight for a panicked Naomi's face. I jump to hit it, just as she jerks away, and I end up punching her right in the face, before we both fall and I nearly crush her under my weight.

Way to make a great second impression, dude.

"Ohmigod, Brandon!" Naomi shrieks. "You hit me right in the face. I'm going to bruise."

My chest tightens. "I'm sorry. I was trying to help."

"Help what, blacken my eye?" Everyone comes running over, and Tank crouches and helps Naomi to a sitting position. She eyes me, checking my pupils like I might be drunk. I can understand that, considering our first time out.

"You'd better get some ice on that," Tank says.

I brush the sand off my shorts. "I can help."

"No, it's okay." Naomi puts her hand on my shoulder to stop me. "You stay and play. Tank, can you help me?"

"Uh..." He glances at me, like he's waiting for my permission and I nod. He turns back to Naomi. "Okay, sure."

Feeling like a total asshole, I stand there as Tank takes Naomi back to the cottage. Shit, why is it I can't do anything right around her?

Are you purposely fucking things up, Brandon?

Okay, while there might be a part of me that could be doing that, I'd never purposely hit her or anyone for my own selfish reasons. It was an accident.

The game picks up again, and I'm not in the mood to play, but I do anyway, and when we lose, I do my best not to sulk like a poor sport, especially when I spot Daisy and Sebastian high-fiving each other.

Congratu—fucking—lations.

The rest of the day turns out to be as shitty as the first half. I go from one activity to another, with Daisy always siding with Sebastian. I try my best to be happy. I love having my friends here, but there's a tear in my heart that keeps getting bigger and bigger as the hours slip by. By the time the sun sets, and we're all sitting around the barbecue, Naomi joins us and I pull my chair close to hers, and check her eye.

"Are you okay?"

"It doesn't hurt as much as it did."

"I really am sorry."

"I know. I think I overreacted. I'm sorry about that." She smiles at me, and I catch Tank studying the two of us. Is Tank interested in Naomi? Even if he was, he'd never go after her if he thought I was interested. We have a thing called bro-code.

"Burgers up," Sanders, whose cottage is beside Sebastian's, announces, and I glance at Naomi.

"Burger?"

"Are there any vegetarian options?"

"I'll check."

I step up to the big barbecue just as Daisy is taking a big bite of her burger, ketchup dripping down her chin. "So messy," I tease.

She laughs, her voice light and she looks so happy. Is it Sebastian who's making her shine? But as I look closer, *really* look —okay, not now, she's turning away from me—I'm not sure that smile reaches her eyes. "How's it going?" she asks.

Before I can answer, Sebastian suddenly appears and is wiping the ketchup off her chin and laughing. I turn to Sanders. "Do you have any vegetarian?"

He nods and I grab one for Naomi. There's not a damn thing wrong with vegetarian or not eating carbs or avoiding dairy, but it does make me realize just how different we are. And yes, of course, there is something wrong with not wanting to ride on my handlebars. That just sort of puts a huge chasm in between us. How could I ever be with a girl like that? Honestly, Naomi seems less than enthused with me too. Not that I can blame her.

What the fuck am I going to do here?

Soon enough we all eat, and with darkness upon us, groups break off for a walk, or swim, or bonfire, and I actually lose sight of Naomi. I also lose sight of Daisy as Sebastian leads her toward his place. I swallow, trying to tamp the fire raging inside me.

With everyone busy, I walk the beach, and finally come across Chase. "Hey bro, where is everyone?"

"Sawyer and Piper went inside to dry off. Then we're going to have a bonfire. You joining us?

"Yeah, sure." I glance around. "Have you seen Naomi?"

He takes a big breath and drops down onto the sand. "I think she's walking the beach with Tank."

I drop down beside him. "I fucked everything up."

Chase angles his head, and beneath the moonlight, I catch the concern in his eyes. "Yeah..." is all he says. "Then I guess you better figure out how to un-fuck it."

He looks down the beach, to where I assume he saw Naomi and Tank last. "I don't think I can."

"If you want her, you should go get her."

"It's not Naomi—"

"I know."

My entire body stiffens. "You know?"

"What Sawyer was trying to tell you about Daisy making mistakes...well, the mistake was Daisy agreeing to help you get Naomi."

"Why did Sawyer think that was a mistake?"

He slaps my shoulder. "Because Daisy loves you, man. Just as much as you love her."

I swallow. Could it be true? Daisy has always been there for me, wanting to help with the book, wanting me to take her virginity, helping me get Naomi...because she loves me so much she just wants to see me happy?

Am I the guy on the team she likes?

Or is all this absolutely fucking ridiculous, and just wishful thinking? But if it's not, and I do have a chance...

"Bring it back to the same spot," I say mostly to myself.

"What?"

My gaze flies to Chase's and I quickly shake my head. "Nothing. It's just something Daisy said to me about my book."

"Your book?"

I take a huge breath, and as I let it out, I can almost feel the weight falling off my shoulders, because I'm going to tell Chase...everything. "I'm a romance author. I like writing books. I like it more than hockey."

He sits there staring at me for so long, I begin to shift. His gaze leaves my face and he glances around like I might be playing a weird trick on him and yeah, this is all coming at him fast and it's a lot to take in.

After a short while, he gives a slow nod. "Like your mom. I like it, bro, and I can't wait to read your books when you get them published."

My racing heart begins to slow. "Really?"

"Yup."

Things are really going way different than I thought they would. I'm not sure I ever expected to hear him say Daisy loves me like I love her. I didn't even know he knew anything at all. But I really expected him to laugh or tell me I was crazy when I admitted I was a romance author. Although he's not an asshole and is a supportive guy. Maybe that was just me projecting my own insecurities. Now that it's out there it feels good, and his reaction makes me think I could tell my folks.

"You need to tell her, dude," he says quietly.

I dig my heels into the sand. "Yeah, you're right. But Naomi..."

"Ah, I think she's into someone else." I follow his gaze as Naomi and Tank come into view, and from the way she's gazing up at Tank, it's clear she's into him. Tank keeps trying to move away, especially when she weaves her arm through his. "Tank won't let it go anywhere. Not if he thinks you like her."

"I know. I'll talk to him, let him know it's okay. Naomi is clearly into him." I shake my head and give a half laugh, half snort. "I never saw that coming."

"Maybe they had a moment in the cab ride here." Chase falls quiet. "You should go talk to Daisy. I'll talk to Tank."

I nod and push to my feet. I walk down the beach as the stars fill the night sky. I really hate that I haven't seen much of Daisy today. We were all busy with the games and she always seemed to be on the opposing team. Assuming she's still at Sebastian's place, I head there, worry and fear and love and need all battling for control inside me. I hear Sebastian's voice as I walk up the stairs.

"So, are you going to put it on for me or what?" I go still at the door, my hand poised to knock as Sebastian continues with, "You know I've been dying to play doctor with you for years."

"Sebastian, I really like you—"

"Dude, we're out of beer. Grab me another will you." I turn at the sound of Nick's voice. Shit I was so focused on finding Daisy, I didn't even see him standing over the fire.

The screen door opens and I find a surprised Daisy standing there, Sebastian behind her, the doctor's coat he bought her as a gift draped over his shoulder. Jesus, what the fuck am I doing? She's into Sebastian—she just told him she liked him.

"Brandon?" she says, confusion on her face. "What are you doing here?"

"I uh, getting Nick another beer," I say as the world crashes in around me.

Sebastian hands me a six pack of cans. "Here you go, dude."

"Thanks." I stand there for a second. I want to tell her everything. Spill my guts, and beg for her to be my girl. I'm a selfish bastard. That much is clear, but for once in my life I can't be selfish. If Daisy wants this with Sebastian, I want it for her. She told me she'd help me get Naomi, simply because she wanted me happy. I want her happy too, which is why I back up and say, "Um, okay, bye."

"Bye, Brandon," Daisy responds and the finality in her words —the truth that what we had is gone, probably forever—hits my face like a runaway puck and nearly knocks me to my knees. But as I walk away, other words she'd once spoken to me ring loud and clear in my ears. While I don't want to be a selfish bastard, I also don't want to be a guy who spends his life saying *what if*.

25

DAISY

You know, deep down I always knew Brandon was a thief, because last night, he totally walked away with my heart. I roll over in my bed and stare at the cloudy sky, a fitting match for my mood, and the honest to God's truth is, this isn't on him. He asked me to help him get a girl. I was the one who agreed. I didn't have to, nor did I have to have sex with him. Hell, I wanted that. It seemed like a good idea at the time. Now, not so much.

I check my phone and find a bunch of messages asking about my flight. I reply with a group message to let the others know I'm going to spend an extra night here at the beach. Ending my vacation wallowing in self-pity is a hell of a lot better than getting on a plane and seeing Brandon and Naomi together. How I even thought if they hooked up it would help me move on was beyond me. With Naomi in med school with me, and now that she's part of our circle of friends, there's no way I can avoid the two.

Yup, totally a masochist.

But I can't think about that right now. It reminds me of the playroom we found and how it ignited heat between us and led us down a path I knew better than to travel. I roll over and stare at the ceiling and work to quiet my racing brain, especially when my gaze lands on a picture of Brandon, Chase and me. Maybe there's a part of me that always knew I'd lose him, which is why I was always afraid to tell him how I felt. I wasn't enough for my own mother, for God's sake. Why on earth would I be enough for Brandon?

I glance at my phone and see three dots coming in from Brandon. It's a private message, not a group one, and my heart stops beating. Maybe he's going to tell me Naomi was a mistake, and that it's me he's always loved and that he wants a future with me. His words finally puncture my screen, and my entire world pretty much falls apart as I read.

Brandon: Safe travels, Duke.

I stare at those three innocuous words until they blur before my eyes. It's not what I was hoping for, but he is wishing me safe travels, and that's nice. Normal. Like we haven't been having sex. But we have been and as much as I don't want to admit it, I always knew he could never be mine, and now... well, now things are different and wrong. How the hell could they not be?

I roll back over and will sleep to come, but soon enough, car doors are being opened and closed, as my friends jump in cabs to go back to the airport. I'll miss a day of classes tomorrow, but I don't really care.

Honestly, I never should have come to Seattle with him, never should have read his sex scenes, and never should have followed him into the neighbors' cottage where things certainly took a different turn in our relationship.

Seagulls squawk in the distance, and when outside falls quiet, I push to my feet and pad to my window. I open it and let the morning breeze wash over my skin. At the other end of the beach, I spot Sebastian cleaning up outside his place. Maybe I should help him. I could use the distraction.

I make a quick trip to the bathroom and clean my face and teeth. I tug on shorts and a T-shirt and lock the house behind me. Sebastian has a confused look on his face by the time I reach him.

"What are you still doing here?"

I shrug, and try to make light of it. "I wasn't quite ready to go back yet." He nods and puts a few empty cans of beer into a garbage bag. I search around and start tidying up.

"Has Nick gone back?" I ask, simply to make conversation.

"Sleeping. We take off in a couple hours."

I nod again and smile, trying to appear happy and light when I'm actually dark and sad. I move with an enthusiasm I don't feel, and nearly trip over a log simply because I'm a hot mess.

"Okay, sit."

I lift my head to find Sebastian staring at me, as he shakes his head. "What?"

Yeah, I get it, I'm pitiful.

"Sit, Daisy."

I plunk down on a log, and he sits opposite me. I hold his gaze and take in his handsome face. What kind of fool was I not to go for this guy? He's funny and sweet and...and...he's not Brandon. Last night when he wanted me to put on the coat, I simply told him I liked him...as a friend. I'm pretty sure Brandon heard the first part, and not the second and I left it at that. At least this way he won't try to set me up with some guy on his team, and now he no doubt thinks I'm hanging back to be with Sebastian. I had to be straight up honest with Sebastian, though. I couldn't let him think I wanted more.

"What the hell, Daisy?"

"What?" I ask again, my heart hurting in my chest.

"If you like him so much, just tell him."

Okay, do I play dumb here? I'd bet I'd be really good at it, considering how dumb I've been lately. I blink up at him, and open my mouth.

"Don't."

Okay, so no playing dumb. "He's with someone else now."

"That girl he punched in the face, you mean?"

I wince. "He didn't actually punch her in the face."

"So, her then."

"Yeah, her."

He snorts. "That's who he wants?"

I'm shocked at the weird revulsion in his voice. "Why do you say it like that? There's nothing wrong with Naomi."

"You're wrong. There's something very wrong with Naomi."

I sit up a bit straighter, and I mentally picture the girl who has it all—even the guy I love. "What could—"

"She's not you."

I go completely still, Sebastian's words circling my brain like a runaway puck. "She's not..."

"Daisy, you're the whole package. Why do you think I spent every summer since we were teens trying to convince you to be my girl?"

"I mean, I kind of thought you might like me."

"Kind of thought? I—we—every guy on this beach was crazy about you."

"I didn't really know."

"Do you know why you didn't know?"

"Stunned?"

He stares at me for a second, clearly not expecting me to say that, and then bursts out laughing. "No, you're not stunned. Well, maybe you are. But you've been hung up on Brandon for as long as I knew you."

I sigh, bend forward and brace my elbows on my knees. "I'm pathetic."

"Nah, you just know what you want."

"He doesn't want me, though. He calls me Duke. You know that."

"So."

"So...Duke is a guy's name. He thinks of me as one of the guys."

"If he thinks of you as one of the guys, Daisy, then he's playing for the other team. Trust me, I've seen the way he looks at you and he does not look at Naomi that way. They have zero chemistry."

"Then why did he never try anything with me?"

He angles his head, like he knows something. "Hasn't he?" Sebastian mumbles under his breath, my cheeks warming as he adds, "Maybe he's worried about the friendship."

"I am too."

"I think you need to get your ass on a plane back to Canada go tell Brandon everything you're feeling."

"What if I lose him?"

He reaches out, takes my hand in his and gives it a little squeeze. "You already have."

It's true, I have and you know what, I'm damn tired of running the other way before someone can leave me. Hell, Brandon already left, and I'm not a baby who can't do anything about that. It's time to slay those demons because I'm a grown woman, totally worthy and loveable and if my mother didn't want me, that's on her. Not me. She's the one who missed out, because I'm a queen, not a pawn. Brandon had shown me that since we were kids, and now it's my turn to show him a thing or two. "Why are you so good at this girl talk stuff?"

"My last girlfriend made me watch all the rom-coms with her."

I chuckle as my mind drifts to Brandon's book. "What do I say?"

"I don't know, Daisy. You know him better than I do. In the movies I was forced to watch, there was always the big grand gesture before the happy ending."

"Happily ever after," I correct.

"Whatever. All I know is you need to show him what he means to you, and that you're the girl for him. Otherwise, you'll spend your life wondering, what if..."

What if...

I said those exact words to Brandon once. Fear and panic bursts inside me, prompting me to jump up. I need to say something, do something...I need to at least try and if in the end Naomi is the girl for him, I'll at least know I fought.

I hug Sebastian. "Thank you."

He laughs. "You're welcome, now go."

I move a little quicker as I head down the beach back to my cottage. The first thing I do is check for a new flight, but today is fully booked. That's okay, it gives me time to show Brandon what he really means to me, and I'm going to do that by writing his happily ever after for him—ending his book the way I want us to end—or rather begin.

For the rest of the day, I think, pace, walk, write, delete and start again. Wow, writing is way harder than I ever imagined. How the heck does Brandon do it? By the time I close my laptop, I'm too tired to see and fall asleep on the sofa. I wake bright and early, read over yesterday's words, which totally suck. But I have the flight home to revise.

I run around the cottage and tidy up, and it's midafternoon by the time I get an Uber to the airport. Only problem is, there's a storm moving in and I'm a bit worried about delays.

My phone pings, and it's a text from Sawyer checking in on me. I resist the urge to ask her how Brandon is doing. I don't want to tell anyone my plan, in case everyone is mistaken about Brandon and it's not me he wants. For all I know, he could have been lip-locked with Naomi since Saturday night. If that's the case, then fine—well not really—but I have to see this plan to fruition.

The airport is crowded and loud with flights being canceled all over the place and I find a corner to sit, wait and write. My heart races faster as the hours tick by and I check my phone over and over to see if Brandon had reached out to me. Nothing. I guess he's back at practice with no time for anything else—although in the past he always made time for me. I'm missing practice too, but for me, my future doesn't depend on hockey like his does, so it's not quite as bad.

Day turns to night and it's Tuesday by the time I get on my plane for the long trip to Halifax. It's not a direct one, either. Booking last minute means stopovers and now I'm worried I won't even be home until mid-week. I'm sure the others are wondering what's going on, so I send a message to the group chat, to let everyone know of the delay. Everyone responds, including Brandon, telling me to travel safe. Wow, I guess from the nonchalant responses, no one is too concerned.

By the time I get home, it's the middle of the night, which means I'm going to have to wait until Wednesday to see Brandon. While I'd like to go straight to him, he'll be up for practice early and I don't want to ruin his game or chances at the NHL because that's what he plans on doing, even if it isn't what he really wants.

Is Naomi still what he wants?

I crawl into bed, and Alysha moving around downstairs wakes me. My heart leaps, knowing I'm going to see Brandon today, and I hurry downstairs to find a very concerned Alysha when I enter the kitchen.

"What?" I ask.

She swallows. "There's something wrong," she blurts out.

"What's wrong?"

"It's Brandon."

I grab a chair and sit. Is Brandon hurt again? Is he concussing? "What?" She narrows her gaze. "Alysha, what is it?"

"I think you should go see for yourself."

I stand on wobbly legs. "Where is he? Is he at the hospital?"

She angles her head like I just suggested the most ludicrous thing, and I remind myself she doesn't know about the concussion.

"He's at his place."

Leaving my purse and everything else behind, I hurry out the door and start running down the street. His place isn't that far and a car would have been faster, but when fight or flight mode hits, I ran. The sound of my feet hitting the ground rings in my ears, and I don't slow until I round the corner, and see Brandon's place in the distance. I soon hear more pounding sounds, but it's not coming from my feet. What the heck is going on?

As I get closer, I realize the noise is coming from Brandon's backyard. His parents own this place, they bought it as an investment for Brandon to live in while he was here, and to rent to students afterward. Are they renovating or something?

I step around the house and come to a resounding halt at the scene unfolding before me. Okay, Alysha was right, something is wrong, very wrong indeed.

"Brandon," I call, the ground wobbly beneath my feet as I take a tentative step closer. I eye him as he turns to me and uses his forearm to wipe a bead of sweat from his face. I swallow and continue with, "What are you doing?"

"Building a treehouse." He says it so casually, like it's something he does every day, a new burst of worry travels through me and grips my throat.

"Okay." I nod, simply to placate him, but I'm still a bit lost here. I glance at the piles of wood, nails and equipment. Why the hell isn't he in class or at the rink? Why didn't one of our friends message me to let me know he's not doing so well. "It's nice," I say for lack of anything else as my brain races. I should contact Chase first. Yeah, Chase. I grab my phone and quickly shoot off a message to Chase, pleading for him to get here ASAP.

"It's for my ending," he says quietly, and I swear to God, I've now seen all sides of Brandon but I've never seen this sad, lonely...worried side.

"Ending?"

"Of my book."

Still a bit confused and wanting to keep him talking until Chase gets here, I say, "I've been thinking about your ending too." I glance at the hammer and nails in his hands. "I've been working on your ending, you know...for the book? I even did some research into publishers." His eyes go wide and I try to see his pupils. I quickly shake my head. "No, I did this on my own, not through your mother. I would never tell anyone. I... I just thought...you never had a happily ever after and I wanted to help." Okay, this grand gesture is going way differently than I imagined after Sebastian put the idea into my head and I hatched a plan back in Seattle. But I want to keep him talking.

He swallows. "You did that...for me?"

"You sound surprised."

"I shouldn't be." The hammer taps against his leg as he swings it.

"This treehouse....it's about your happy ending?" Making light I say, "Do the nails have something to do with nailing your happy ending?"

He goes dead serious. "Daisy, where did we meet?"

"In a treehouse."

"Where was the first time I scared you? Sorry about that, by the way."

"In the treehouse, and no, you're not."

He grins and this is the first time since coming around the corner that I can breathe. "The first time I put my mouth on you?" he asks his voice a bit husky now.

I swallow and my body heats in remembrance. "In the treehouse, and it was the first time I put my mouth on you, actually. The first time you put your mouth on me was the neighbors' playroom."

His eyes dim, like he too is remembering. "The first time I fell in love with you?"

Naturally I'm about to say the treehouse, as it's been the answer to his questions, but my brain kicks in and I ask, "...you love me?"

"I love you, Daisy. I think I always have, but blocked it because you were my best friend, and I was fucking terrified of losing you. I couldn't think of you like that..." He shakes his head, and blows out a slow breath. "Until I couldn't stop thinking of you like that."

My pulse is thudding so fast, I'm not sure I'm hearing what I think I'm hearing. "Concussion?" I touch my head. "Changed your personality."

He shakes his head. "I could never finish my book because I had no idea what happily ever after looked like. You once gave me advice to circle around to the beginning. Put my characters in the same spot doing the same thing as when they met, but this time, feeling differently about it." He drops the hammer and nails and puts his hand on a big two by four piece of lumber. "That's what I'm doing here."

Tears prick my eyes. Is this really freaking happening? "Brandon," I begin. "I haven't been honest with you. I've been keeping a whopper of a secret and that secret is that I've been in love with you since I first set foot in your treehouse. I was terrified of losing us." He takes my hand in his, brushing rough callouses against my flesh and I warm. "I helped with the ending of your book. I wanted to write out an ending. To show you that I'm here for you, and love you. No matter what. I want you to have the future you want...and more importantly, I want to be in it. I planned to tell you all that, but then Alysha told me to get over here, and you...you were one step ahead of me, trying to put us back together with a...treehouse."

"Sebastian..." he murmurs, his voice shaky. "I heard..."

"There is no Sebastian, and I know what you overheard. What you didn't stick around to hear was me telling him I liked him as a friend." Warmth and love move into his eyes. "It's you I love, and this is our happily ever after," I say, tears choking me up. "You're a real-life hero, Brandon. This is better than any romance novel ending."

His jaw works as he clenches, like he's fighting back tears. "This...this will be our treehouse, Daisy. No one else allowed." He swallows as he struggles to talk. "As far as my concussion, I don't think it changed my personality. All I know is you were the girl who was always by my side and when you came to Seattle with me to put me back together, I couldn't keep what I felt for you under wraps any longer. I saw you for who and what you really were. The girl I've always loved. I guess in the back of my mind I figured if I fucked things up, I could blame it on the concussion, Duke."

"Duke," I say quietly that one stupid word hitting like a punch to the face. I stumble back a bit, and he reaches for me.

"Hey."

"Brandon, you called me Duke." I shake my head. "I'm not sure you really do see me as anything other than the tomboy who was only girl allowed in the treehouse."

His face pales as he stares at me, and then as if he has an epiphany, he laughs and steps back into me, holding me tight, so I can't break free. "Don't you get it. You wore those daisy dukes. Those sexy denim cutoffs that fueled my teenage fantasies."

Now it's my turn to stare. "Wait…" I grin, the pieces starting to fall into place. "Ohmigod, that's why you call me Duke?"

"Yeah, and I had to call you Duke to remind myself I needed to treat you like one of the guys, but holy hell, Daisy, you were as sexy as fuck and you still are and I fucking love you with all my heart and I want a future with you."

"I…I want that too." I turn at the sound of footsteps and spot Sawyer and Chase, Kennedy and Matt, Piper and Beck, and my roommate Alysha standing there. Alysha is all alone, naturally, since her soon to be fiancé is in the Hamptons. I shake my head as they all grin at me. I guess this is why they've all been so quiet and distant. They were all in on this. I grin at them, and my friends all give me big smiles. That's when I spot Ryan, and the way he just moved in beside Alysha.

There has to be something going on between them, but I can't think about that right now, not when Brandon is squeezing my hand. I turn my attention back to him, and let it all pour out of my heart. "You once told me med school was the most important thing in the world to me," I say. "You were wrong. You are. You've always been more important than anything else, and I love you and want a future with you."

"You've just made me the happiest guy in the world, and I want to write, Daisy. I'm going to tell my parents."

My eyes go wide. Did he just admit he wants to write in front of our friends?

"It's okay. I told them everything, even how much I love you, but they already knew that." He exhales hard, and a grin plays with his lips. "Okay, now let me get this damn treehouse finished, so we can climb in, make out, and start on that future!"

"Oh, come on," Chase says. "We didn't need to hear that."

Everyone laughs as he hugs me tight.

Okay, this is even way better than what I put in his book, which is why he's the writer and I'm not. "Now this is the perfect ending, B."

"No, it's not," he says, and I frown in confusion. "It's the perfect beginning, but don't worry, when I get you alone, we're going to talk about that ending you want."

"Oh?"

He winks. "It's time we nailed our happy ending, Duke."

I laugh out loud as he spins me around and kisses me with all the love he's been holding inside him. "I don't think we have to wait until the treehouse is built." I take his hand, ready to drag him inside. "Come on, let's get started on our future, and I'm definitely into showing over telling, so how about you show me exactly how you're going to nail that happy ending."

EPILOGUE

Brandon

Christmas production.

"You're not supposed to be back here," I say to Ryan as he comes backstage, moving in and out of cast members as Sawyer has last minute words with the actor—she wrote the play that's taking place here at the Academy. Kennedy is with the band going over their last-minute music, and Piper is helping with the costumes. Daisy is floating around, working to keep everyone calm.

"And you are?" he asks me and punches me on the shoulder.

I flex my bicep and say, "They needed the guns."

"Yeah, that's why I'm here. Daisy asked me to help out."

"Since Chase, Matt, and Beck are running around doing last minute prep, probably to hide from doing the hard lifting, get on the other end of this sofa. We need to move it to the stage." The guys aren't really hiding out. We've all been at it all day. This Christmas production is so important to our women, as they all have a part in its success, and we all want it to be an amazing performance.

Ryan lifts the other side of the sofa, and all is going well as we carry it onto the stage, until he sees Alysha practicing for her solo. His fingers slip and his end of the sofa comes down hard. Jumping back before it crushes his foot, he curses, and I let my end go.

"You okay?"

"Yeah, uh..." He tears his gaze away from Alysha. "Just thought I saw a mouse."

"That's the best you can come up with, and since when have you been afraid of mice, anyway?" Our house had plenty of them running around. I'm glad I moved out of Storm House second year. It's full of new guys now, and the partying scene is behind me. I love the little downtown house I plan to buy from my folks. They invested a couple years ago, but now Daisy and I live there together, and since I have no plans to go to the NHL, and Daisy and I are working on publishing my novel, they decided to sell to us instead of renting it out to students.

"What is going on here?"

I turn at the sound of Daisy's voice and my heart does a little somersault. Corny and cliché, I know, but what can I say, and yes I would use that line in a novel.

"Hey babe." I lean into her and kiss her soft mouth, but she has her eyes on Ryan as he scrubs his face and tries not to stare at Alysha. He's not doing a very good job of it.

"Ryan, are you okay?"

"Yeah, great."

"You seem...distracted."

"He saw a mouse," I tell her.

She softens even more. "It's okay. It's probably more afraid of you than you are of it."

"I'm not afraid of mice, it just caught me off guard."

"More like Alysha in her tight dance costume caught him off guard," I say under my breath, which earns me an elbow to the gut from my lovely fiancée.

Daisy turns to Alysha as she stumbles. Concern moves all over Daisy's face. That's just like my sweet, Duke. Always concerned for everyone else, which is why I do my best to take care of her.

"I'll be right back." She hurries over to Alysha, and Ryan picks up the end of the sofa again. We position it on stage, and I notice the quiet, intense way the two girls are talking. I'm not sure what it is, but Alysha is very upset about something. We move a few more items around and as soon as we're done, Sawyer claps her hands.

"Okay everyone, go grab your seats," Sawyer says. "Let's get this show started."

I wait for Daisy backstage, and there is deep concern all over her gorgeous face. "Hey," I say and pull her in. She melts into me like she always does and my heart soars. God, to think about how close we came to messing up 'us' still makes my stomach tight. I put my hands on her shoulders, and inch back. "What's going on?"

"Alysha doesn't want me to say anything, but we—"

"Have no secrets." It's true, we don't. We were both holding back secrets that could have destroyed our future, but never again.

"She's worried about going home for Christmas."

"That's strange." From what I understand, she comes from a great family. Hell, her dad just bought an NHL team that I'm sure a few guys at the Academy would kill to play on. Alysha kept that quiet, though. I like her modesty. We actually found out from Coach Jameson.

"Apparently she's sure her boyfriend is going to ask her to marry him."

Two thoughts hit at once. "I thought she was already engaged."

"As good as engaged, is the way she put it."

Second thought is, "Um, why doesn't she want this?"

Daisy shrugs. "She's not sure she's ready."

"What's she going to do?"

"I have no idea, but she's definitely off her game tonight. I told her to put it out of her mind, and when the show was over, we'd go for a drink and talk about it."

I hug her again, as Sawyer glares at us. "We need to get to our seats."

We make our way to our seats and Ryan is seated beside me, taking up half my chair. "Move," I say and shove him, but he doesn't budge. He's a barrel of a guy—a nice asset for the hockey team, and on his potato farm.

"Shh," Daisy says, and we both fall quiet.

The curtains open and for the next hour we're all lost in the production. Every time Alysha comes onto the stage, Ryan shifts beside me. There is absolutely no doubt in my mind that he has a thing for her, but he's not a guy to touch another man's woman, and Alysha has made it clear that she's as good as engaged.

The end of the performance is Alysha's last dance, and I glance at Ryan, who is totally enthralled.

"Something is wrong," Daisy whispers and I turn to her.

"What is it?"

She shakes her head. "I don't know. She's wobbly. Look at her movements."

As soon as the words leave her mouth, Alysha twists her ankle and drops to the floor. Gasps can be heard through the entire auditorium, and I jump to my feet. So do the rest of our friends, but its Ryan who's on stage, gathering Alysha into his arms before any of us can make a move. The curtain closes and as chatter erupts, and the lights come on, we all hurry backstage.

"Alysha," Daisy murmurs worriedly and drops down to check her ankle.

Tears form in Alysha's eyes. "It's just a sprain." She winces as Daisy touches her.

"I actually think you might have broken something." Daisy glances at me. "We need to get her to the clinic."

"I'll drive," I say.

"No," Ryan interrupts firmly. "I'll take her."

Alysha puts her hands up. "No, please. I'm okay. I can walk it off."

We all hesitate as she reaches for Ryan's arm, and he helps her to her feet. Everyone holds their breath as she puts her foot down and applies pressure, but her yelp of pain has Ryan picking her up again. He carries her to a chair, and we all surround her.

"I'm so sorry," she murmurs quietly. "I ruined the show."

Sawyer, Kennedy, Piper and Daisy all speak at once, assuring her the show was perfect and that her well-being is way more important than anything. It's so nice to have such a tight, caring group of friends.

"Hey, it's going to be okay," Ryan whispers.

"It's not that..."

Everyone frowns, clearly confused, but Daisy and I know what's going on. Not that we'd say anything. "It's just...I'm supposed to go home tomorrow."

Ryan goes deathly quiet, and while he's a big, tough guy, he's kind of a gentle giant and when he goes quiet, it means he's in deep thought.

"Alysha," he asks pointedly. "Do you not want to go home?"

She sniffs, and with the smallest movement, shakes her head.

Ryan gives a curt nod, like he just solved world hunger or something. "It's settled then."

"What's settled?" Alysha asks, just as confused as the rest of us.

"Everyone will be with family for Christmas," he begins. "And you're not staying here alone over the holidays."

"It's okay. I don't need to be with family for Christmas."

"Yeah, you do, and you will be, because you're coming home to Prince Edward Island with me."

Alysha stares at Ryan like he might have just sprouted hockey sticks from his skull. "Ryan—"

"It's a good idea," Daisy interrupts. "My guess is you're going to need a boot for your foot, and flying will be a nightmare. You can't fly with a big boot on, Alysha?"

I look at my beautiful girl and realize she's giving Alysha a way out. Just when I thought I couldn't love her any more. I pull her to me and drop a tender kiss on the side of her head.

"Um, yeah..." Alysha agrees, looking very much like a deer in the headlights as the puzzle pieces fall into place.

Ryan nods, and picks Alysha up. "It's settled then. You're spending Christmas with me."

As he carries her offstage, I lean in and whisper to Daisy, "Hey, maybe now we'll find out why Ryan was camped out on her sofa during reading week."

* * *

Thank you so much for reading Daisy and Brandon's story. I hope you enjoyed it as much as I loved writing it. Stay turned for SHUT OUT, Ryan and Alysha's story, December 2022. Please read on for an excerpt of The Playmaker!

The Playmaker

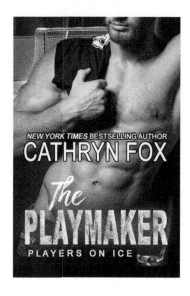

NINA:

Fat drops of spring rain pummel my head, wilting my curls as I dart through Seattle's busy traffic to the café on the other side of the street. My best friend, Jess, is inside waiting for me, undoubtedly hyped up on her third latté by now.

I step over a pothole and search for an opening in the traffic. I hate being late, I really do. I totally value other people's time, but when the email came through from my editor, asking me to write a hot hockey series, my priorities took a curve. I've worked with Tara for a couple years now, and I know her like—pardon the pun—a well-worn book. To her, hesitation equals disinterest. She's a mover, a tree-shaker, and it wouldn't have taken long for her to offer the opportunity to another author. She wanted a quick reply and I had to give it to her.

I got this!

Yeah, that was my response, but what did I have to lose? I've been in such a rut lately, thanks to my fickle muse, deserting me when I needed her most. I swear to God, sometimes she acts like a hormonal teenager. I need to whip her into shape so I don't lose this gig. The royalties from a series will help make a sizeable dent in the bills that are piling up high and deep.

High and deep.

I laugh. One of those self-derisive snorts that crawls out when you'd really rather cry. Yeah, that pretty much sums up the *I got this* response I emailed back. High and deep, like a big steaming pile of—

A car horn blares, jolting me from my pity party. With my heart pounding in my chest, I step in front of the Tesla and flip the guy off. I safely reach the sidewalk and once again my mind is back on my job, and off the impatient jerk in the overpriced car.

I step up on the sidewalk and lift my face to the rain, the cool water a pleasant break from this unusual spring heat wave we're having. Pressure fills my throat. The hum of traffic behind me dulls, leaving only the sound of my pulse pounding in my ears. Panic.

Why the hell did my editor think I, former figure skater turned romance novelist, would want to write a series about hot hockey players? Yeah, sure my brother is an NHL player, but that doesn't mean I'm into the game. I hate hockey. No, hate is too mild a word for what I feel. I loathe it entirely. But you know what I don't loathe? Eating. Yeah, I like eating. Oh, and a roof over my head. I really like that, too.

I draw in a semi self-satisfied breath at having rationalized my fast response.

Except my reply was total and utter bullshit. I don't *got this*. In fact, I...wait, what's the antonym of *got this*? All that comes to mind is, *you're screwed*. Yep, that pretty much describes my predicament.

Why didn't I just stick to figure skating?

Because you took a bad spill that ended your career.

Oh right. But seriously, a hockey series... Ugh. Kill me. Freaking. Now.

I reach the café, pull the glass door open and slick my rain-soaked hair from my face. I quickly catalogue the place to find Jess hitting on the barista. Ahh, now I get why she picked a place so far from home. I take in the guy behind the counter. Damn, he's hotter than the steaming latté in Jess's hand, and from the way she's flirting, it's clear he'll be in her bed later today.

I sigh inwardly. It's always so easy for her. Me? Not so much. Men rarely pay me attention. Unlike Jess, I'm plain, have the body of a twelve-year-old boy, and most times I blend into the woodwork.

I pick up a napkin from the side counter and mop the rain off my face. Doesn't matter. I'm not interested anyway. From my puck-bunny-chasing brother to all his cocky friends, I know what guys are really like, and when it comes to women, they're only after one thing, and it isn't scoring the slot. I roll my eyes. Then again, maybe it is.

And of course, I can't forget the last guy I was set up with. What he did to me was totally abusive, but I don't want to dredge up those painful memories right now.

I shake, and water beads fall right off my brand-new rain-resistance coat. At least something is going right for me today. Semi-dry, I cross the room and stand beside Jess.

"Hey, sorry I'm late."

Jess turns to me, smiles, and holds a finger up. "I'll forgive you only if you're late because you were knees deep into some nasty sex, 'cause girlfriend, it's been far too long since you've been laid."

Jesus, what ever happened to this girl's filters?

Thoroughly embarrassed, my gaze darts to the barista, who is grinning, his eyes still locked on my friend, looking at her like she's today's hot lunch special and ignoring me like I'm yesterday's cold, lumpy oatmeal.

Ugh, really?

"Non-fat latté," I say, and scowl at him until he puts his eyes back in his head. I might be an English major but I have a PhD in the death glare. Truthfully, I'm so sick of guys like him, one thing on their minds. Then again, Jess only wants one thing from him, so I really shouldn't have a problem with it. Why do I? Oh, maybe because Mr. Right, my battery-operated companion, isn't quite cutting it anymore, and it's left me a little jittery and a whole lot cranky.

Jess is right. I *do* need to get laid.

Jess's lips flatline when she takes me in, her gaze carefully accessing me. "What?" she asks, her mocha eyes narrowing.

God, sometimes I really hate how well she can read me. "Nothing."

She straightens to her full height, and I try to do the same, but she dwarfs me, even without her beloved two-inch heels.

I square my shoulders, but it's always hard to pull off a high-power pose when you're only five foot two, and teased relentlessly about it.

"Come on," she says, and guides me to a corner table. I peel off my coat and plunk down. Jess sits across from me. "Spill."

I point to my forehead. "Do I have 'idiot' written here?"

She looks me over, and cautiously asks, "No, why?"

My phone chirps in my purse, and I reach for it. Great, it's my editor wanting to set turn-in dates. "How about never?" I say under my breath.

"Uh, Nina. You're talking to your phone. You better tell me what's going on."

"You're not going to believe what I just agreed to."

"Do tell," she says and leans forward, like I'm about to spill some dirty little sex secret. If only that were the case.

I grab my phone and hold it up, showing her Tara's message. "I just agreed to write a hockey series," I say, and toss my phone back into my purse, mic-drop style—without the bold confidence.

Jess pushes back in her chair, clearly disappointed. She lifts her cup, and over the rim, asks, "I don't see how that makes you an idiot."

My mouth drops open. Jess and I have been friends since childhood. She of all people knows how much I hate hockey. "Are you serious?"

She shrugs. "You're a writer."

Mr. Sexy Barista brings me my coffee and he shares a secret, let's-hook-up-later smile with Jess. "And...?" I ask when he leaves.

"Writer's write and make things up. I know you hate hockey, but what does that have to do with anything?"

"I can't come up with a plot, or write about the game, if I don't know anything about it."

She shakes her head. "And I can't believe your brother is a professional player and you never once paid attention to the game."

"I was busy pursuing a professional skating career, remember?"

She reaches across the table and gives my hand a little squeeze. "I know. I'm sorry."

My tailbone and neck take that moment to throb, a constant reminder of a career lost.

I didn't just lose my dream of skating professionally the day my feet went out from underneath me, I lost my confidence, too. A concussion will do that to you.

Good thing I majored in English in college. Once I hung up my skates, I began to blog about the sport and sold a few articles. I joined a local writers group, and after talking to a group of romance writers, I tried my hand at one. Much to my surprise, it actually sold. I went from non-fiction to fiction, in every sense of the word. Happily ever after might exist between the pages, but it certainly doesn't in real life. At least not for me.

I take a sip of my latté, and give an exaggerated huff as I set it down. Jess instantly goes into problem-solving mode when she sees that I'm really stressed about this. As a brand-new high school guidance counselor, she can't help but want to fix me.

"Okay, it's simple," she begins. "You have to learn the game."

"How am I supposed to do that?"

"Turn on the TV and watch."

"I can watch a bunch of guys chase a stupid puck around a rink all I want, I still won't be able to understand the rules."

"How dare you call my favorite sport stupid."

"Jessss..." I plead. "What am I going to do?"

She crinkles her nose. Then her eyes go wide. "I've got it. Shadow your brother."

I give a quick shake of my head. "No, he's on the road, and he won't want me hanging around."

Jess goes quiet again, and that hollowed-out spot inside me aches as I think about Cason. I miss my brother so much and wish we were closer. Cason and I grew up in a family where there were no hugs or words of affirmation. I know Mom and Dad loved us, but as busy investment bankers, work consumed their lives. Sure, they put me in figure skating, and Cason in hockey when we were young, but they never shared in our passions, or really supported our pursuits.

I guess I can't expect my brother to display love, when none was ever displayed to him.

"Why don't you teach me?"

"It might be my favorite sport to watch, but I don't really know all the rules. I think you'd be better off getting your brother or..." She straightens. "Wait. I got this," she says, and

I cringe when she tosses my three-word email response back at me. A warning shiver skips along my spine, and I get the sense that whatever she's about suggest, is going to take me right down the rabbit hole.

"What about Cole Cannon?"

I groan, plant my elbows on the table, and cover my face with my hands. "Never," I mumble through my fingers. "Not in a million freaking years."

Jess removes my hands from my face. "Why not? He's your brother's best friend. I'm sure he'll help you."

"Cocky Cole Cannon, aka, The Playmaker. Do I need to say any more?" I reach for my latté and take a huge gulp, burning the roof of my mouth. Damn.

"I know you hate him, Nina, but—"

"Of course I hate him. You remember the nickname he used to use when we were kids—Pretty BallerNina. I was a figure skater, not a ballerina," I could only assume he was mocking me about being pretty too, but I keep that to myself.

"At least he worked your name into the moniker, and hey, it could have been worse. He could have called you Neaner Neaner, like Cason did."

I glare at her and she holds her hands up. "Okay, okay. I get it. But Cole's been home for a month, recovering from a concussion, and his team—the Seattle Shooters, in case you don't know the league's name," she adds with a wink, "are probably going to make it to the playoffs, so you know he's watching all the games. You don't have to like him to ask him to explain a few of the plays, right?"

"I suppose."

Wait! What? Am I really thinking about asking The Playmaker to help me? I reach for my latté and blow on it before I take another big gulp.

"And if you ask me, while he's helping you learn the plays, I think you two should hate fuck."

I choke on my drink, spitting most of it on my friend as the rest dribbles down my chin.

OMFG, how embarrassing. All eyes turn to me. Mortified, I grab a napkin and start wiping my face, but Jess is laughing so hard, I start laughing with her.

"Couldn't you have waited until I swallowed?" I ask.

"That's what she said."

"Ohmigod, Jess. How are we friends?"

She waves a dismissive hand. "You know you love me because I'm hellacioulsy funny."

"I do, just stop cracking jokes when I'm drinking."

She leans towards me conspiratorially, and I brace myself. "I wasn't joking. You and Cocky Cole Cannon should hate fuck. He's as sexy today as he was when he used to hang out with Cason at your house when we were teens." I give her a look that suggests she's insane. She ignores it and wags her brows. "He's explosive on the ice, but do you know why they really call him the Cannon?"

"Because it's his last name."

"Yeah, but that's not the only reason."

Don't ask. Don't ask.

"Okay, then why?" I ask.

"'Cause he's loaded between his legs."

Yeah, okay, I totally set myself up for that.

"You don't know that," I shoot back. My mind races to my brother's best friend, and I mentally go over his form. He's athletic, tall and—as much as I hate to admit it—hot as hell. The perfect trifecta. Could he be packing too? Working with some top-notch equipment?

Jesus, what am I doing? The last thing I should be thinking about is Cole's 'cannon'.

"Come on." Jess grabs her purse. "I'll drive you there."

I flatten my hands on the table. "I'm not going to his house, especially not unannounced."

"Give him a call then."

"No."

She sits back in her chair and folds her arms, a sign she's changing tactics. "And here I thought you liked your condo and food in your cupboards."

I groan at the direct hit.

Her voice softens and she touches my hand. "But you know you always have—"

"Fine." I stop her before she brings up my trust fund. Yeah, sure, Mom and Dad set money aside for me, but I don't want to use it. I want to live by my own means, make it on my own merit. Besides it wasn't their money I wanted, then or now, it was their attention, their love. I moved out years ago and only ever hear from them on my birthday or at Christmas.

I pull my phone from my purse. "I'll text him. If he doesn't answer, we don't talk about this again." I go through my contacts and find his number, having stored it years ago when he called to check on me after my injury. The call had taken me by surprise; so did his concern. Maybe my brother put him up to it. I don't know. Nor do I know why I kept his number.

My fingers fly across the screen, but in no way do I expect him to respond. At least I hope he doesn't. I read over the text. *Sorry to hear about your concussion. I was wondering if you could help me with something*. Then hit send.

I set my phone down and look at Jess. "Happy?"

"Hey, I'm not the one who's going to be homeless."

Point taken. Maybe I should be hoping he *does* text back.

My phone pings, and we both reach for it. Jess gets it first, and from her smirk, I guess my wish just came true—Cole responded.

Careful what you wish for.

"What does it say?" I ask, afraid of the answer.

"It says, sure what's up?" Jess's fingers dance over the screen as she responds for me.

"What are you saying?" I ask, panic welling up inside me. "So help me, if you're telling him I need to get laid..."

The phone pings again and she holds it out for me to read.

"I asked—I mean *you* asked if you could stop by his place, and he said sure."

"I don't know whether to kiss you or choke you," I say.

Jess laughs. "I think you'll be thanking me." She stands. "Come on."

We make our way outside, and the rain has slowed to a light mist as I follow her down the street to her parked car. I hop in and question my sanity. Am I really going to ask Cocky Cannon to teach me the game?

Jess starts the car and the locks click as she pulls into traffic. Guess so.

"You remember where he lives?" I ask. I think back to when he bought the house. He had a big party to celebrate. I was invited but didn't go. Why would I? Watching the hockey players with their bunnies was not my idea of a good time.

"Of course." She jacks the tunes and sings along off-key as she drives. Twenty minutes later, she pulls up in front of his mansion. It's a ridiculously big house for one person. I stare at it, and once again question my sanity.

"Go," Jess says.

"I'm going," I shoot back. I open the door, and smooth my hand over my mess of curls. Why the hell did I do that? It's not like I'm trying to make myself presentable or impress him. We don't even like each other.

I force my legs to carry me to his door, and I'm about to knock when it opens. My breath catches as I take in Cole, standing before me shirtless and barefoot, dressed only in a pair of faded jeans that hug him so nicely.

God, he is so freaking hot—and I never, ever should have come here.

As we stare at each other, like we're in some goddamn Mexican standoff, I can't stop thinking about his 'cannon'. My gaze drops to the lovely bulge between his legs, and a moan I have no control over catches in my throat as Jess's words come back to haunt me.

You two should hate fuck.

Thank you, Jess, for planting that idea in my brain. Christ, I should have choked her when I had the chance.

* * *

If you want to find out what antics Cole and Nina get up to check it out here.

The Playmaker

ALSO BY CATHRYN FOX

Hands On

Hands On

Body Contact

Full Exposure

Dossier

Private Reserve

House Rules

Under Pressure

Big Catch

Brazilian Fantasy

Improper Proposal

Boys of Beachville

Good at Being Bad

Igniting the Bad Boy

Bad Girl Therapy

Stone Cliff Series:

Crashing Down

Wasted Summer

Love Lessons

Wrapped Up

Eternal Pleasure Series

Instinctive

Impulsive

Indulgent

Sun Stroked Series

Seaside Seduction

Deep Desire

Private Pleasure

Captured and Claimed Series:

Yours to Take

Yours to Teach

Yours to Keep

Firefighter Heat Series

Fever

Siren

Flash Fire

Playing For Keeps Series

Slow Ride

Wild Ride

Sweet Ride

Breaking the Rules:

Hold Me Down Hard

Pin Me Up Proper

Tie Me Down Tight

Stand Alone Title:

Hands on with the CEO

Torn Between Two Brothers

Holiday Spirit

Unleashed

Knocking on Demon's Door

Web of Desire

ABOUT CATHRYN

New York Times and *USA today* Bestselling author, Cathryn is a wife, mom, sister, daughter, and friend. She loves dogs, sunny weather, anything chocolate (she never says no to a brownie) pizza and red wine. She has two teenagers who keep her busy with their never ending activities, and a husband who is convinced he can turn her into a mixed martial arts fan. Cathryn can never find balance in her life, is always trying to find time to go to the gym, can never keep up with emails, Facebook or Twitter and tries to write page-turning books that her readers will love.

Connect with Cathryn:

Tik Tok: @cathrynfoxwriter
Newsletter https://app.mailerlite.com/webforms/landing/
c1f8n1
Twitter: https://twitter.com/writercatfox
Facebook: https://www.facebook.com/AuthorCathrynFox?
ref=hl

Blog: http://cathrynfox.com/blog/
Goodreads: https://www.goodreads.com/author/show/91799.
Cathryn_Fox
Pinterest http://www.pinterest.com/catkalen/

Printed in Great Britain
by Amazon

22865288R00179